IN THE GARDEN OF EDEN

A Detective Marcus Jefferson Novel

PETER STOCKWELL

Westridge Art
PO Box 3847, Silverdale, WA 98383

Published by
Westridge Art
PO Box 3847
Silverdale, WA 98383

First Printing 2019
Copyright © by Peter Stockwell
All rights reserved.

20 19 10 9 8 7 6 5 4 3 2 1

ISBN-13: 978-0-9886471-7-6

Printed in the United States of America

Publisher's note
This book is a work of fiction.
Names, characters, places, and incidents either are the product of the author's imagination or are used fictionally, and any resemblance to actual persons, living or dead, business establishments, events, or locales is entirely coincidental.

Cover Design by Peter Stockwell
Images from Shutterstock.com

Interior Design by Timothy L. Meikle - REPROSPACE

Distributed by
Westridge Art
and Ingram

OTHER WORKS BY PETER STOCKWELL

ADULT FICTION
Motive series
Motive
Motivations
Jerry's Motives
Death Stalks Mr. Blackthorne

NONFICTION
Stormin' Norman – The Sermons of an Episcopal Priest
Volume I
Volume II

DEDICATION

This book is dedicated to my friend and fellow author, Mark Miller, for being a constant companion to my crazy ideas and plans.

"... SO MAY STRIFE PERISH FROM AMONG GODS AND MEN, ANGER THAT SETTETH A MAN ON TO GROW WROTH, HOW WISE SOEVER HE BE, AND THAT SWEETER FAR THAN TRICKLING HONEY..."

HOMER'S ILIAD, BOOK XVIII

REVIEWS

"Peter Stockwell cranks out mystery after mystery with electrifying ability to keep readers on the edge of their seats."
- **S. E. Beall, editor**

"The latest novel by Peter Stockwell is the best story in the series about detective Marcus Jefferson and his war with a drug cartel. "In the Garden of Eden" is a page-turner with continuing twists and turns, making it hard to put down. Filled with tension and visual stimuli, readers intently follow the Jefferson family as they battle to maintain safety and survival. Detective work runs strong in the blood of each Jefferson as they work together sifting through elusive clues to an unexpected conclusion."
- **RJ Bauer, author and poet**

"I have been reading your book on my free time and so far, it has made me smile and cry. You are such a great and amazing writer."
Adelina Vargas, Pochutla, Oaxaca, México

TABLE OF CONTENTS

CHAPTER

1

Detective Marcus Jefferson's mind wandered through the history of the Alaskan cruise vacation disrupted prematurely by the death of an internationally known author. The cityscape emerged from the overhanging cloud cover of a summer rainstorm. Puget Sound and Seattle rose up to capture the Alaska Air Boeing 737-800 as it approached SeaTac International Airport. He turned to Joan, his wife, and remarked, "I have another week of vacation which should have been on the Salish Sea. Since I'm not due in the office for another ten days, Fellington can just wait his turn."

Joan smiled, "I agree. We've had enough excitement." He stared out the window at the lights passing beneath the plane. The dream cruise in Alaskan waters metamorphosed into a nightmare of ferreting out evil. Five people died as a result of the attempts to end the career and life of Kitsap County Sheriff's lead detective. Marc, wounded, and his two sons, Marcus and James, both kidnapped and assaulted, needed time away from crime. Nothing indicated any existed.

Two of his children sat across the aisle. James slept while Sarah stared out the window. The first-class seating, courtesy of the American Pacific Cruise Line, afforded room and attention none of them had experienced. American Pacific offered the seating because of Marc's involvement. Assaults killed author James Blackthorne, a steward name Iskandar, another crew member, Commodore Cayde Thorsen, and Cruise Director Jarina Camacho. Marc became the target of crew members who used the ship for smuggling illegal drugs and other contraband from Vancouver, British Columbia to Seattle, Washington. After he and his father and uncle crushed a drug cartel operating in Everett, Washington, they sought revenge. He and Security Chief, Dag Ingersol, worked to contain the violence and neutralize threats to crew and passengers. The journey ended half way complete. A grateful management team needed to compensate innocent passengers and crew.

His head carried the mark of a bullet which grazed his skull. James survived poisoning by the same substance which effected a fatal heart attack on the author. Marcus, their oldest son, had endured a similar poisoning and assault by two identical women who had managed to escape the ship undetected.

He watched the city lure him to another investigation fraught with unknown dangers. Would two lethal females follow him from Anchorage bent on terminating his future?

Fellington could wait. He needed time for post-traumatic stress disorder to abate. Joan needed to have family together again. Children needed to be home without threats. Beginning an investigation into the source of the material with lethal toxins challenged any time for rest.

A final announcement regarding the connecting to other flights, collecting baggage, and remaining seated until the plane came to a complete stop at a gate interrupted his brain. His hand reached for Joan who clasped it and smiled a weak happiness. Who was next to come after them?

⋊⋉ ⋊⋉ ⋊⋉

Gabriella Jefferson, Lydia Jefferson, Marcus Jefferson, and Delinda Middlebury stood near the TSA exit from the C gate which passengers used to enter the unsecured side of the airport. Marcus and Delinda held hands and kept space between them small.

Mother, aunt, son and girlfriend crowded the doorway anxious to see those who completed the contested journey to Anchorage. Marcus and Delinda had begun therapy to help them through the mental rigors of kidnapping, rape, and poisoning. They developed a bond which they meant to foster for life.

Marc's mother and aunt had returned with them to Seattle as the cruise ship sailed north from Skagway, Alaska. Father and uncle remained to fish for theories regarding the ingredients which proved powerful enough to render death.

Greeting the travelers from Alaska corrected the wrong done by Jefferson clan enemies. They disrupted a criminal entity and battled for the safety of a couple thousand unwitting participants. Home was an achievement. Togetherness brought safety in numbers.

Gabriella Jefferson spoke first, "How was the flight in First Class?" Lydia nodded as Marcus and Delinda held tight and passively waited their turn.

Marc answered his mother, "Fine. The cruise line was quite generous to see we came home in comfort and style. It must have been quite a shock to find the depth of the corruption aboard the ship. Captain Lars Dalgaard, second mate Cayde Thorsen, cruise director, Jarina Camacho, and the head steward were all part of the ring which smuggled material to Andrew Pepper in Everett. By the way, when are Dad and Uncle Jerry arriving home?"

Lydia responded, "Jerry called and said they were arriving tomorrow afternoon." A horde of people descended the escalator to the baggage claim area to retrieve luggage. The Jefferson luggage came home without fees. Another benefit afforded the Jefferson family for enduring injuries and attacks. Silence injected itself as passengers shuffled to the carousel to await bags.

Marc acknowledged her comment with a nod. His mind, lost in thought, cared more about finding the source of death-dealing honey and tea. Death which infected a cruise ship. Death which stalked an author and stalked his family. Death delivered by people affiliated with Andrew Pepper. Death delivered by a drug dealing cartel in Everett, Washington, which lost a battle with the Jefferson clan and Snohomish and Everett police.

He traced the grim reminder of fatal actions pursued by members of the crew, who misused the good graces of the American Pacific Cruise Line. An innocent writer of thriller fiction became a victim like a character of his own creation.

Marcus approached his father while Delinda stayed with mother and aunt. "Dad, I know you want to close this part of our family history, but don't give those killer twins any chance to harm anyone else." Marc grabbed a red bag with a striped ribbon tied to it. Marcus retrieved another. "You're the strongest person I know. You and Mom." A third suitcase approached, and Marc reached for it. Bending sent a twinge of pain across his wounded head. He grunted. Marcus intervened and pulled the last three bags from the carousel.

Standing with the women and children, Marc said, "Let's get home. I need to rest." Joan pulled the handle up to pull her suitcase. Marcus grasped the suitcase which had not accompanied him to his grandmother's house earlier in the week. James and Sarah collected their bags. Lydia placed a hand on Marc's as he pulled up the handle.

"I'll take this for you. You've had enough stress and strain." He acquiesced and smiled. The family ascended the escalator to the next level and traversed the walkway overpass to the parking area of SeaTac. At the van which Gabby drove to pick up her son and his family, Marcus stacked suitcases in the back as passengers seated themselves.

Lydia also had driven a vehicle, so enough room existed for transporting all members of the family to the home of Tiberius and Gabriella Jefferson. Delinda and Marcus rode with her. The caravan of two departed the confines of the fifth floor and headed north to Ballard and home.

Joan sat in the front seat while Marc sat with Sarah and James in the middle seat area. He asked, "Did you have any problems getting home?" Joan glanced at him as if to say, "leave it alone." He rocked his head and grimaced. Sarah saw her father's motion but not her mother's. James had his eyes closed, escaping any interaction for the moment.

"No, Lydia helped with Marcus, and Delinda is a delightful young woman." The conversation died for lack of interest in confronting Joan. After the hour-long drive on Highways 509 and 99 to the Viaduct and Western Avenue, the cars arrived at the home in which Marc spend most of his youth. The group carried bags into the house and to guest rooms for the evening stay. Aunt Lydia bade a good night and left for her home in Snohomish.

Standing with his mother and Joan in his boyhood bedroom, he placed suitcases on the queen-sized bed which replaced his twin. "Marc," Gabby asked, "are you doing alright. I hated leaving you in Skagway to deal with those dangerous people. I feared for your life." Turning to Joan, she said, "And that includes you and Sarah and James. Those people wanted you harmed and Marc dead."

Marc faced his mother. "The end has come. No one is left to cause any problems." His words did not match his thinking. The twins had somehow evaded capture and remained a threat. "Let's forget about what happened in Alaska. It's over, and we survived." He opened the suitcases and took some items from it, held them a moment and then dropped them on the bed. Joan followed his actions by removing her personal items for the bathroom down the hall. Gabby turned to leave. Marc closed the bedroom door, holding the knob to be sure he and Joan remained alone.

"Your mother is right, even if you deny it. You said it, we survived. It wasn't enough. We should have enjoyed a freedom from investigations and medical needs. How long before one of those lethal girls shows up to cause conflict?"

CHAPTER

2

Marc awakened after a restful night, trying not to disturb Joan. Slipping on a tee shirt and sweat pants, he left his boyhood bedroom to find coffee to brew. In the kitchen he found his mother preparing breakfast for his family. "Good morning, Mom."

"Good morning, Marc. I hope your sleep brought you peace and comfort." Her joyful demeanor stirred memories of growing up in the house with his two sisters and brother. They had scattered to other parts of the world with less stress-filled jobs and families of their own. Gathering the tribe had become a monumental challenge for holidays and coordinated vacations.

"We slept well." Searching for a pot of black elixir, he asked, "Any coffee made?"

Gabby pointed at an urn on the counter by the refrigerator. Cups assembled like soldiers in formation, individual and yet part of the unit. "Help yourself."

He studied the cups and picked up one which had a Seattle Police logo and sergeant stripes. "I forgot about this cup." His mother looked at him and smiled. "I'll be glad to have Dad home. He and Uncle Jerry were very generous in helping finish off the rest of that nefarious gang of cutthroats. I hope they enjoyed some time together in Alaska."

"He called last night. They provided the evidence which indicated you were the target to the Alaska State Patrol and FBI. I'm so sorry for the family of that author who died."

"Yeah, I just hope Sarah will forgive herself for suggesting the gift basket with the toxic tea and honey was meant for him when the cartel really wanted us to get sick and die." Marc filled his cup and wrapped his hands around it to warm them.

"Give her time. She's a resilient young lady. And speaking of young ladies, your son has met a most enchanting person. I can see why he fell in love with her."

"Mom, he's only eighteen and hasn't experienced life. I don't want him tied to a relationship which keeps him from attaining what he wants." He sipped his coffee. His mother placed the spatula in her hand in the bowl she was mixing and faced him. Time for a lecture, he thought.

"Your father and I met when we were barely older than he is now. Do you think we didn't attain what we wanted?" Marc settled back on the counter to listen to words of wisdom. "We married right away, and you came along almost before we had begun our journey. I have no regrets and Marcus and Delinda will have none, as well." He grinned. "And wipe that smirk off your face."

"Yes, mother." He kept smiling. "I know you're right. I just wanted him to reach for the stars and finish school as I did." Joan wandered into the fray and glanced at Marc and then Gabby.

"Am I interrupting something?" She folded her hands behind her and waited.

Marc answered her, "No, we were discussing our son and Delinda's future which may have arrived already."

"Marc thinks they're too young to be a happy, successful couple. I reminded him of his father and me."

Joan laughed and said, "Yes, Marc, what is it about a relationship in which you pursue and stalk a young nurse until she acquiesces and breaks off a relationship of her own, just to appease you?" Marc shrugged his shoulders and grinned again.

"Guilty." Marcus and Delinda entered the kitchen followed by Sarah and James. His family resisted the assaults on the ship and stayed intact. His life was truly blessed. "Good morning to all of you. Let's have breakfast and enjoy a great day."

As they sat at the dining room table and consumed scrambled eggs, ham, bacon, muffins and juice, Marc reached for Joan's hand below the table. An exchange of looks and smiles relieved his anxiety for the moment. He worked his eyes around the table watching the conversations of the others. Nothing about the experiences aboard the cruise ship to Alaska interfered with the enjoyment of kinship.

Concentrating on Marcus and Delinda, he decided his mother was correct. They were a couple, and the idea of their being such an item held no negativity. He accepted the union and knew a future together was better than separation and a broken heart.

"Dad, you okay?" Marcus asked when he noticed his father staring. Other voices rested to await an answer.

Marc blinked out of his trance. "I was admiring you and Delinda. You have been through more than most people endure in a lifetime and you share a strength I didn't have when I was your age. Delinda, your father is very proud of you and misses you. As soon as business is finished in Anchorage, he is coming here for you. He's going to need you to be strong for him and help him accept the truth." Marc stood and raised a glass of water. "I propose a toast to all of us for being who we are and fighting for the survival we have within us." Glasses of water and juice clinked in agreement.

With breakfast concluded and dishes cleared and washed by hand or machine, Marc and Joan returned to his childhood bedroom to pack their clothing and prepare for a return trip to Kitsap County and home. He had his life back and a head scarred but intact.

Joan stopped collecting her clothing. "Are you and your dad and uncle going to find the source of that toxic honey?" Marc remained silent, so she waited. He slowed his progress and pondered a respectful answer.

"I don't know where to start looking. It's the proverbial needle in the haystack. We need to find one or both twins and then ferret out the information of how they acquired it. They're not going to return here unless they're still bent on revenge." He sat on the bed. "We'll have to be diligent."

Joan sat with him and clasped his hands. "Death may still exact a cost no one wants to pay."

"I'm going to find Marcus and Delinda," he continued. "We need to get some idea what they want from each other and us. He starts school in another three weeks." Joan nodded a silent agreement. They halted any further packing and together searched for their eldest child. The University of Minnesota had accepted Delinda, and her father wanted her to return with him to their home. Long distances tended to interfere with closeness.

Finding them in the family room watching television, Marc and

Joan sat with them. A game show played on the screen. Marcus looked at his father and asked, "What's up?" Marc started to say something and stopped. "You're wondering about me and Dee, aren't you?" A nod answered the question.

"What kind of relationship can you have when separated by a thousand miles or more?"

"Mr. Jefferson, I've decided to apply to a school here in Seattle." Delinda's smile belied the travesty Marc believed awaited her decision. Randolph Middlebury was a lonely father unwilling to accept a daughter's summer romance as a long-term relationship. "Dad's going to have to accept that I'm a woman and of an age to make my own decisions."

"Where would you live? How are you going to pay for a school here? Will your father being willing to support you and your decision?"

Delinda smirked. "All good questions. I'll find an apartment. I have a college fund already. And my father's ideas of support are not necessarily mine."

Joan intervened, "Delinda, Marcus is living in a fraternity when he begins school. If you were thinking of living with him, it might create a complication. As for school, we have a community college in Wendlesburg which is a great place to begin your studies. Marc and I are willing to provide you a place to stay." Marc's eyebrows rose as he heard the statement.

"That's very nice of you, but I like being on my own."

"And you want to be closer to Marcus. He does come home, you know. Besides he's going to be busy with frat requirements and studying. He may not have time to date." Joan's voice carried a parental sternness.

Marc listened, not convinced he wanted a replacement child. Although, as he thought about the situation, another female near Sarah's age might have positive results. Neither his nor Joan's working schedule included domestic oversight of their children. What harm came from Delinda living in Wendlesburg and attending school while being available to keep an eye on children?

"We'll finish this discussion as soon as your father arrives from Alaska." Marc sounded as if an edict had been professed and was destined for obeyance. But was he too late because the maturation of Marcus defeated such thinking?

CHAPTER

3

Tiberius wrapped an arm around his brother's shoulder. "I will be so happy to get home and relax." Jerry laughed and flipped the arm from his body.

"Your son, my nephew, has an uncanny knack of finding trouble where no one expects. I'm glad we concluded the cartel's business."

"But it doesn't explain the murder weapon. I never would have believed honey could be lethal."

Tiberius nodded. A speaker announced boarding for Seattle on Alaska Air. They joined the queue awaiting the cattle call for the back of the plane. Tiberius cell phone buzzed. Checking the caller, he showed it to Jerry.

"Middlebury," he said and clicked the green button to answer. "Hello, doc. What's up?"

"I just called to let you know I will be on the next flight to Seattle. I had hoped to get on sooner, but the FBI had more questions for me than I expected. Olivia Breckenridge was helpful, though."

"I hope we get to meet her. She played quite a role aboard your ship."

"When you get home, please let my daughter know I miss her. I tried calling but was unable to connect."

Tiberius asked, "Did you try my house?" He gave Dr. Middlebury the number. "Call Marc on his cell."

"Thanks, I'll be in touch when I arrive tomorrow."

"Where are you staying in Seattle?"

A hushed breath indicated a blushing moment. "Olivia is with me. She invited me to stay in a spare room she has."

"Ah yes, the accommodating FBI and undercover nurse. I want to meet this woman." The called ended with an agreement to gather at Tiberius' house.

Jerry asked, "How's he doing?"

"Seems fine. He and that nurse FBI gal are traveling together tomorrow. He's missing his daughter, though."

Jerry laughed, "I bet your grandson isn't." The line slithered toward the ramp doors where a young man accepted their boarding passes and bid them a good day. The walk down to the plane was uneventful as was the flight to Seattle.

As the plane taxied to the gate, Tiberius called his wife, Gabriella, to inform her of their arrival. He listened to her as she informed him that Lydia had arrived at the cell call parking area to await picking them up. Jerry called her number.

The intrepid officers gathered their bags and waited for Lydia at the baggage claim ramp.

Jerry kissed his wife and said, "You are the best spouse anyone can have."

"I am. Let's go."

Tiberius leaned in so Jerry could hear. "She always has been a bit pushy." He grinned.

"I heard that. He wouldn't be here today except for me." The truth revealed.

The pair of Spanish eyes watched Tiberius and Jeremais as they gathered their suitcases. She was young and beautiful, lethal beyond anyone's imagination. Her flight had arrived an hour before along with another plane on which contained a twin image, just as lethal and magnetic.

As her sister approached, she smiled. "They're so cute together."

Kerrine nodded, "Yes, but they're only leading us to the other one who should be dead and is not."

Kaliana folded her arms. "Does he need to die?" Her eyes followed the pair of officers. They exited to a lady with an awaiting car. They assumed her to be a wife of one of them.

"You are still living in a fantasy. You had no success with Jefferson, but I did with that doctor. He succumbed as quickly as any of the others."

"Jefferson has flaws. I need to find one which breaks his resolve."

Curling an arm in her sister's, Kerrine reflected on the comment. "Resolve is not one of your strongest traits."

"I missed traveling with you." Kaliana cupped her hands over her sister's hands still wrapped on her arm. "Where are we staying while we're in Washington? I didn't receive any information other than my passport and a ticket. Flawless items, I must say."

"We are headed to Wendlesburg and a small house near our target. Do you have your bag nearby?" Kaliana pointed to a paisley carry-on suitcase. "Good, I'll get mine, and we can pick up the car which is in the garage on floor 5." They traversed the walkway over the departure roadway, clogged with automobiles. Waiting by the elevator to ascend one floor, two young men approached. Kerrine smiled with a coy glint in her eyes. Kaliana watched, wary of the fate of the two men.

The taller of the Nordic looking men spoke first, "Hi, did you just arrive here?" Kerrine remained quiet but nodded. "From where?"

"We are from California, visiting some family members in Tacoma. Where did you fly from?" She asked.

The other man stepped nearer to Kaliana. Her demeanor, meant to halt his advance, challenged his attempt to speak with her.

Tall Nordic continued his conversation. "Can we drop you somewhere? The rental shuttles are on the 3rd floor, but I guess you have a car in the garage." Kerrine touched his lips with a finger.

"Stop talking," her voice whispered. "We are all set for transportation. But what are you doing for the next couple of hours?" His eyes widened.

The other man and Kaliana exchanged glanced at the other pair and with each other. She shrugged and raised one eyebrow. Her mouth curled as if to say, "Why not."

Tall Nordic stammered, not believing the apparent offer. "I don't know. We were heading to Bellevue for a conference, but I think we can delay for a while. What'd you have in mind?"

"Can we have an early dinner and then a nice cozy, private dessert at your place?"

"Ah, sure, I guess." He glanced at his friend who stared in disbelief. With a plan to meet later in the afternoon constructed, the two pair of millennial travelers parted. Kerrine and Kaliana entered the elevator as the men left to descend the escalator to the shuttles.

Kaliana spoke as they approached the Toyota Prius, "Sis, I enjoy a hook-up as much as you, but do we need this distraction? Are you planning to be lethal when we finish with them?"

"You worry too much. No, I don't plan on killing them. I just want to have some fun. We can enjoy their company for the evening and disappear from their lives." At the car, she continued. "If you don't want to share time with them, we don't have to do anything. We can leave them wondering what happened."

Kaliana opened the trunk of the car and placed her bag in it. "Let's head to Bellevue and their hotel. No harm in a little dinner and dessert." Kerrine put her bag in and closed the back.

As they drove down the circular ramp to the exit, Kerrine asked, "What do you want from Jefferson? He's not going to leave his family for you. If you only want to screw with his life, I get it. If you want more, then it should be his demise."

Kaliana stopped at the cash gate and paid the attendant. As the pike rose, she closed the window and answered her sister, "He needs to understand what he did on the ship and in Everett was most distasteful. He ruined a perfectly good business and murdered our friends. I think killing him doesn't make him suffer enough. He needs to hurt. He needs to fall from that pedestal people put him on and lose the people he most cares about."

"And then he can grovel to you, and you can have your way with him. He becomes a submissive who begs forgiveness for his sins. Sometimes I think you're more conniving than I am." Kaliana bared a Cheshire grin.

As they drove along Interstate 405, traffic slogged to a crawl near the "S" curves. The afternoon rendezvous time suffered a delay, but the sisters concluded that their dining partners were experiencing a similar fate. They slowed to a stop in the HOV lane and discovered the reason for the afternoon traffic jam. Blue lights flashed ahead of them, and a siren wailed from behind them. Cars cleared a path for the ambulance and another state patrol car.

"I hope no one is seriously hurt?" Kaliana said. A path opened for the traffic to bypass the three vehicles which blocked two outside lanes. The cars in the HOV lane sailed past the damage and picked up speed. Kerrine monitored the cars as they drove on.

"If our dinner is lost among those wrecks, I will be unsatisfied."

At the Bellevue ramp to 4th Avenue, Kaliana followed the GPS suggestion which indicated their route to downtown and the Hyatt near Bellevue Square. At the valet parking area, a young woman came to them and asked, "Are you checking in?"

"No," Kerrine said, "we are meeting friends for dinner." She took the parking slip and handed the girl a ten-dollar bill. "Take good care of our car." She winked as if to imply that a female would be better than a man at preserving the automobile.

They entered the sliding glass doors to the reception area. Inspecting the atrium, they found a bar in which they were to meet their conquests. The time for dinner was an hour away, so they ordered drinks and sat. Black widow spiders lure their victims to the web for procreation and a meal. Kerrine and Kaliana were only interested in one of the two goals.

Nordic and his shorter friend arrived at the appointed time and signaled a waitress. As they sat with the sisters, eyes flitted from one to the other. Nordic stammered, "I didn't realize how much you two are alike. Are you twins?" His friend punched him in the shoulder.

"Sometimes you're an idiot. You didn't notice at the airport?" He sat next to Kaliana. "I apologize for Ryan's inability to observe the obvious. His brain locks up whenever a pretty girl speaks to him."

Ryan Wittingham sat near Kerrine and confessed, "He's right. I saw you and wanted to meet you. I am surprised you two showed up. Most girls I meet promise and don't deliver."

Kaliana chided him. "And what do you think we promised?" His face flushed, and Jeremy Caldwell laughed.

He said, "All I know is, we are buying you dinner and then having dessert served in our hotel room. But as to what the dessert may be, I will await the delivery." The waitress addressed the need for beverages and left.

"Smart boy. Let's eat dinner and then adjourn to the consumption of whatever promise may be implied and delivered."

Ryan asked a question neither man wanted to entertain but thought prudent to ask. "How much are your services going to cost?"

Kerrine frowned, "I do believe you have mistaken us for someone in a different vocation. We are not engaged in the practice of solicitation. We offered to share a meal and see what the evening brings us. You are attractive men, and we are accommodating sisters when we want to be. Do not believe we are exchanging any money for services promised or delivered." Both men nodded as their drinks arrived.

The afternoon waned as they ate dinner in the Eques. After assigning the meal to the room, the four young people left for the 23rd floor and an evening of entertaining each other. Little did the boys know the extent of the promised show.

CHAPTER

4

Marc and his father, Tiberius, sat in the Seattle Police office of the Assistant Chief for Criminal Investigations. All the materials gathered during the nightmare cruise of the Salish Sea about Andrew Pepper and his criminal organization using the cruise line for smuggling sat on the desk of Chief Vanessa Christine. As she thumbed through the evidence, her head rocked from side to side.

"Tiberius, you took time for a vacation, but you were working with your son as a representative of Seattle Police. I wish you had informed me of your intentions."

"Ma'am, I don't think that would have endeared me to the department. After we took down Pepper last spring in Everett, my captain was supportive of our accomplishments. But heading to Alaska was not done as a lark, nor was I representing Seattle. I did use my credentials to access certain Alaskan law enforcement departments. The material we gathered demonstrates that we still have a problem."

"Detective Jefferson, you were aboard the ship. I understand several members of your family were assaulted and nearly killed, including you."

Marc straightened. "Yes, my wife and family and I had earned vacation time and did not expect to be subjected to the conflict directed at me because of our destruction of Andrew Pepper and his criminal enterprise in Everett. What surprised those aboard who were not part of the cartel, was the use of an ordinary food product which had lethal properties. As you can read in the folder, honey which is made exclusively from rhododendrons and azaleas was used for the harming of humans. We suspect someone has created a hybrid plant which is more toxic than usually found in our backyards."

Turning her attention to Tiberius, Christine asked, "What do you want from us? Isn't the FBI already involved in an investigation to find the source?"

"Yes, an undercover agent worked with the crew and the members of the cartel. She was present at the raid against Pepper's warehouse, was not detained, and ended up aboard without anyone suspecting her double life. Olivia Breckenridge was instrumental in the destruction of the smuggling operation which my brother, Jeremais Jefferson, of the Snohomish Sheriff's Office, had not uncovered in his investigation of Pepper prior to the raid."

"What do you want from us?" Chief Christine repeated as she closed the folder.

"We need to open any cold cases in which people died for unknown reasons or from suspicious circumstances and have our forensic people reexamine bodies for grayanotoxin, the substance in rhododendrons and azaleas which sickens animals and humans who consume the plants."

"How do you propose covering the expense of such an investigation?" She interlocked her fingers and placed forearms on her desk.

"I don't know. The involvement of several jurisdictions might help to defray the expense Seattle would incur."

Marc interrupted. "This is important to me because two of my children were subjected to the toxin and nearly died. We do not know the source of the honey, but I suspect that a major wholesaler of plants may be able to guide us. I have a friend in Kitsap who sells honey and knows many people in the beekeeping business and manufacture of honey. Two ladies escaped from the ship and may have returned to this area to finish what they started in Alaska."

After gaining assurance of limited support for an investigation, Marc and Ti departed the office. As they passed his captain's office, Ti stopped. "We should update my boss." He turned to face Captain Morgan's secretary. "Is he available for a quick update?"

"He's not in the office until tomorrow. Do you want to leave a message?"

"Tell him I'll update our finding from the Alaska trip as soon as he's available." The two men left the Seattle headquarters for a stop at home and a check on the arrival of Middlebury and Breckenridge.

"Sergeant Jefferson," a young woman said to them as they entered the motor pool, "I'm glad you're back from Alaska." She offered her hand which he took.

"Officer Varona, Glad to see you made a full recovery from your experience of being shot."

"The vest was very helpful. Thank you for your concern. That's not why I stopped you. I did some digging into the raid you and your son orchestrated in Everett. I think you said something about this cartel being like an octopus. Many arms and cutting one off does not end the beast which will grow back the missing limb." Marc folded arms together and waited. Tiberius rested hands on his hips.

She continued, "The people who were detained for their involvement and expressed an interest in turning state's evidence may have played us and the prosecutor. They gave up some of the people we wanted and received reduced sentencing or probation, but like the arms of the octopus others are still out there which we have leads on and no direction from our friendly felons."

"Give me what you've uncovered. We'll add it to what we have from Alaska and Vancouver. And stay in touch with me. Our training sessions may be over, but your education should continue. Are you still in our department?"

"Yes, sir."

"Good. We can use as much street help as possible. Let's meet when your shift ends so I can fill you in on what transpired up north." Another handshake ended the conversation.

Marc interjected, "She was with you when the truck cut you off, and the guy shot at you. That was a few days before our raid in Everett. Wasn't it?"

"Yes, she took three to her vest. I'm just glad it wasn't career ending for her. She has more potential than most of the recruits this last year. She can be a lot of help to us."

As they drove out of the garage, a black sedan tailed in behind them but turned away a couple of blocks later. Tiberius said, "Every time I see one of those cars, I think another tail is on us. Just like in Everett."

"Paranoia, Dad? But I get your drift." The rest of the trip to Ballard and home was uneventful. At the house, a strange automobile parked on the street. The license was a government issue. "I guess Breckenridge is here. I wonder if she brought Middlebury?"

"Let's find out." Tiberius pulled into the drive. Before they could exit the car, Sarah and James greeted them from the front porch.

"Grampa, Dad, the doctor is here and the FBI lady," Sarah spoke while James said nothing.

Entering the house, they found their friends from the ship in the kitchen drinking coffee and eating newly baked cookies. "Greetings from Alaska," Randolph said as he shook Marc's hand.

"Greetings to you, as well. Where are Delinda and Marcus? I figured you'd want to see your daughter as soon as possible."

Gabrielle answered the inquiry. "I sent them to the store just before Olivia and Randolph arrived. They should be returning soon." A rush of caution filtered through Marc's brain. They had been kidnapped in Skagway when they were away from the family. He kept his discretion to himself. After all, this was Seattle.

Chit chat continued about the trip in from Anchorage and the investigation by FBI and Alaskan State Patrol into the misuse of a cruise ship and the peril of two thousand passengers and crew. The closeness of fatality of innocent lives was not lost on Marc or Dr. Middlebury and his nurse, albeit, FBI agent, in keeping the lid on such an explosive situation.

The back door to the kitchen opened, and a pair of eighteen-year-olds entered with recyclable grocery bags in hand. "Dad, I am so glad to see you." Delinda placed her two bags on the counter and grasped her father in a bear hug to keep him from escaping her. "I missed you."

"I'm so glad you are well. The Jefferson family took good care of you from what I can see." Randolph glanced at Marcus who still held two grocery bags. A stilted smile crossed his face. Marcus was not the enemy, but a daughter lost to a summer shipboard romance did not improve his emotional state of what was to come next. Would he be leaving for Minnesota with his daughter or was she grown to the point of being an independent woman with a future in the arms of another man?

Delinda released her victim and set her teeth and mouth. "Dad,

I don't want you to dread what I'm about to say, but I have made a decision about this fall and going to college." Randolph braced for the disappointment he expected. He knew he had to let her make up her mind. No amount of debate would change the results.

"You want to stay here. You found someone to replace me, and he's not going to Minneapolis." The atmosphere of the room cooled as quickly as a storm front crossed Puget Sound.

"I'm not replacing you. I'm adding to our family. I love Marcus, and he loves me. We'll attend school here in Washington, and when we deem the time to be right, we'll decide about getting married." The words hit him like a ton of bricks fell from a wall in Pioneer Square after an earthquake. His chest seized and breathing halted. The magic of seeing his daughter after almost two weeks apart melted away. He had news to impart, but the timing fractured for the moment. Silence reigned.

CHAPTER

5

Eden Montague closed and locked the refrigeration unit in the basement cavern of her warehouse. Word had come from a reliable source that law enforcement may have questions for her regarding the raising of bees and the pollination of rhododendrons and azaleas. She understood in a moment of reflection what that meant. Tracing the honey her wholesale nursery produced was not difficult. She marketed it around the northwest. Varying tastes required certain plants to be targeted by her bees during the spring and summer growing months.

"Bernice, what's the situation with our bumbles?"

"The boxes are in the warehouse with the chrysanthemums, cornflowers, phlox, and asters. The honey bees are working the flowers, as well. Our honey production should be above average this year. You sound as if you're concerned about something. What is it?" Bernice Harapat worked for Montague Nursery for more than twenty years. Her knowledge of beekeeping was second to none in Washington State. Her reputation across the country was impeccable.

When Eden's husband, Malcolm Varian, died and she took over the business, the request for special handling of certain species of bees and the pollination of certain plants during seasons of the year did not surprise her. The product of the bumblebee's exclusive spring and early summer visits to luteum azaleas and hybrid rhododendrons had sparked a curiosity about the honey. The creation of "Mad Honey," as many people called it, was mixed with other types of clover, dandelion, and wildflower honey to create a brand unique to the nursery. Bernice relished the idea of using her bees to develop kinds of honey the buying public would find nowhere else.

"Some news came to me about our production of honey. I don't want you or Chris to be concerned. An inquiry will not soil our reputation." Chris Colella held the position of nursery supervisor and field manager. Hiring him from another of the large wholesale houses had been a coup for Eden. She needed help, and he provided the very assistance for overseeing which plants needed the greenhouses and which could be outdoors. He ran the crew of 47 with ease and efficiency.

Bernice scowled, "What inquiry are you talking about? I've heard nothing about problems with honey production here or at other growers."

"I don't want to alarm anyone."

"Alarm anyone? You just did." Bernice's arms stretched out with palms up. "Explain the inquiry. Nothing about the practices of our farm should alarm anyone, as you said. So, who wants to cause alarm?"

Eden set a straight line with her lips. "I don't know. I received a note yesterday from an acquaintance who says honey has been used to kill people. The only honey which can come close to doing that is our production of 'Mad' which is mixed with other honey to take the sting out and enhance the flavors of different types." She turned away from Bernice and sat at her desk.

"Don't leave me out. I can help if you think the police are coming. We have nothing to hide." Eden said nothing. Bernice continued, "Have I done something which goes against the ethical production of consumable honey?"

Eden looked up, anger filling her head, but she controlled it. "We are not guilty of killing anybody. As you said, we have nothing to hide. Now leave me, please." Before Bernice could depart, Eden admonished her. "Say nothing to anyone about this. I mean it. Nothing." Her apiarist left her to the task of finishing paperwork and bookkeeping.

As the afternoon waned and before darkness consumed the remaining light, she traipsed the grounds around the three massive greenhouses which housed the seedlings and grafted plants before their introduction to Mother Nature and the whims of weather.

Entering the first building, she found Garcia and Jocelyne mixing soils and preparing planting boxes. They acknowledged her as she entered the office of her supervisor.

"Chris, are you in here?" The office had three rooms for secretaries and the boss. Her voice echoed off the walls. She turned to leave, but Chris stood in the doorway.

"Eden." His soft words soothed her troubled mind. "Did you need something?" He leaned against the door jamb, waiting for a response. She tapped his shoulder.

"Just wanted to be sure all was running smooth as silk."

"You know it is. I can't fail you. You're the best friend I never had growing up. All the fall plants are producing. We deliver to the retailers this week and cash in."

"Thanks. I finished the books for the week, and the cash on hand at the bank will tide us over the next month. Order what you need for the fall and winter grows."

"Already done." He reached for her waist and pulled her to him. "When are we going to close our business? You know how I feel about you." She caressed his cheek.

"I know." She wriggled free and left the greenhouse. She was not interested in gaining another partner for her nursery or her bed. The one liaison she shared with Chris had been good but a disaster for her mental state. She closed the opening and refused to yield to his pleas.

Her mind returned to the note in her pocket. She pulled it out and read it again. "Detectives are looking into the deaths of several people from what appears to be plant toxin. You may get a visit within the next few weeks. Be careful what you say or admit." Her sister's signature ended the communication. They were unable to see each other often even though they lived less than 75 miles apart. Each occupation restricted freedom for frivolous partying. She folded the note and placed it in her pocket.

She had nothing to fear. She repeated her mantra, aloud. "I have nothing to fear." Darkness finished any additional wandering around the grounds. Tiredness strangled further activity, so she entered the large manse her father had built nearly seventy years ago. Sleep became a priority.

She knew the news of a Seattle based cruise ship evacuated

in Anchorage because of the death of crew and passengers, including a famous author. The report about grayanotoxin afflicting several people scared her. And now the note. What could she tell investigators? That she grew rhododendrons and azaleas to produce honey to kill people? Her records indicated the deliberate pollination of Rhodies and azaleas by bumble bees. They were the only apiary species capable of surviving the making of honey. Bernice had proved that fact to her.

She read about 'Mad Honey' and the intoxicating nature of it. She read about animals and children who ate the plants and became sick. She studied the tragic Greek army slaughtered by Turks centuries ago after eating gifts from the local people of honey made from luteum azaleas. Now an investigation was coming to her, and she had nothing to hide but much to fear. Would she be mistaken for a murderer? She had never killed anyone directly. But what if her honey was the culprit? What if her sales to persons who came to the wholesale house was not a legitimate purchase? What if she could not prove her innocence?

Sleep was fitful. Maybe a good romp with Chris would have relaxed her. No. She was not going to start down that path. She drank enough vodka to slur thinking and crashed into bed with her clothes strewn on the floor. The bamboo sheets slithered against her naked body as she collapsed into the arms of Morpheus and raced through dream after fearsome dream.

"To whom are you selling this honey? Why are you making such a deadly batch of honey? Your honor, we the jury find the defendant guilty. Guilty. No. I've done nothing wrong. I didn't kill anyone. I'm innocent. I sentence you to fifty years for the murder of passengers. The jail door slammed shut. The silence of the night haunting her incarceration."

Morning came with an alarm from her side table. "Shut up," she whispered and cut the sound with a single slam on the button. Her arm fell to the side of the bed. A migraine struck her head as she raised it. No. Not a migraine. A hangover. Checking the clock which rudely brought her to consciousness, she read the digital red numbers. 6:00 am. "Ugh. I don't need this today. Why did I drink so much?" Pulling back the sheet and blanket, she lay naked for a moment before rising and heading to her bathroom.

She could declare a sick day and call in for rest and relaxation time. But who was she to call? She was the boss, and nothing stopped her from performing her duties. She had a loyal workforce. All of them were in the country legally or had been born in the United States. She paid well and did not relax but acted as an example of the benefits of hard work. She paid bonuses every year. She showered, letting the warm water cascade across her body, her head, her face. As she sobered, she recalled the note. What was to be her fate?

CHAPTER

<u>6</u>

A knock alerted Chief Christine her next appointment had arrived. "Come in." She stood to greet an old friend. Shaking hands, it was not proper to hug at work, she pointed at a chair. Olivia Breckenridge sat down as did Vanessa.

"Seems you've done well," Olivia said. "Chief of Criminal Investigations." Her head nodded acceptance of the job.

"Thanks, the work can be rewarding. But let's talk about your latest experiences. You met one of our police officers in Alaska, Tiberius Jefferson."

"Yes, and his son, Marc. Quite an experience, as you put it."

"How did you get involved with Andrew Pepper in Everett?" Vanessa leaned in to listen.

"The FBI had been tracking sales of drugs in Snohomish for a while and needed someone on the inside to gather intel. My nursing degree and experience seemed the best cover, so I volunteered. I went to his office and applied for a job."

"Why does an import/export business need a nurse?"

Olivia folded her fingers together. "I presented an idea which he accepted. I would help patch up anyone who got hurt, so no one was reported to authorities about gunshot wounds or suspicious injuries. At first, I'm sure he suspected me of not being real. His background check of me uncovered my nursing degree, but not my time at Quantico."

"And then the raid last spring changed all of that. You must have been rather upset; all of your work had been blown up." Vanessa sat back.

"It threw a monkey wrench into the plan, but I had uncovered the smuggling operation and accepted the position of nurse aboard the Salish Sea. The American Pacific Cruise Company had approached the FBI about suspicious activities. My boss asked me to get on the ship. I knew the cruise director because of her connection to Pepper, which made it easier to get hired."

"And the death of a famous author?"

"James Blackthorne was the unfortunate victim of a mistake. A basket meant for the Jefferson family, who were aboard on vacation, was given to him. It contained the honey and tea laced with grayanotoxin. Did you read the report I sent you?" Vanessa picked up a folder from her desk and handed it to Olivia.

"Yes," she said. "The folder also contains a report from Sergeant Jefferson relating his investigative support of his son, Marc, aboard the ship and his brother, Snohomish deputy Jeremais Jefferson's, involvement. Tell me about the doctor. Middlebury?"

Olivia glanced away. "He's a competent medical practitioner who suffered a loss and was the ship's doctor to get away from his troubles." She looked at Chief Christine. "He suspected right away the author had died from poisoning, but he was instructed by ship security to keep it under wraps. No need to report it to the FBI as a murder. That was hard for me to remain silent, but he contacted Mrs. Jefferson who, it turned out, was a nurse and had seen the body." Olivia glowered, "Then things got really dicey."

"The honey trail has gone cold, though," Vanessa said. "What's next?"

"Nothing. With no suspects and no idea who would produce such a product, it's like looking for the proverbial needle in the haystack." Olivia stood. "I must go. It was a pleasure to see you, again. You're looking well. I think being a chief agrees with you." With the door closed, a hug commenced.

"Let's get together for dinner outside of work."

"Let's. Contact me when it's convenient for you. My FBI schedule is flexible, right now." Olivia left the office.

Vanessa sat at her desk shaking her head. Olivia had not been as forthcoming as she wanted. Everything she related was in the report. But was the trail cold or did it lead somewhere? Somewhere which could be a danger to another person close to her?

⨾⨾⨾ ⨾⨾⨾ ⨾⨾⨾

Randolph Middlebury sat at the kitchen table in the Jefferson household, drinking coffee and listening to the banter of a family with few concerns and plenty of love. He missed his wife, and a fit of mock jealousy swirled in his head. In reality, not jealousy, but a sense of missing out on the redemptive side of life. Marcus and Delinda were a beautiful pair of young teenagers embracing life after nearing death in Skagway. Sarah and James Jefferson had a future filled with hope and anticipation. Joan Jefferson was as competent a nurse as he had ever encountered and had the fortitude of a veteran warrior. Meeting Gabriella Jefferson had allayed any fears that his daughter would be in any danger.

Leaving the ship after the assault on her life had been the right decision, although he missed her terribly. She was a woman, now, and a future away from Minnesota and home lurked around the corner. His news awaited the return of Marc and Tiberius. Olivia promised to come to the house as soon as she reported to her FBI office. His announcement would wait.

"Dad," Delinda sat across from him. "I want to apply to schools here in the Seattle area. I'm not returning to Minneapolis. Please know I love you, but I have to get on with my own life."

"I shouldn't have taken you on the cruise with me," he lamented.

"I know I didn't want to go, but it became the best thing I could have done. I miss Mom as much as you. But I have Marcus and a future as bright as you had."

"I'm not stopping you. I have decisions to make, myself." He sipped his coffee.

Joan entered the conversation. "Randolph, there are positions here in King and Kitsap Counties for experienced doctors. You could get your credentials with the state and start practicing with a hospital or clinic." He smiled.

"We'll see," was all he offered.

The door opened, and two intrepid officers of the law entered. Gabriella hugged her husband and son and then handed them mugs of coffee.

"We have some assurances from Seattle to help track our elusive honey supplier." Tiberuis seemed upbeat. Marc kissed Joan and sat next to her.

"Did the chief understand the importance of the connection to Pepper in Snohomish County?" Joan asked. "I want them stopped. They tried to kill the men in my family."

Tiberius answered her, "I think so. Jerry's talking with Sheriff Granger in his office in Snohomish. I don't think it will take much to convince him since Under-sherriff Allen and his secretary compimised his department."

"I'll speak with Fellington in Kitsap about what happened. I'm sure he's wondering if I fell off the earth. But I'm supposed to be on vacation still."

Gabriella interposed a question." What of the FBI and Canadian Mounties? Are they part of the search for your honey source?"

"Yes, Olivia and Regina are reporting to their offices today or tomorrow," Tiberius answered. "By the way, Randolph, you traveled here with Olivia. When is she showing up in our lives?"

Middlebury flinched. "She's coming here, today. But I'm not keeping tabs on her." His gruffness caused a startle among the crowd in the kitchen. No one remarked.

The doorbell rang at the front of the house. Marc stood, "I'll get it." He returned with Olivia Breckenridge in tow. "Look who I found." He smiled and winked at Middlebury.

"Hello everyone. It is so nice to see you all in such a better atmosphere." Gabriella poured a mug of coffee and offered it to her. She accepted but did not drink. She leaned and whispered something to Randolph. He shook his head in a slight movement intended not to be noticed.

"So, what does the FBI have to say about your escapades in Alaska?" Tiberius remarked.

"I just turned in my report. My supervisor was very positive about my working with all of you to uncover the source. The cruise line will get a report about the Salish Sea incident later today. I am to receive a commendation for the undercover work I did. Not that I relish any recognition."

Randolph stood and whispered in Olivia's ear. She beamed and held his hand. "We have something to announce," he said.

CHAPTER

7

Ryan and Jeremy escorted the twins to the elevator for the 23rd floor and their two queen-bed room. They had ordered desserts and had them sent to the room. As they waited, Kerrine wrapped an arm in Ryan's right arm. Kaliana held Jeremy's left hand. Separating them empowered the girls to control the situation.

When the door opened, three people evacuated before the two couples entered. The doors closed and the magical marathon for Ryan and Jeremy began. Neither had experienced such a celebration. Neither man spoke so as not to jinx the fantasy. As the doors opened on the correct floor, Kerrine and Kaliana exited first and waited for Ryan and Jeremy to escort them. They maintained a perfect spirit of excitement to instill the same in their companions. Neither girl planned an overnight stay and figured an hour or two of eating chocolate mousse and cheesecake and then sating male libidos was enough.

In the room, Ryan asked, "Shall we break into the mini bar?" He opened the cabinet which consisted of several individual bottles of various hard liquors and mixers. He pulled out a vodka and a rum. As he held them in his hand a knock on the door interrupted his intended charming of the twins. Jeremy answered the notification, and a cart entered with four desserts, an apple pie, a chocolate mousse and two cheesecakes with strawberry sauce. He handed the valet a ten-dollar bill.

"Thank you," he said as the man left. With the door closed, he engaged the privacy lock. "I would like to have a rum and coke."

Ryan picked up the clue. "I will have a vodka tonic." Directing the next question to their companions, he asked, "What would you like?"

Kerrine picked up the mousse and answered him, "Just this, thank you." She began a sensual licking of lips and deliberate, slow pace of ingesting her food. Kaliana chose a cheesecake and mimicked her sister. Shallow breaths escaped the two men, still holding tiny bottles. Tossing the bottles to one of the beds, each of them secured their preferred after's.

Kerrine placed her plate on the dresser and took Ryan's dessert from his hand. "Sit, and I will feed you." He climbed onto the bed with his head resting on the wall. She straddled his legs and licked her lips again. "Eat each bite slow and deliberate." She placed small portions in his mouth. Jeremy and Kaliana watched the foreplay as they finished their plates.

With nothing left to eat, Jeremy took the empty dishes and put them on the tray. As he turned to find Kaliana, she caressed his face with her hands and kissed his mouth slipping her tongue across his lips. "Do you want more dessert?" She said as she led him to the other bed. Removing her blouse and pants, she clasped his hand. Kerrine finished feeding Ryan and unbuttoned his shirt.

⋙ ⋙ ⋙

As they descended the elevator to the lobby of the Hyatt Kerrine asked, "Do you think they enjoyed their dessert?" Kaliana smiled and held her sister's hand.

"We did give them a night to remember. Who did you enjoy more?"

"Ryan was a little hasty. Jeremy spent a half hour with you before bursting forth in a gush of satisfaction."

"Yes, but Ryan slowed after his time with you. He was more attentive with me as was Jeremy with you."

"I do believe we met their needs for the evening. The pleas for us to stay the night were juvenile, though." As the doors opened, an idea emerged in Kerrine's mind.

"I wonder what conference they are attending? Maybe we should ask if it is here?"

"Wonderful idea." They approached the concierge desk and asked. No conference was scheduled for the meeting rooms, but a forensic training was at the Bellevue office of the King County

Forensic Investigative Services. The man stated that the hotel had a block of rooms set aside specifically for the attendees. "Thank you for the information," Kaliana said. They stepped outside to the valet and presented their ticket.

After paying and leaving a healthy tip, Kaliana drove away with Kerrine punching in the address for the house in Wendlesburg. She said, "According to this we should be at the house in an hour and 54 minutes, barring any unforeseen impediment."

The car's clock registered the time as 11:34 pm. The evening had stretched beyond the amount of time the twins had wanted to use, but the interlude had supplied a desired sating of appetites for food and fun. An early morning arrival in Kitsap County was not the original plan. Punching the number for the cell phone at the house, she waited for an answer.

"Where are you? I thought you were to be here this afternoon."

"We were waylaid by another incident. Nothing dangerous or alarming to our goals, but we are on our way and should be at the house in a couple of hours."

"Picking up stray dogs, again?"

"You need not worry about us. We are more than capable of handling our affairs."

"Yes, and affairs they are, but if you jeopardize our plans, there are consequences neither of you will want to endure."

"Do not threaten us," Kerrine said with a lowered timbre. "You are not our mother, nor our employer. We are coming to finish what was begun in Everett and on the cruise. You hired us and we will comply with our contract. But be assured you do not want to become an adversary." She clicked off the call.

"Problems at the house?" Kaliana said without glancing at Kerrine to see what her face exhibited. She knew the expression. Silence was the response as she drove 405 to I-5 and a run through Tacoma to Highway 16 and Kitsap County.

After a few minutes, Kerrine fashioned an answer. "She doesn't awaken well, I'm guessing. That and the fact we altered our arrival and upset her. She will learn or settle for a nice cup of tea and honey." Kaliana peeked at her for a hint of why she expressed the threat.

Interstate 5 had few vehicles on it as they drove past Federal

Way and Fife. Construction of the new lanes in Tacoma altered the route they expected, but the GPS unit flawlessly guided them to the proper exit.

Approaching the Tacoma Narrows Bridges, Kaliana spoke, "What if we decided to forfeit this contract and leave before anyone can trace us? What if we start in another area with clean slate and fresh names? We have plenty of money stashed away in the Cayman Islands. We have new passports and identities. Avoiding the Jefferson clan could be healthier for us."

Kerrine smiled, "That may be true, but we must complete what we start, or our reputation will be sullied. Our monetary compensation will not maintain a life style we want to have. Remember our goal. Accumulate enough funds so we can retire and become normal, average housewives and mothers when we are in our thirties."

"Yes, and I agree. However, if we are not successful in our pursuit of emasculating Mr. Jefferson and harming his family, our reputation may not matter."

"Are you worried or offering alternative scenarios for consideration?"

Kaliana glanced at Kerrine. "Just offering alternative scenarios." But her mind carried the worries of a failure of success and the consequences of a shortened future or one of incarceration. She desired neither. Her mind carried another trope of a future with a man who imperiled her life but excited her imagination of possible alternative scenarios.

Flashing blue lights appeared in the rear-view mirror. Kaliana checked the speedometer. The cruise control held the car at 63 miles-per-hour. The state patrol blared past them at better than 80. "Must be something happening ahead. I do hope we are not delayed."

Kerrine's eyes flashed open from the short nap she began after they crossed the bridge. "Nothing will stop us." She closed her eyes again.

At the Tremont exit to Port Orchard, several blue flashing state and county cars presided over a two-car accident on Tremont. "Someone forgot to stop at the sign."

Kerrine blinked, "What?"

"Nothing. Go back to sleep." At least she was garnering rest, thought Kaliana. The evening escapade had expended energy which now requested a nap for her, as well. She fought through the temptations of sleep.

As Highway 16 ended at the end of the bay and Highway 3 began, the remainder of the trip to their destination was quick. At the house, they entered to find the voice on the phone standing in the doorway. Her black hair and dark eyes shadowed in the porch light. "About time you arrived," she admonished.

Kerrine responded, "I'm not in the mood for a fight." They entered.

Kaliana asked, "Have the Jefferson's returned to their house?" The other woman shook her head. "Then we have time to prepare for their return."

CHAPTER

8

Randolph beamed. "We have something to announce." The crowd smiled a knowing smile but remained quiet for the news. "Olivia and I have decided to pursue a relationship. Delinda, I am staying here in Seattle. If you want to live with me, I'll find us a place to rent while I close everything in Minneapolis. Surprise?"

Delinda grasped her father and Olivia. "Thank you, Olivia. You have saved my father from the doldrums of life on a cruise ship."

"We started talking about a future together aboard the ship. On the plane, we continued to talk and decided we were better together than apart. I called my clinic in Minneapolis to say I was extending my stay in Washington. My partners were not happy but acquiesced. I'll return soon to sell my part of the practice to them and find a Realtor to sell my house. Joan, who do I contact to get my practice started here?"

Joan pondered a moment and then said, "I guess the Department of Licensing is as good a place as any. They can set up your medical credentials, a business license, and whatever is needed." He nodded.

"Thank you for everything. Delinda, we can discuss housing as soon as I can make arrangements." Olivia smiled.

Marc asked, "Well, misdirection, what are your plans for your future employment. I hear the FBI needs to find a honey manufacturing place. I also know the need for highly competent and experienced nurses."

"I am staying with the FBI."

"And, if I may be so bold as to ask, is Olivia Breckenridge your real name or an undercover alias?" Her brow furrowed, and eyes stared at Marc. He surmised her answer would shake up the group. After all, what undercover person uses a real name. Even Tim Knudson called himself Wiley when undermining Andrew Pepper in the investigation with Uncle Jerry in Everett, Washington.

"My name," Olivia paused, "is what you know it to be. I kept my real name for the nursing business. The FBI cloaked my identity from public records because the purpose of my training was for covert operations. I will be keeping the name unless a certain doctor desires a change in our status in the next few months."

Joan looked at Randolph. "Do you intend to desire a change in names?" Her grin belied the seriousness of the question.

"That's a bit fast for me. We haven't been out on a real date or consummated our future."

"Then ask her out." The chorus of voices blended in a harmony of tune to convince his query of her to commence.

Randolph remained quiet. Eyes widened as mouth gaped. Delinda finished the task. "Olivia, will you accept a dinner date with my father. If you wish an escort to provide nominal cover of the covert activity, Marcus and I will accompany you." Laugh burst from the others.

Marcus chimed in on the frivolity. "I do believe we would be chains of restriction, Dee."

Randolph answered before Olivia could respond. "I would be delighted to dine with you this evening." Turning to his daughter, "Without an escort."

Olivia answered, "I accept. We can celebrate the building of a great relationship and the satisfactory conclusion of a desperate voyage. Delinda, I agree with your Dad. We will not need an escort. I do think you two should have a quiet dinner together at a favorite spot. Marcus, a waterfront dinner at Anthony's Pier 66 and Bell Street Diner is deemed a respectable reward for enduring hardships no person should experience. My treat."

With arrangements made for two of the couples, a grateful mother proffered a third date. Gabby said, "Marc, you and Joan need time together without children. Your father and I will oversee Sarah and James while you two have a date night."

"Can we go to Red Robin?" James' plea for a night out met an affirming nod. All was set for the evening. The survival of the voyage from Hell delivered unity for more than just Marc Jefferson and his family. New relationships, forged in the fire of Vulcan, welded separate people into one component, comprised of alloys stronger than original metals. The challenge remained, however, of what future travesty would confront each of them.

Randolph and Olivia sat next to a window in the Salmon House on the north side of Lake Union, observing the lights of Seattle and boats as they motored through the channel to Portage Bay. He gazed at her as she watched the activity on the water. "Why me?" His question, filled with doubt, or more accurately, disbelief, attracted her attention. "Why did you want to pursue a relationship with me?"

Olivia smiled, "You dredged up my angst for sharing. I, like you, did not have someone in my life. You lost a wife to disease. I lost a companion to murder." Randolph's jaw dropped. "He was in the FBI when I met him. A bad guy shot him, and he ended up in my hospital in Cleveland. It wasn't a serious wound, and he recovered quickly. He asked me out, and I accepted. We were together for three years, long enough for me to have a daughter."

"What happened?"

"One night on a stakeout, three men confronted him and his partner while they sat in their car. They didn't even get a chance to draw their weapons. Both died of multiple wounds. I confronted his supervising agent about the safety of agents in the field. He understood and sympathized. His answer to me about encountering danger led me to apply to become an agent. He assisted with the application process, wrote a glowing reference, and convinced someone that I was what the FBI needed. That was sixteen years ago. My daughter and I moved here to Seattle, and I began working the criminal underground."

Randolph sat and stared. Olivia comprised more than an efficient nurse and woman. She was an enigma. A mystery to unravel. Fear and longing blended into a sensual desire to blurt out his love for her. But was it love, or his lack of verve to initiate his encountering of loss?

"I don't know what to say?"

Hands clasped him as she continued, "Say nothing at this moment. After dinner, fulfill our unrequited union, and then we can reflect on the consequences of being together." They ate Alaskan cod and salmon with wild rice and a concoction of various vegetables. Foregoing dessert, they split the bill, at her insistence, and returned to her house in Broadmoor. Olivia's daughter, Alanna, attended the University of Washington but lived at home rather than on campus. Insurance, gained with the death she and her mother endured, covered tuition and school expenses. Growing up without a father was a condition Olivia rued for Alanna. The house echoed the longing for another male to be part of their lives.

"Do you love me?" His question, begging a lie to support sharing the night with her, was more to assuage his hunger than to elicit truth.

"I suppose not, but that doesn't mean something sown in such fertile soil can't germinate. Do you love me, or are we playing the hook-up game?"

"I spent twenty-two years with my wife. She was the part of me I couldn't fill before I met her. Delinda is so much like her that I never confronted the possibility of another person replacing her."

"I will not replace her any more than you will replace Franklin. We are in a different chapter of life. Let's enjoy the moment and continue enjoying moments until we decide time is deflecting our true direction." Olivia led him to her bedroom.

"What about your daughter? You said she lives here. Won't she be confused by my staying overnight?"

"She is staying with a girlfriend at my request. She knows about you and wants me happy and content. She is not a prude about what adults do, nor is she unaware of who you are."

As they lay in the bed after consummation of the evening, each feared to say any word which might corrupt the perfection they constructed. Sleep overcame a lack of communication. Holding tight to naked warmth, each built resolve in dreams of being with each other and for each other. A summer cruise fling had blossomed into a field of wildflowers caressing a mountain hillside.

In the morning they showered and dressed. "Randolph, when I offered a spare room for you, I was playing innocent for an audience other than Alanna. I want you to share this room."

"Thank you. It makes my next request that much easier." He held her hands and asked, "Would you be my partner in life while we decide whether to legitimize our relationship or not?" She laughed and nodded.

"We're rather old to be acting like teenagers." She kissed him.

"Delinda and Marcus started it. Watching them become engrossed in their love for each other at such a depth in so short a time, caused me to reflect on why misery detained my moving forward after her death. I was frozen until they blazed a trail for me to follow. You were on that trail."

The conversation ended, and they made their way to the kitchen to find what remained of any foods which might be in the pantry. Was the larder filled or empty? Was their future?

CHAPTER

9

Olivia left the house, leaving Randolph to finish cleaning up the breakfast. A noise alerted him to another body roaming the house. He guessed Olivia forgot something and returned to retrieve it. He called out to her, but the person who appeared in the kitchen doorway was a younger vision.

"Hello," Alanna said. "You must be the doctor. Welcome to our home." Randolph blushed at her discovery of his being present.

"I'm sorry. This is an awkward way to meet you." She came in and sat in a chair at the table. "Yes, I'm Dr. Middlebury. You must be Alanna." She held out a hand which he clasped with reluctance as the blush covering his mortification departed.

"Do you and Mom like each other?" He sat in a chair across from her.

The warmth of his face extended to more of his body. She was as beautiful as any female he had met. Although her hair was lighter than her mother's and longer, her face imitated Olivia. Her blouse hung loosely across her bodice, the top three buttons unhooked.

"I think so. We want to explore a future together. Would you be upset?" She reached out her hands and stroked hair from her face.

"No. I would rather like to have a man in the house. It's been a long time for Mom to be alone. I don't remember my father although her stories revealed much to me of how she felt about him." Randolph flinched at her openness.

"My daughter thinks we make a cute couple." Her hand slid away to rest in her lap. He inhaled a gasp of air.

"I understand she's here in Seattle with a guy she met on the ship. Does she plan on living here?" A coy smile appeared as if she discovered the possibility of gaining a sister.

His breathing shortened and shallowed. "We haven't worked out those details." She stood and moved toward the door.

"I apologize. Mother is not against sharing." Her whisper confused him. She departed without saying another word. Alone, he stayed to be sure he was truly alone. Silence reigned as he sat pondering the young woman who did not flinch at a stranger invading her home. Driving the rental vehicle to the Jefferson house, he parked and sat pondering his next move with Delinda.

He opened the door and faced the challenge inside the house. Was he sure he could convince all the women in his life? He knocked and waited. Waited for a chance to run. Waited for an entrance.

Gabbie appeared. "Welcome, Doctor Middlebury. Please, come in." She stepped aside for a clear path to purgatory.

"Is Delinda awake?" He had much to say and little confidence. His night with Olivia rebuilt a sense of worth missing far too long.

"She and Marcus on out on a morning run. They should be back soon."

He sat at the kitchen table as Gabby poured a mug of coffee. "Are Marc or Joan here?"

"They're upstairs. They're leaving for the ferry to Wendlesburg within the hour." He stood and carried his mug to the stairs, hesitated, and then decided to wait.

Returning to the kitchen, he asked Gabby, "How serious a person is your grandson?"

"That's an odd question. Are you worried about how he will treat Delinda? He's a smart young man and appears to adore your daughter. He reminds me of his father when he chased Joan around until she caught him." He furrowed his brows and then smiled.

"I have a housing solution for us, I think. I must clear it with Olivia, but I don't think she'll mind. Oh, I met her daughter, Alanna. Very confident person for an eighteen-year-old. Very much like Delinda."

The door blasted open, and two sweaty, panting people entered. "Hi, Dad." Delinda declined a hug to keep her father dry. "Been here long?"

"No. Can we go somewhere alone and talk?"

"Let me shower and change clothes. I want to talk with you, too." She disappeared, leaving Marcus drying with a paper towel. His hushed demeanor confused Randolph, who watched him, frowning.

"Dr. Middlebury," he said, "you have a great daughter. I want you to know. I would do anything to protect her from harm. What happened in Alaska can't happen here." A closed, straight mouth and slight nod was the response. Randolph had doubts. Safety was compromised on what should have been a safe and secure cruise ship. He wanted her with him while he lived at Olivia's house.

Marc and Joan joined the crowd after placing suitcases in the foyer. Sarah and James followed. "Mom, thanks for housing us. We're leaving as soon as our ride is here. Where's Dad?"

"He's meeting with his captain to begin the search for suspicious deaths. He'll contact you later about his findings." She handed an envelope to her son. "He asked me to drive you to the ferry."

Marc turned to his son. "Are you coming home tonight?"

"It depends on what Delinda wants. I want to stay with her. Or can she come over with me?"

Marc and Joan understood their relationship had a physical component. They looked at each other wondering about thoughts of sleeping arrangements in Wendlesburg. Joan answered, "Yes, bring her along." Randolph frowned.

"I was hoping to spend the evening with my daughter," he said.

"Oh. Of course, I'm sorry." Joan placed hands together in front of face. Marc signaled to migrate to the car with luggage in tow. After goodbyes and promises from Marcus to return to Kitsap with or without Delinda, they left. The house calmed to an eerie, awkward silence between Randolph and Marcus.

"I'm going to get cleaned up. I don't hear the shower, so I'm guessing Dee is done and I can use the bathroom." He left Randolph sitting at the table.

Taking out his cell phone, he punched the quick dial for the clinic in Minneapolis. He left a message with the receptionist for either of his business partners to contact him. Delinda appeared from the hallway. She sat with her father, no smile, fingers interlaced and arms on the table.

"That was the clinic," he explained. "I'll need to go home and make arrangements."

"I'm not going with you." Her face retained a steeled countenance.

"I didn't think so. However, I want to ask Olivia if you can stay with me at her house until I can get us a place." He waited for a response. None came. "She has a daughter who is the about same age as you. Her name is Alanna. I met her earlier this morning."

"Are you sure you want me in the middle of your life with Olivia? Don't get me wrong, because I think she is the best thing to happen to you in the last year. I want the same thing with Marcus." His dimples cracked in as his mouth firmed. She unfolded fingers and placed hands in her lap.

"I have to ask her first. She went to work. You'd like Alanna. She attends the University of Washington."

"Dad, I want a place of my own, so I can come and go as I please. I don't want you to worry about me. What happened in Skagway is over. Marcus and I are seeing a psychologist, and we are getting through it together. I can stand on my own."

Randolph's eyes stared at the floor. "You've been stronger than me ever since your mother died. I wasn't sure I could stand on my own. I'm still not sure. Please, let me talk to her. Maybe you can attend school at a community college and enter a four-year school at semester or next fall." He stood, as did Delinda. He placed his hands on her shoulders. "I almost lost you. I can't live without you in my life. How can I live if I lose the one person whom I know best?"

Delinda put her arms around her father. "You won't. You need to know Marcus better. We are a couple and will not be separated."

"Oh, the proverbial I'm not losing a daughter, I'm gaining a son?" They split and laughed at the comment. Marcus arrived freshly washed and dressed in jeans and a polo shirt.

"Did I miss something?" Delinda kissed him and smiled.

"No, Dad and I were talking about where I should live."

"Mom offered you our house. You can stay in my room since I'll be here in Seattle."

"Dad wants me with him. He's going to find us a place."

Marcus perked up. "Here in Seattle?"

She turned her head and eyed him at a slant with one eyebrow raised. "Why yes, I do believe that is the intention."

Randolph snorted, "You make a fine couple of young lust-filled teenagers. At least her mother would have approved of you, Marcus. I'll have to get used to the fact my daughter is no longer a little girl."

"Yes, sir. I do believe she is no longer a little girl."

The confab ended with Randolph leaving the house for Broadmoor and Olivia's house. He saw little reason to chaperone his daughter. She was unwilling to be away from Marcus. How was he to fair? He had so much change happening. He wondered if he was making the right decisions about moving, about the clinic, about Olivia.

CHAPTER

10

The Washington State Crime Lab forensic conference commenced with a small sampling of case studies which baffled local officials. One case involved a man in his thirties who died of an apparent heart attack. He had no history of pulmonary problems, was physically fit, and died in a motel in Edmonds, Washington, alone. A woman, the manager had seen with him, had disappeared and was a person of interest.

Another case included the deaths of two drivers for a floral delivery service at an Aurora Avenue motel. Recordings of the arrival showed two women with the men. The women left alone less than two hours later. The men were found dead of apparent heart failure.

Three deaths with no true reason for the occurrences. Ryan and Jeremy listened intending to learn what evidence existed and what trails had yet to be followed. They had arrived from Portland, Oregon to discover three cases of mysterious deaths from suspected heart failures. Despite the previous evening human activity with two of the most beautiful women they had ever met, the focus for the day cleared their heads of the images of the naked bodies and their creative actions.

Forensic science had new tools and procedures for the elimination of cold cases or the frustration for the lack of closure. Ryan had graduated from medical school at the University of Oregon, completed his residency and began his internship with the Portland forensic lab. Jeremy was back home as a graduate of the University of Washington School of Medicine. He found a practice in Tigard, Oregon which hired him to help with difficult illnesses and subsequent deaths. The work directed his attention to forensic science.

As the conference waned in the early afternoon, several of the attendees decided to meet at a local watering hole and forget about investigating anything except alcohol and the opposite sex. Most of them were male, but several intelligent, talented investigators were female. Ryan and Jeremy stated they would join them later.

"Why'd you want to stay here?" Jeremy asked.

"Don't you think this is interesting?" Ryan answered.

"Yeah, but we're missing out on the fun." Ryan waved off the comment. He picked up the folder containing the evidence of the two drivers. As he fingered through the pictures from the video surveillance, his jaw fell. Jeremy noticed the reaction. "What is it?" Ryan held up a blow-up of a scene from the video feed. Jeremy studied it for a moment.

"Do you see it?" he waited for his friend to discover what he thought he had found. "Look at those girls, closely."

"Yeah, I see, but the picture isn't very good."

"They are identical." Ryan snatched the picture from Jeremy. Picking up a magnifying lens, he pondered an idea which filled his mind with a curious thought.

"What are you thinking?" Jeremy stared at his companion. The density of any memory of what Ryan conceived from the observation eluded him.

"Jeremy, the two ladies we entertained last night could pass for these two." He pressed the picture into his face. "Look." He handed the glass to him. Rummaging through other pictures, he found one with the body shapes. The curves were a mimic of their late afternoon and evening hookups.

Jeremy shook his head. "Lots of girls could pass for our dessert companions. I don't see what you see."

"Alright, I'll ask one of the detectives who they think the women are." He left to corral one of the speakers.

Jeremy studied the pictures again. He wished they had been smart enough to photograph the ladies from dinner. An idea trailed his remorse for the lack of thinking in his head last night. He had been interested only in dessert.

Ryan returned with a detective who looked as if Ryan was a kook. Jeremy handed him the folder of the Seattle crime scene. "This is one of the cases I'm working. Your friend here thinks he knows these girls."

Jeremy responded with a short shake of his head. "I can't be sure, but I have an idea." He gritted his teeth and looked at Ryan. "We picked up twins at the airport last night. We had dinner together and then dessert in our room later. Neither of us thought to memorialize our rendezvous with pictures." Ryan frowned as he realized where this was going. "What if the Hyatt has a security system which has them and us on it?"

"Good idea," the detective said. "I leave it to you to follow up on this lead. It'll probably be nothing, but I've solved cases with less."

"I guess this means we're not going to the party," Ryan said. They returned to the Hyatt to search for a manager or any person who had authority. Asking at the concierge, they were directed to the management office on the upper concourse. When the two men introduced themselves, they displayed badges for an authoritative quality to convince the secretary they needed a manager. The afternoon was passing, and office hours were ending. They had to get to security.

"May I help you," a tall man with a European accent said.

"Yes," Ryan interjected a tone of impatience, "we are with the forensic science conference at the King County office here in Bellevue. We were studying a case which happened earlier this summer in Seattle. A picture containing the images of two women marshaled a memory in me of two women I saw here last night. I want to compare them with the photo evidence." He explained the need to watch security footage.

"This is a rather unusual request," the manager said as he hesitated to accede to allowing them access to the recordings.

"Do you need any other item to compel a proper response to our legal request for cooperation in a criminal investigation?" His badge hung from his shirt as if he was lead detective. The manager nodded and led them to the security station downstairs and away from visitor traffic. "Thank you."

They directed the security technician to play the recording of the previous afternoon lobby. Jeremy yelled, "Stop. Stop there." He pointed at the screen which showed the main entryway from the valet area. Two women with identical features walked across the floor to toward the concierge. One looked at the camera as if to say, 'Take a good look.' "Can you print a frame from that time?"

The technician nodded. After deciding the best showcase of the women, he produced a picture. Ryan and Jeremy thanked the person and left.

Returning to the forensic conference, they found the detective and gave him the picture. Comparing the two frames was not conclusive. Although features had familiarity, no court of justice would have accepted the argument they were the same people.

"Does this development mean anything to you?" Ryan asked the question as a way of entering the search for possible decisive role in the hunt for the killers of two men. Or as the detective might say, alleged murderers. No one was sure the women had done anything to them. The evidence displayed sexual activity and no struggle or fight. The room was neat, clean, and did not indicate a female presence. Evidence of tea, honey, and crackers remained. Had the deaths been foul play? The case for murder was inconclusive.

"What if the bodies are reexamined? Any toxins or drugs found in their systems?" Ryan folded his arms, a habit formed in childhood as he tried extracting information for his satisfaction.

The detective opened the folder and read. Closing it, he said, "No drugs, nothing but remnants of the foods they had eaten and the coffee and tea they drank."

"Did they have any medical history which indicated any weaknesses?" The detective handed Ryan the folder.

"You're the doctor. You read it." He move to leave but turned back. "And put the folder back on the table, without the new picture. It's not part of the package." He departed.

Together the men read the medical examiner's report which had less information than either thought appropriate. No drugs. No standard toxins or poisons. Nothing but the usual leaving after eating a snack and having a sexual encounter. Neither dead man was out of shape or unhealthy. Something didn't add up.

Jeremy concluded his perusal and offered an opinion. "I think we have found the right women in the motel photo. All we have to do is find them."

Ryan expressed a lighthearted guffaw. "Yeah, we'll call them up and ask for another date. After we bang for a couple hours or an entire day, we arrest them on suspicion of murder. Our single problem is a lack of knowledge of their whereabouts." He sat in a chair. "Forensic science has not been used effectively by us. I feel like such a dupe."

"Me, too." Jeremy sat next to his friend and fellow idiot. So close, and yet still they remained far from having any chance of riding the evidence to the end. Where were they? Who were they? "Why were we singled out for their evening tryst?"

CHAPTER

11

Delinda stood at the door as she watched her father leave. When the car was gone, she closed the door, staring at it, wondering. Her father was important to her. She watched his descent into a languid life deprived of joy after her mother's death. "Marcus," she said, "I don't know what to do. He wants me as a companion, a reminder of what we lost when Mom died. A reminder of Mom."

Marcus held her hands. Venting fueled his passion for being her companion, a soul mate. She had lost a mother, an event he wanted to never endure. He suffered his father's recent near-death experiences at the hands of people aboard the cruise ship. In the spring a war with a drug cartel in Everett involved several shootings. A kidnapping of both father and grandfather was as close as he thought prudent to relive.

Their kidnapping, rape and attempted murder in Skagway brought all her emotions to a head. His mind carried scars, as well.

"He'll be fine. I think he wants to be sure you're safe. He almost lost you."

"And your parents almost lost you, too."

Sitting in the living room, nothing credible about a positive future for them fostered ideas. The only thing which mattered was the partnership they formed aboard the Salish Sea. A partnership welded together in travesty and death. Suffer together, not alone, seemed the proper mantra. The time making love to each other was short, fulfilling, and momentary. Fears returned to her as much as to him.

Delinda asked, "Do you really love me as much as you say? Do you want to have a life together? Will you be for me as much as with me?"

Marcus reacted as if wounded in his heart. "I said what I meant. I fell for you almost the first moment I saw you. When we made love for the first time in your cabin on the ship, I knew then I wanted a future with you. This is not some guy fling with a beautiful girl and then on to then next conquest. You have conquered me."

"Then make love to me. I want what Mom and Dad had. I want what I see in your family. I want to be the kind of parents we have. I know nothing is guaranteed in life, but we have now, and that is the only time we have."

He stood and offered a hand. Delinda accepted and stood. They ascended the stairs to the room they shared. No one had questioned the relationship as anything less than permanent. Marriage was not required for sharing a bed. Reality proved a better consummation than any religious ritual. They removed their clothing and lay on the bed, holding each other as one body, one mind, one soul. Making love was more than a physical act. They enjoyed the passion of sex, but now was more about relishing the promises of future days and months building into years and decades.

No fear of reprisals from a grandmother soon to return or a father, whose own passion had acquired new meaning, interfered with a slow and deliberate sating of something more than lust. They were one being.

In the afterglow they remained still, listening to the silence enveloping the house. Peace and safety bridged the chasm from fear and angst attributable to surviving a vacation in Hell.

"Marcus, Delinda, I'm home." The voice registered in the far reaches of minds wandering fields of cosmic openness. They rose, dressed, and joined Gabriella.

"Where's your father?" Gabby asked Delinda.

"He said he was going to Olivia's."

Marcus added, "Mom and Dad got on the ferry without any problems, I'm assuming."

"Yes. They want you to come over tonight and celebrate a last hurrah of summer. All about making peace with the cruise and what happened." Gabby paused and then said, "It wasn't much of a vacation for your Aunt Lydia and me as our husbands tried to convince us it was. They wanted to help your father and taking us assuaged guilt."

"Grams, I'm glad you came to Alaska. We would have remained targets to push Dad and Mom into a non-survivable situation. You and Aunt Lydia are the best."

"Mrs. Jefferson, I agree. You have been a most gracious host for someone you hardly knew. I love you and your whole family." Delinda squeezed Marcus's hand. "Especially, this one."

"I have been a cop's wife for a long time. I've watched danger flaunt an ugly appearance with my husband, my son, my brother-in-law, and my nephew. To have you two absorbed into the underworld became a Hell I was unwilling to submit to." She hugged them, letting them go because life continued. The hug was a reminder of all the love which others challenged.

Delinda asked, "Marcus, will you take me to Olivia's. I want to see if the arrangement can work for us. Then I want to find a school and apply."

They left the house oblivious to any dangers which lurked around them. Perceived or real, life was not a comfort zone of safety, once a mainstay of both their lives.

"Do you have an address?"

"Dad gave me one this morning before he left. It's in Broadmoor."

"Ooh, that's a nice neighborhood. I've driven through it but never had a reason to stop."

They arrived to see a smaller house with a neat yard and well-kept gardens. The rental car sat in the driveway. Nothing appeared ominous. No other cars were in the street or other drives. Marcus surveyed the area.

"What do you think?" Delinda asked.

"I think I'll move in, too."

Parking and vacating the car, they walked to the front door and rang the bell. Randolph opened it and grinned. "Want to live here?" Delinda scowled.

"Not so fast, Dad. Let me look around." They entered the foyer and discovered a small living room, dining area, and kitchen with a breakfast nook. A hallway led to bedrooms.

Marcus stepped into the living room surveying the decor. As they explored the house, other people arrived.

Olivia and her daughter found three startled beings in a back bedroom. "Hello, everyone," she said. "This is my daughter, Alanna. Alanna, I would like you to meet Randolph and Delinda Middlebury, and Marcus Jefferson."

Alanna spoke next, "I met your doctor earlier this morning." She held out her hand "Pleasure to make your acquaintance." She shook Delinda and Marcus's hands.

"Well, what do you think of my humble abode?"

Marcus offered, "You live in a very nice neighborhood. Pretty upscale for a cop." He grinned, knowing his own family lived in a better part of Wendlesburg.

"Yeah, I took bribe money and invested it." She winked. Delinda gasped. Marcus chuckled.

Randolph rocked his head back and forth. "One shouldn't joke about that. You were able to accept money from those killers on the ship. Did you? As well as taking a salary from American Pacific? How long have you lived here?"

Alanna entered the fracas. "Don't yell at my Mom. She was telling a joke."

Olivia waved her hand in a calming manner. "I make good money as a Federal Agent. You needn't worry about any money from Pepper or anyone else in the cartel. To keep my integrity intact, I placed all the money in a fund. Insurance proceeds from the death of Alanna's father assured my financial future. I invested and have been using the dividends as a cushion for extraordinary expenses such as this house. Are we clear about my honesty?"

Randolph nodded. "I apologize. I had no reason to doubt you. Can I still live here?"

Marcus realized a challenge festered with his romance of Delinda. Each came from different histories, but the problem lay in the world in which they now lived. How self-reliant could they be? Was their relationship sturdy enough to handle everyday common situations if they disagreed? Should they rely on each other in their living arrangement and not borrow problems from family?

Alanna spoke, breaking his train of thought. "Mom, if Dr. Middlebury is to live with us, is his daughter moving in also?" Reading her intent of the question was hard. She masked any disapproval or annoyance. Marcus looked at Delinda and her father, then at Alanna. What arrangement had they discussed? He had been with Dee all morning. Nothing suggested a problem until now.

Olivia answered her. "We haven't made any arrangements. Randolph living here is temporary. He needs to return to Minneapolis and close his medical practice and dispose of his house."

Randolph interceded, "Alanna, we do not presume to be a burden to you or your mother." Facing his daughter, "Would you be willing to live here until we find a place of our own?" Without looking at Olivia, he asked, "Olivia, would it be acceptable to you?" He did not see the furrow forming above her eyes. Marcus did. Dee squeezed her eyes, shutting out any confrontation forthcoming.

A chink in the armor of Delinda Middlebury? Marcus feared a fault line would create a chasm of anger between father and daughter. Was he next? Did the doctor and nurse/FBI agent uncover a fester which might derail a future with Dee?

CHAPTER

12

The ferry arrived in Wendlesburg with little fanfare. The Jefferson clan walked the few blocks to the sheriff's office where the car remained while they sailed to Alaska. As they placed suitcases in the trunk, Marc said, "I'm going to check in, then we can head home." He started for the door.

"Don't let anyone talk you into working." Joan admonished. Marc rocked his head. Entering the building, he headed for the division commander's office.

"About time you returned. We got word of the tragedy aboard your cruise ship. I'm glad you survived." Undersheriff, Brian Driscoll, stood from his desk and planted a warm welcome hand on Marc's shoulder. "We kept an eye on your house as requested, but nothing happened. As for your other request, to gather deaths on the peninsula that were ruled as naturally occurring but had possible suspicious causes, we found only two."

"That's good. I'll check them out from my office when I return tomorrow or the next day. I'm supposed to be on vacation. Fellington know I'm back?"

"Not yet, but I'm sure it won't be long."

"Thanks, Brian. I appreciate the discretion. Someone in our area is supplying a deadly form of honey and tea to contract killers." He left the office for his car and family and a ride home to his sanctuary. His call for help in pursuing the only lead he had, would come at a difficult time. Joan wanted him to seek a counselor, something she was going to do. Sarah and James would be part of her sessions. A debrief of the cruise from Hell could only help.

When he returned to the car, Joan asked "No work?"

"Nothing yet. I'm on vacation." The group laughed.

At the house, they unpacked the car and entered through the kitchen door, disarming the alarm system. Sarah and James left for their rooms and unpacking. Marc and Joan closed the door of their room and emptied suitcases. As they moved about, Marc smelled a familiar scent lost to his brain for a moment. The lingering effect of something triggered nothing for him to recall, but he figured the closed rooms contained remnants of forgotten bouquets.

"Marc, I'm going to call the senior center to check in. I promise not to work." Her hand rose in a boy scout pattern. He chuckled.

Their lives returned to a familiar pattern as quick as a play concludes its run. Slow and steady.

As the morning progressed to afternoon and lunch became an aim for kids, Joan declared each person was on their own for foraging what remained in pantry or refrigerator/freezer. Peanut butter without the benefit of jelly sufficed for two teenagers. Individual chip bags augmented the fare. Marc found a frozen pot pie.

"James, please clean up the kitchen for your mother. I'm going outside and work in the yard. Sarah, you help your brother." Groans accompanied his edict.

Outside plants bloomed in gardens and grass needed mowing. As Marc prepped for cutting the grass, flower scents assaulted his nose and remembrances cleared of an odor of jasmine. A fragrance from a cruise fraught with peril caused by two women whose focus was to kill him. He thought, "Funny how the brain works." He dismissed memories from the ship as meanderings of his head wound. The ache remained although the flesh had healed. Joan had stated the crack in his skull might take more time. Jasmine? Where were they? Kerrine and Kaliana faded from the scene in Anchorage. Dock crew members must have aided in the escape, but little evidence meant no arrests.

As he completed mowing the lawn and put away the equipment, he thought Joan might like to have fresh cut flowers. Roses bloomed, and chrysanthemums and zinnias displayed their colors. Rhododendrons and azaleas grew in several places in the yard. Wondering about the report the Alaska Crime Lab sent home with Tiberius and Jerry, he thought about the toxin which is present in the leaves, flowers, stems, and roots of the plant. No one he knew had ever been sickened by the bush. The common knowledge was; the rhodie could make an animal or person ill. What type of plant did he have in his yard? He clipped a few samples to be examined and clipped other flowers for the bedroom to offset memories. His mind wondered where those twins had gone?

Movement on the computer screen showed Joan in the bedroom, alone. Marc had placed his clothing in the laundry basket, or drawers and closet as needed. He had left her alone, and another screen showed him talking with his children. Kaliana muted the volume on the computer. He then went to the backyard and began mowing the lawn. She mused about his domestic tasks.

"He looks so vulnerable thinking we're gone." Her sister stood by her and watched for a minute. Turning to look at her, Kaliana continued, "When do we want to implement our plan?"

Kerrine moved away, "Soon. But patience is needed for them to relax and let down their guard. We'll keep watch on them for now."

The third person living in the rented house three blocks from the Jefferson house spoke, "As soon as we can complete the elimination of that man, the better."

"True, but we should wait. Forcing him out before we are ready would result in another disaster like on the cruise ship. I am sorry about what happened to your sister. I liked Jarina." Cassandra Camacho slipped a tear at the mention of the name. She wanted to accomplish as much as Jarina had. Now, she wanted revenge.

A view of the children's bedrooms revealed more than expected and yet the rooms needed cameras despite the possibility of inappropriate video. Bathrooms were monitored, also. The twins relished the expected nudity of adults but not the children. They wanted only to follow the movements of the family to implement a plan to acquire a time when someone was vulnerable to kidnapping. Their plan needed the information.

"He's done outside," Kaliana said. "He clipped some of the Rhododendrons in his yard." She faced Kerrine. "Do you think he knows?"

"Knows what?"

"About our honey?" Kerrine studied the video again. She watched Marc fondle the leaves and stems as if testing them for information. He then clopped off a small branch from each of three different bushes.

"So what? He doesn't know we're here. And when he finds out, it will be too late." Kerrine clicked the live feed on again.

Cassandra watched with an underlying rage at the man responsible for Jarina's death. American Pacific Crusies contacted her when the Salish Sea docked in Anchorage five days ago. She asked that her sister be shipped to a California mortuary. When funds transferred, the proper paperwork was completed and faxed.

The scramble to rent a property close enough to the Jefferson house before the venture on the high seas required a finesse garnered from years of working land and home deals in northern California. Cassandra was only six years older than the twins and a decade removed from her sister. She was smart, educated, and skilled at several business ventures. Now she focused attention on the one venture consuming days and nights.

With the aid of a friend who shared occasional nights with her, she installed the video and audio in the Jefferson house. Breaking in without tripping alarms had instituted a skill she gained in real estate ventures when home system operations remained active after sellers vacated. Bypassing a power source to neutralize the code box without tripping the alarm was not easy. A few previous trial and errors because of her agent status with house owners prevented any fear of failure.

Marc showed up inside the house and delivered the roses and other blooms to Joan. She kissed him and followed him into the bathroom. The three women played voyeurs for the shower scene and the accompanying action of a soft porn movie when Marc stripped and turned on the water. He convinced Joan to join him.

Later, the twins finalized a timetable of actions to isolate a member of the family. Blackmail now became an option. What better way to forge an agreement than through threatening to expose the movie to the Internet? Children videos required some intervention by other remaining members of Andrew Pepper's cartel. Few had freedom, and some were now deceased. No trail remained of the lethal drug cartel which collapsed after the invasion by the Jefferson family.

Marc, his father, uncle, and a cousin caused more havoc than any other law enforcement group. Snohomish County sheriff deputies had been on the payroll and looked out for invaders. They, too, were history, incarcerated in prisons, isolated from the criminals they had arrested.

Jeremais Jefferson's undercover sting crashed without financial support. His death, a suicide, had been the solace afforded to Pepper and his cohorts. But Marcus and Tiberius Jefferson unmasked the fraud perpetrated on the illicit group. Jerry had faked his death, and the resulting assault on the warehouses destroyed the cartel.

A vacation aboard a cruise ship by Marc and Joan with their three children happened to be on the one vessel used by the cartel to smuggle material into Seattle from Vancouver, B. C. Somehow, the quickly constructed plan to poison the family ended with the inadvertent death of a guest lecturer and author, James Blackthorne. Modifications of the plan resulted in the destruction of the smuggling operation and the death of three crew members and the capture of the captain.

The twins' hearts pulsed with anticipation of exacting revenge.

CHAPTER

13

Jeremy and Ryan studied the picture of the twins from the hotel security camera and the official image of the suspects in the death of two floral van drivers. "What can we do next?" Ryan asked. "We think we have the right girls and no way of finding them or connecting them to this investigation." He flapped the folder holding the remaining pieces of information.

Jeremy nodded. "That detective wasn't very polite about sharing. He brings it to the conference to demonstrate the complexity of forensics but refuses to get new ideas."

Returning to a class about poisons, the intrepid investigators listened to accounts of odd uses of naturally occurring plant and animal toxins which history bore witness to inventive people eliminating obstacles to their insidious goals. The Washington State Patrol Forensic Laboratory director Donovan McAvoy directed the listening crowd to think 'outside of the box' when certain convoluted cases popped into the hopper.

Ryan whispered to Jeremy, "Trite statements. But so true." The air cooled as the HVAC clicked on. A twitter of complaints wafted through the room. McAvoy stopped speaking. Was he waiting for the machines to stop humming or for the negativity to wane?

The lights dimmed as if a video was to begin. Nothing happened. An odor of rotting garbage polluted the air. The smell tasted of over-aged cheese and other refrigerator anomalies.

After what seemed to be minutes but was only thirty seconds, the room heating returned, the lights came on, and the odors abated. McAvoy scanned the room. Ryan and Jeremy tracked the direction of his views. Several of the attendees eyed others near them. Had they witnessed a diabolical plot to ruin the lives of investigators or a planned distraction to enliven the conference?

"So, what did you all observe? What senses did you empower for discovering the reasons for what just happened?" McAvoy scanned the audience again. A murmur arose. "Well? Anybody have anything to say?" Silence enveloped the cavernous room.

Jeremy shrugged shoulders and glanced at Ryan. "Sir," he said as he stood, "outside of the box, this was an attempt to get us to clear our heads and reflect on the situation presented to us. I don't agree with the assumption it was outside of any box."

Donovan McAvoy uttered a loud, gruff cough. "And who might you be?"

"My name is Jeremy Caldwell, sir."

"Your analysis is that this was a ruse of a sort?"

"No sir, not a ruse. I think we witnessed an attempt to awaken our brains. To me, that is not outside the box." Jeremy glanced again at Ryan, who shrugged his shoulders.

"What do you consider to be outside the box, Mr. Caldwell?" All eyes focused on the young forensic analyst. Heat rose in his cheeks and neck. A drop of perspiration dribbled beside his left eye.

"Sir, Mr. Wittingham and I have a possible link to a case which occurred in Seattle less than a month ago. We are not privy to the notes of the acting detective, so speculation as to the involvement of two women we met yesterday has to be outside the box."

Ryan stood to assure Jeremy. He spoke, "We met and had dinner with a set of twins who are possible persons of interest in the case."

"And you know this because...?" McAvoy planted his hands in vise grip upon the podium.

"A picture from the security video at the crime scene has a remarkable similarity to the twins. The picture shows two women who look alike. Same dark hair, body structure, and facial features. Although the graininess of the enlargement is not crystal clear, I believe, as does Mr. Caldwell, that the women we met may be the same as the video feed."

"Do you know these women's names?"

Eyes locked on each other and then the floor. They answered simultaneously. "No, sir."

"I do believe you are correct, Mr., ah..."

"Caldwell, sir. And my friend is Mr. Wittingham."

"Yes, Caldwell. I do believe you are outside of the box and outside of any possibility of a future involving this case. No names. You had dinner. And I am assuming, outside of the box, a liaison for extracurricular activities. And no names. Did you get any information about them which might have been useful? Besides their names?"

Each of the young men shook heads and sat. They remained quiet for the remainder of the session, another half hour.

As the gathering dissolved upon the final analysis of the events which appeared before Jeremy's fateful experience, McAvoy signaled Jeremy and Ryan to come to him. Reluctant to hear another tongue thrashing, they hesitated. A second gesture convinced them to acquiesce.

The forensic director finished packing away materials used in the session. Ryan and Jeremy waited. As he placed the last of his things in a box, McAvoy asked, "What do know about the deaths of two men in a hotel on Aurora Avenue in Seattle?" Ryan and Jeremy looked at each other and then Donovan McAvoy.

Realizing to which case he referred, Ryan spoke, "Not much. We saw the case file earlier and spoke with the lead detective."

"These two women you enjoyed accompanying, why do you believe they are important?"

Jeremy answered, "Sir, we saw the picture from the security feed and thought they were a match. We asked at the Hyatt to see the video feed from their security cameras. We printed a picture and compared it to the crime scene photo. We believe they're a match."

"And the detective? What did he think? I assume you showed him."

"Yes, but he dismissed it."

"Too big a problem in some departments. Not so much a lack of investigation as a lack of effort. Too many cases and not enough human recources."

Ryan asked, "Is this an important case? It seems to me that the death of two men is a routine matter. I sense a need for more intensity, more vigor for resolution."

"Several people have died mysterious deaths, and these two are the latest. I have a friend in Snohomish County who was investigating a crime group in Everett a couple of years ago. The group employed twin hit persons - young women with the ability to lure a person to their fatal meeting. We were not sure of the reason or method of killing until recently. Now we need to find these women and trace the source of their lethal weapon."

Jeremy pondered the situation. "Our ladies are the twins you seek." Donovan nodded.

"It is imperative to get as much as we can. If you have a clear picture of the twins, we have improved the odds of finding them. They are masters at hiding in plain sight." Ryan removed the picture from a folder he carried and handed it to the director.

"If these ladies are our perpetrators, this may help. May I keep this?" A nodded answered his query.

"Sir, what if we are unable to locate them? We met them at SeaTac airport. Would the security feeds there help?" Ryan said.

Jeremy added, "Maybe they flew in from someplace and tracking their flight could help."

"I need you two to stay in Seattle. You're from Portland, right?" They bobbed heads wondering how he knew. Visible name tags solved the mystery. "I'll contact your office and see about you assisting us here. These pieces of information may be crucial. You see, thinking outside the box has improved our odds."

As Ryan and Jeremy left the ballroom and headed to the Hyatt during the break, and idea exploded in Jeremy's head. "They had to have driven here. Maybe they parked with the valet and left another trail."

Ryan slapped his friends back. "You're a genius. A license plate number may be just the ticket, so to speak."

"We should check for fingerprints in the room. They may have left some behind. Although, Director McAvoy alluded to their ability to stay incognito."

As they crossed the street, another thought invaded Ryan. "What if we could lure them out of hiding? What if we used social media to include all of King County to search for them? Someone must have seen them or knows who they are. Let's run through proper channels to get permission, so we aren't infringing on anyone's territory."

The men headed for the valet and more leads. At the window, they asked who they should see to get parking records. They were sent to the same office as before when they wanted to see the security video. Excitement enthused their quest. Nothing in Portland had measured up to the quest now engaging them.

In the business office, they found the same secretary who asked them to wait while she connected with her boss. Time crawled along as if a slug found an alluring bit of sustenance and slithered toward it. After several minutes, the same man with the European accent joined them. "How may I be of help to you now?"

14

Eden approached her beekeeper, Bernice Harapat, and asked, "Do we have any honey left from the last rhododendron flowering?"

"I don't think so. Chris sent the last batches to the processors for mixing and clarification. Did you need some?"

"No. Just checking inventory." Eden walked on past the beekeeper. She eyed the boxes of bees wondering whether they understood their role in the world of food finance. Her head rocked imperceptive to Harapat, who held a water bottle which she inserted into the top of a hive.

Returning to Bernice, she asked, "When do you decide to switch the hives in the small greenhouse? You know, from bees to bumbles? How soon do you decide?"

Bernice continued inserting water bottles as she answered, "Usually Chris lets me know he wants bumbles only in the warehouse when the rhodies and azaleas are isolated."

"I figured as much. I wanted to clarify in my mind the time table."

"Ms. Eden, I know you trust me to do my job, and I do. Do you want to become more involved in the process? You haven't had much interest in the past."

Eden folded her arms across her chest, sighed and exhaled. She breathed in the air with a faint hint of honey. A bee landed on her arm, stayed a moment and flew away. She flinched. She wasn't afraid of being stung but had an aversion stemming from a traumatic swarming as a child. Her friend had incurred nearly fifty stings and a trip to the nearest hospital.

"No, I haven't, and I think I made a mistake. Ever since my husband died, I concentrated on the financial side of this business. Leaving all the flowering and pollinating to you and Chris. I've made a mistake." She paused as another bee flew close to her ear. The buzz startled her. She brushed it away with her hand. The slight movement didn't interrupt Bernice. "Teach me how it works."

They agreed to schedule time for her education in the apiary world. She observed Bernice placing the water bottles on the top of the boxes. Her first lesson. "Why the bottles?"

Her mouth curled before Bernice answered. "They use water just as we do."

"Of course." Eden rolled her eyes and shook her head. "I've much to learn." She walked away with thoughts of bees swarming around her. They weren't attacking or stinging. She was the queen, and they attended her needs. Along the way, she spoke with workers tending rows of flowers and trees. She decided she hadn't paid proper attention to the daily routines of her family business. Her father, Giordano Montague, had tried to teach her, as did Malcolm. After being abandoned to run acreage alone, she relied on Chris Colella for the operations. She concentrated on the books and attaining retail customers at stores, nurseries, and flowers shops. Business boomed, and money rolled in. She cared for success without realizing the daily routines. That was to change.

In the largest warehouse seedling trees and bushes were attended by migrants, hired for the season of preparing young plants for transport to businesses which marketed to the public. Trucks bearing the Montague logo awaited the packing and loading. Within a few hours, dozens of places would receive these plants. Checking the operations and looking as alluring as he had after Malcolm's death, Chris directed the work with ease and efficiency.

He looked up from a clipboard, saw Eden, and smiled. "We're sending out the fall sales. Looks like you've garnered enough business for a tidy profit." She nodded. Her regular contacts sent requests like clockwork. She had added fifteen new businesses to her list in the last few weeks. The nursery uptick in work scrambled schedules for the migrants, but they were given revenue shares above the usual wages to keep them happy and on the property.

"Looks like it," she answered. Watching the process, she again thought of the bees swarming around her attending her needs. She did have a swarm of attendants who met the requirements of her success. She placed a hand on Chris's arm and continued. "I've decided I need to be more involved in the daily operations. Dad and Malcolm wanted me to learn. It's been too long with my nose in the books and not in the soil." She removed her hand.

"Are you sure? We have a great operation going. I wouldn't want you bored watching plants grow." He grinned at his attempted humor.

"Funny. Almost as funny as watching money grow."

"Welcome to the daily operations." She stood beside him as he directed workers with the tasks for sending Montague plants around the Northwest. She watched the effectiveness of his directions as trucks filled with yearling trees, trays of tiny flowering shrubs, and bulbs of spring flowers for planting in household gardens this fall.

Her mind wandered to the note in her pocket. Her ally in Seattle warned of impending danger. Alert to the needs of her business being safe from any untoward activities, she decided to become more involved. Events around her hinted at an operation clear of any irresponsible actions, but what was happening elsewhere had prompted her sister's dire warning. Digging into the soil of the business could presumably dig into nascent ideas in her head of nefarious dealings. Graft had not been part of any profit and loss statements. Embezzling money from the gross receipts had not been detected. Plants, donated for various reasons, accounted for a small and legitimate activity. All was proper. So why the warning?

Chris finished with loading the trucks and drivers left for deliveries across the state of Washington. Some of the trucks headed for nearby airports for transfers to Oregon, Idaho, and California, such was the reputation of Montague Wholesale Nurseries.

"That wraps up our work for now," he said in a loud voice. Startled, Eden gasped. "Are you alright?" He grabbed her arm.

She removed his hand. "I'm fine. You shocked me." She began to walk away, but he touched her arm again. "What?"

"I thought we could go to town and celebrate your success. The day is getting late. I can send the workforce home, and we can have a pleasant evening together." She stared at him in disbelief. They had not shared an evening in a couple years. Their liaison after

Malcolm died was short. She deflected any further advances from him, and they settled into a quiet but distant working relationship.

"No. I want to be alone tonight." As usual, she thought. Nobody struck her fancy, nor did she place herself in any situation whereas to meet anyone fancy. "Thanks for the offer."

"May I walk you up to the house? We could have dinner in and see how the evening progresses." She glanced at him and began the trek to her home. He followed.

"Okay. Dinner and nothing else. Get Bernice to come as well." She left him, not looking back. What was he thinking? "Still pursuing me after all the rejections?" she thought. Noting the need for his services as a supervisor, she dismissed the idea of allowing him to caress any part of her or worm his way into her isolation. She wanted only to live out her life and leave her estate to philanthropic organizations. Montague Enterprises would die with her.

At the house, she directed her chef to prepare a meal for three. Pacific salmon with rice, fresh vegetables grown in the gardens of the property, and garlic bread, became the decided repast. She wanted something resplendent to reflect the shipping of plants - an award to her and her management staff.

A shower and change of clothing were deemed appropriate. Dinner was set for seven and word sent to Chris and Bernice to be prompt and well accoutered. She ascended the stairs to her bedroom and prepared her body for the celebration. As water cascaded across her body, a vision of another being with her manifested in her brain. He washed her back and buttocks. She moaned as he stroked the front of her pelvic region. Aloud she screeched, and the vision melted into the water and down the drain.

Pulling on a pair of dress pants and a blouse over her matronly underwear, she placed minimal makeup on her face and brushed her hair without any fancy arrangement. She departed for the living room and her soon to arrive guests.

When Chris and Bernice entered, she offered them a glass of wine and hors d'oeuvres. They chatted until the announcement of dinner. Sitting at the dining table, Eden offered a toast, "To all of our success and the future success we will have." Glasses clinked, and drinks were taken.

Chris asked, "Are you sure you want to enter the dirty work of involving yourself in daily operations?"

Bernice added, "And learning about bees?"

"Yes, I need to know what is running around here. I am the owner of a large estate, and I should be more concerned and less self-absorbed." Eden excused herself to check on the progress of the kitchen.

Bernice frowned and asked, "Do you think she suspects?" Chris set his mouth in a line but said nothing. What was his boss thinking?

CHAPTER

15

School at the University of Washington started without fanfare. Marcus attended classes and returned to the Phi Delta house for his freshman requirements as a pledge. He missed Delinda but remind himself she was not far away. Her father, Randolph Middlebury, and Olivia Breckenridge were truly a couple. Dee lived with them and Olivia's daughter, Alanna. Although the tolerance of teenage girls sharing a bathroom and a bedroom raised questions about the arrangement, she had not returned to Minnesota when her father departed to close his practice and sell their family home in Edina. He saw her when a break in schedule allowed.

Seeing his parents in Wendlesburg was more challenging. He had no real reason for visiting except during school breaks. The next vacation was Thanksgiving, over a month away. He studied and lamented joining the fraternity.

On a warm October day, a young woman approached him and asked for his name and number. It seemed unusual to him, but his fellow frat brothers spoke of the openness of college girls to be what he considered rather forward. He asked for her name before expressing any answer to her query. She said her name was Rose and had seen him around campus and found him attractive. Flattered, he gave her the information she requested and asked again for her number. She gave him a number he figured was phony.

She looked older than other freshman women and exotic, her dark skin flawless. He thought of Delinda and her beautiful face and skin. As Rose departed, he rued his decision to share his information. If she ever contacted him, he would decline to accept any invitation to dinner, party, or sporting event. Guilt wracked his emotions, so he called Dee to inform her of the contact. Hide nothing from the one woman with whom he wanted to share life. Her phone clicked to message. He told her to call as soon as possible.

Another class held his attention, so he dismissed his meeting Rose, the exotic. The subject matter of the class drifted from his concentration. Rose appeared before him. His mind fought to focus on Delinda, but Rose was as real as any other person in the lecture hall. A voice droned upon the stage about math basics. He paid little attention. From behind another voice spoke to him. A familiar voice. His brain sharpened. The vision had been real. He turned, and the exotic smile scared him. Was she stalking him or was she a member of the student body attending math?

"Hello, Marcus. I couldn't leave without asking about your relationship with your father." She rose and signaled him to follow. His father? What was her end game? Another beautiful woman luring him to an unhealthy end? He followed her from the auditorium.

Alone with her in the hallway, he stopped her, physically grasping her arm and turning her to him. "Who are you and why have you contacted me?"

"I do apologize for the brusque nature of this meeting. I was asked to connect with you because a friend of mine has information which I fear has negative ramifications for your family." *Cryptic*, he thought. His apprehension raised hackles, alerting him to be careful of false information.

"Explain what you want. I'm not going with you until you tell me what this has to do with my family." Fingers curled into fists, as muscles tensed. He waited as she handed him a note. He opened the paper and read. Looking at her before finishing, he noted her lips, the set of her mouth. She appeared relaxed. He finished reading. His heart beat harder, and his face warmed with controlled rage.

"Do you believe the note?"

"Have you read it?"

"I have."

"I am not one to believe the words of an insane person."

"Insanity is personal to some. I do think you should be careful about ignoring these words. Your family is under surveillance and any movement they make will determine what happens to them. If you cooperate and allow for these actions to occur, they will be safe from harm."

Marcus doubted the words emanating from her mouth. "Are you friends with the twins?" His question, intended to upset the outcome, drew no hint as to the depth of her involvement.

"Come with me now or be informed later of the harm incurred by your sister or brother." Her threat fueled his desire to save them from any injury or death. She turned, and he followed.

In a parking lot next to the cavernous building, she unlocked an SUV and opened the passenger door, signaling him to enter. She moved around to the driver side and sat. He hesitated, knowing the result could be his death. Could he sacrifice himself for the safety of his family? He entered the car, but did he await a fate worse than Skagway?

Alanna and Delinda arrived at the house together from separate places. Alanna opened the door and waited for Dee to enter. Following her in, she asked, "How was your day?" Dee dropped her backpack in the hallway and faced her roommate.

"Class went well. And how about you? How was school for you?"

"It was fine." Little tension existed, but neither one desired conversation. Alanna proceeded to their bedroom and Dee entered the kitchen. Her plans to meet Marcus for dinner and spend an evening at a motel room with him focused her mind. They had made this a routine for at least once a month and planned to increase the time to once a week. She wanted him. She needed him. Their history aboard the Salish Sea and the kidnapping in Skagway cemented her relationship with him. He acted with intelligence and regardless of fear made sure he saved her from death. She adored him and wanted a life with him. She was willing to wait until they finished their education, but not a moment longer.

Alanna entered the kitchen and foraged for food. "What do you have planned for the evening? Another date with Marcus?" Delinda nodded. "I envy you, I guess. He is as handsome as any guy I know and smart as anyone I've met."

"We've been through a lot together. He is as strong a person as his father, and as compassionate as his mother."

"You do love him, don't you?" Delinda smiled as the conversation stalled. Alanna took a container from the refrigerator and sat in front of the television to watch the news.

Delinda checked her watch and noted the time. She walked down the hall to their room and removed her clothing. She placed her robe on her body and headed for the bathroom they shared and a cleansing of body and soul. The water relaxed her body, but her mind furnished a wonderful liaison with Marcus.

Clean and refreshed, she dressed in spotless lacy underwear, covered by jeans and a blouse. She had plugged in her phone to assure enough power. Clicking Marcus's number resulted in immediate messaging. Not what she expected. He was to meet her at their prearranged restaurant. Her father left the keys to the car he leased from a local dealer.

She drove to the restaurant and waited for him to show. After an hour she decided to go to his fraternity to uncover his delay. "Have you seen Marcus Jefferson? Has he returned from class?" Her question prompted a search of the house to no avail.

A senior in the house stated he was not present and was last seen in the morning when he left to attend three classes. Another student of the house stated he saw him in the math class they shared, but he left with a woman before the end of the class. He described her as enticing, oriental, but intimidating.

Delinda returned to her car and left for Olivia's house, hoping to find the FBI agent home. She needed help. She feared the worst. She could not even hope for the best. Tears formed as she sat waiting for a light to change.

A honk behind her awakened her to move through the intersection. She drove in a slow pattern. Her phone remained beside her on the seat but did not buzz with Marcus's number. As she arrived at the house, she tried once more to connect with Marcus. Nothing.

Running into the house, she searched for Olivia. No one was home. She tried Marcus once again and received a message without any ringing. A rash decision to pursue another route crossed her thinking. She called Marc and Joan. "I can't reach him," she cried. "I get an answer on his phone to leave a message. He's not at the fraternity, and one of his frat brothers says he left class with an unknown woman, he described as intimidating. It can't happen again; can it?"

She heard reassurance from his parents that he could handle himself, but the situation remained. He was missing, and she feared the worst. Had he been kidnapped again. And this time they would kill him to avenge what happened on the Salish Sea?

CHAPTER

16

Joan and Marc stood on the backyard patio of their home in Wendlesburg. Delinda had called. Marcus was missing. He held a small video camera in his hand and wondered how many more existed. He had not searched for it but rather stumbled upon it when he moved an item on a shelf in the living room. Scanning the outside environment revealed more tiny cameras. Someone was monitoring every move they made.

"Let's get in the car. Or walk down to the corner." He guided her off the patio and toward the street. As they passed the house next to them and stopped at the corner, he said, "I found this in the living room and spotted three more outside. We're being watched. I'm contacting Glen to send a sweep crew out to clear the house." Joan remained quiet.

"What about Marcus? Delinda sounded frantic."

"I'll call Olivia after I get the crew out here. He's probably occupied by some unexpected thing." He clicked his phone and called the sheriff's office. After relating the conditions of his house, he called Olivia. Joan returned to the house to free Sarah and James from the intrusion. Marc followed her as he spoke with his FBI friend.

"Has Marcus made any contact with you or Delinda since she told you she's worried?" Olivia answered in the negative. "Well, keep me informed. He's only been gone an hour or so.434345 He listened a moment. "Yes, he is a responsible person, and this is unlike him to not stay in touch." Another moment of listening. "Alright. Thanks, Liv." He clicked off.

At the house, Marc decided to search for more devices. He grabbed a paper and pencil to mark each location. On a lark, he wrote a note on a paper. When he found a camera, he held up the paper for a moment before disabling it.

"That should fix whoever intruded in our lives. I don't know how many days they've been watching..." He turned to find himself alone. He searched the house for his family and found them outside, away from the building. "What are you doing out here?"

"Dad, Mom says someone's been spying on us. Have they been watching everything we do? Are they perverts watching me naked? Ew."

"Sarah, it's not as bad as that." Sarah cringed. James remained his usual stoic self. Marc's phone buzzed. A car approached with blue lights flashing. He checked the caller, who recorded as 'unknown caller." He didn't need some telemarketer. "What," he said. "Who is this?" The sheriff's car stopped in the driveway, and the officer extinguished the flashers.

"Oh Marc, I was hoping we could be more civil with each other. I've missed our encounters on the ship and in Alaska." Bile churned into his throat. His heart raced. He separated from his family as the two sheriff deputies waited for him to finish his call. He signaled Joan to lead them on their quest.

"What do you want?" No one spoke except to purr. "I thought you'd be far away from me by now. If I find you, ..."

"You will. Find me that is. I'll be sure you find me and my sister. We have unfinished business." His rage boiled, but control of emotions had to rule.

"Where are you?" Marc softened his voice so others would not interfere. He observed Joan direct Sarah and James to stay by the squad car, as she led the search team into the house.

"I do believe you meant what you wrote on the paper. I'm surprised it took so long for you to find the camera. Maybe you aren't quite as good a detective as we thought." The voice in his ear summoned up the memories of the confrontation with Kerrine and Kaliana aboard the Salish Sea. They had eluded capture in Anchorage but haunted him now.

He thought of the note pointed at an unknown entity now clearly the enemy he desperately wanted to incarcerate. "You're responsible for ... the cameras?"

"You are a good lover. I'm now truly disappointed I could not seduce you on the ship. And your children are growing into beautiful young people. It would be a shame to pollute their future with nude pictures and videos of them splashed across the Internet." Kerrine stopped to allow her threat to develop.

"What do you want?" His voice, a whisper now that he understood the magnitude of his condition, repeated, "What do you want from me?"

Kerrine growled, "I want what you did not give me on the ship. I want you to die."

"And then you'll leave my family alone?" His mind thought of Uncle Jerry and his fabricated suicide. "Do I just kill myself, or do you want the pleasure of watching me succumb to a dose of your lethal honey and tea?"

"Oh, first we have a close encounter of the physical, and then I get to watch your magnificent body wretch with spasms of paralysis and pain. After I am satisfied with your demise, I release your son, Marcus, and disappear from your family's lives forever." He heard another voice in the background. "Kaliana wants to know if she can have Marcus for herself. She wants to be with you but figures any conjugal relationship over a long period is fraught with danger."

"Where are you?" He couldn't conceive of them in Wendlesburg, but confirmation of Marcus missing in Seattle sent chills up his spine.

Kerrine answered his question with one of her own. "Where do you think I could be? The Internet makes it so easy for me to be near or far. I can be on the next block or halfway around the globe."

"I get it. You tell me. I can come over and complete your fantasy, if you were so inclined."

"I'll be in touch. And keep your father and uncle out of this. And that traitor nurse will be suffering a sad situation soon. I hope she loves her daughter." The phone call ended.

"Damn it." His concentration with Kerrine blinded his awareness of Joan.

"Trouble just follows you around, doesn't it?" Her arms folded across her chest set the stage for another confrontation he did not want. "Was that the person responsible for watching us? Watching us shower, have sex, get dressed, eat meals, fight about things?" A little spittle left her mouth and landed on his cheek. He ignored it.

"Kerrine. She claims to have Marcus." A shriek startled Sarah and James by the car. They stared but did not move.

"Don't panic. She wants to meet with me, so I can finish what they wanted on the ship, my death. They promise to release Marcus and leave you, Sarah, and James alone. They said not to involve my Dad or Uncle Jerry."

"The twins are in Seattle?" Joan dropped her arms as fists formed. A scarlet tinge blossomed on cheeks. "I'll kill them if they harm anyone in this family. It must end, Marc. It has to end." An attempt to hug and reassure her met resistance and a shove.

"Are Dave and Patti about finished with the house?" She nodded as they came out on the front deck. Marc approached them.

Patti, a sergeant with Kitsap County and lead investigator in cases of home invasions and unlawful monitoring, held a large plastic evidence bag containing several small cameras. "We found a total of twelve in various parts of the house. We're going to scan the outside next." Marc directed them to the backyard deck and three more cameras.

"What's the range on these devices?" he asked.

Patti directed Dave to use the equipment to find more cameras. She then answered his query. "They operate on Bluetooth and probably not much more than a mile. Whoever placed them is nearby." Marc dropped the camera he placed in his pocket in the evidence bag."

"Then develop a possible area of reception and find me a house recently rented or purchased or something."

Dave returned with five more micro-cameras which had night vision capability, radio signal transfer, and wide-angle lenses. "That's the last of them," he added. He carried them in another evidence bag.

"Turn them over to the desk office with a note to have Tom Knudson contact me." They left without blue flashers. Joan closed the distance which was acquired as he spoke with his fellow sheriff officers.

"What now, Marc? I want my son back. I want this Everett cartel business ended forever." She walked a bit then turned. "Delinda and I want Marcus back. Do you hear me?" She waved for Sarah and James to follow. They entered the clean, swept house, a stench of probable uncertainty about privacy marring the evening.

Marc knew what he had to do. He had no reason to involve any other family member. He formulated a plot bordering on insanity and dishonor. He had no other choice but to undertake his thoughts. Survival depended on it.

CHAPTER

17

Chris Colella and Bernice Harapat mapped the spring planting and flowering seasons. The small greenhouse set-up for rhododendrons and azaleas and the bumblebees to pollinate them drew work from the staff in March to place the soon to flower bushes inside to isolate them.

The bumblebee boxes moved along with the plants. Each spring the need for preventing other pollens from mixing with the honey production of the bees became paramount. Each spring the small amount of raw honey was processed for one particular use. Bernice bred bees of extraordinary strength to resist the deadly toxin associated with the plants. Each seasonal challenge to produce healthier queens and hives engaged her skills.

Chris used his ability to graft shoots of high-grade flowers for stronger, more potent pollen, leaves, stems, and roots. Seeds from the plants became the future plants with deadlier grayanotoxin coursing the veins of the organisms. The resulting pollen improved the chances of successfully refining honey with a less bitter taste and more potent outcome.

They had worked for several years to intoxicate the honey for unusual but lethal uses. The money garnered from a select few buyers financed accounts separate from salaries earned working for Eden. These nest eggs stayed unrecorded and untaxed. No paper trail of transactions existed. No names crossed lips or phone lines. Sales of small vials of the honey and teabags of mixed oolong and crushed rhododendron leaf added to the excitement of anyone wanting to eliminate a rival or seek revenge for a wrong or avenge an injustice.

Each season the bees succeeded in gathering a large pool of pollen to become honey. New queens, drones, and workers ingested and digested the honey and survived, stronger than before. Each hive created enough material for dozens of small jars for a market which demanded more and more of the elixir of death.

Chris said, "After the production is finishes and we have sent the expected amount to Eden for mixing with the other honeybee production, I will move the cargo off-site to our other place and get the word out to our distributors."

"Eden's going to want an accounting of the stock. You know that. I can give her an estimate and then be sure she gets the expected amount."

"Agreed. But if we can have more for us, then we can increase profits."

Bernice whispered, "Don't become greedy. We've already made a substantial amount of capital gain. Any loss of 'Mad Honey' and she will suspect something is wrong."

"Work it out. She isn't a problem. And if she becomes one. Well, maybe she meets the same fate as her husband."

Bernice scowled, "You'd kill her? Why? That would bring attention to the farm, and we don't need any. No one knows the source of our teas and honey, and we must be sure to keep them apart."

"I won't kill her. Just wondering if she can die naturally, as he did."

"Naturally, as he did. Are you nuts? I've thought something happened which should not have. Somehow he consumed the wrong batch of honey and his heart attack was only natural because the honey was natural." She had never accused Chris of any wrong. She just wasn't convinced he was innocent.

"The seedlings I planted this summer are growing nicely. We should have small bushes ready for the season after this next one which are hardier and more potent than this springs' collection."

They concluded the plan and doctored the records for the sake of keeping Eden Montague happy and satisfied they were doing their job. Each year the reputation of the legitimate refined honey increased. Small stores and individual customers arrived to purchase cases of the sweetener. Each was a testament to the work of her supervisor and beekeeper.

She added the gross proceeds to her account and paid salaries and wages which satisfied all her employees. They made more with her than other wholesalers paid. Loyalty fostered more diligent work which provided the best trees, flowers, and manufactured products to retail outlets and individuals.

Her own salary remained static because of her desire to help her permanent workers, which fostered a medical insurance plan, 401-k plans, and bonuses in banner years. Migrants came and went as the seasons dictated. They were properly compensated.

Bernice reflected on the plans. "Do you think we can keep the twins at bay? Last time we talked with them, they sent that stooge from Edmonds. Then they killed him. When they wanted a larger supply, I wondered how many they planned to erase from existence. We are running low of last year' batch."

"They'll just have to be satisfied with what we have."

Bernice changed the subject. "Eden wants to learn about apiary. I asked her why, and she said she wanted to be more involved in daily operations. Do you think she'll interfere?"

"She told me the same thing. We'll be fine. Let's get back to other chores."

As they left the office of the small greenhouse, Eden approached.

"Oh, good. I've been looking for you." She sounded calm, although Bernice gasped when she saw her boss.

"We were planning the spring season of plants and bees in this greenhouse. I think you'll be pleasantly surprised by our predictions." Chris flashed a manila folder. "As soon as I write this up, I let you have the final copy."

"Thanks, but remember, I asked you to include me in the operations. I want to be part of the planning for each rotation." Bernice's sweat increased and perspiration beaded on her forehead. A sleeve wiped away the moisture.

Chris acted as if nothing had changed. "We'll have to remember. We aren't used to you being outside with us." He smiled, but sincerity remained hidden.

The fall presentation of newly harvested seedlings filled several outdoor canvass canopies. Customers milled about picking favorite colors and styles. Eden enjoyed meeting her loyal fans. She relished adding new-to-the-area people who heard of her plantation and drove for hours to see the proof their neighbors were correct.

She kept meticulous records to contact them for future seasonal acquisitions. Her greatest profits came from retail stores. She sent a small army of trucks and sellers to the businesses to help display her wares in the best possible way. As a result, they became loyal returning customers with each passing season.

Now she watched the crew move saplings and bushes, trays of flowers, and buckets of trees from fields and greenhouses to the small market area she maintained for drive-ins. She had wanted to greet each person or family, but the desire to become involved in the dirty work curtailed much of her hand-swaps.

Bernice asked her, "Do you want to accompany me as I check field boxes?" Eden nodded, and they drove away in a small cart which usually passed for a golf vehicle.

As they went their way to a series of white cubical enclosures, Eden said, "I appreciate being part of your world." Bernice handed her protective gear which they adorned as they neared the boxes. The buzzing fostered memories of her childhood friend and the calamity. Covered from head to toe with clothing or webbing, she relented and stood by Bernice as she raised lids and lifted honeycombs. All seemed right with the product.

Chris had waved as they left. Now he created a scenario in his head which eliminated any opposition to keeping him sated and convincing Eden to be part of his life. If she suspected any part of the operation Bernice and he ran, he wanted to be next to Eden, in the fields, in the house, in her bed. He had to implicate her without her awareness, an insurance policy protecting him from prosecution - an edge over all people who worked at Montague Wholesale Nursery. His alternate cell phone buzzed.

A burner phone, which he swapped out regularly, indicated a call from one of the regulars. He swiped the screen and spoke, "What's up?" He listened to the silence around him and the voice in the speaker. "Listen, you are becoming a liability. Someone is bound to uncover your source of materials and that isn't going to be good for me." He listened as calm as he could. "I'll meet you tomorrow at the same place as before. Bring another thousand or no deal." An agreement struck, he closed the phone and grumbled. The failure to keep deaths out of the light of scrutiny irritated him. His instructions were clear. Make death as natural as possible and leave no evidence.

Kerrine asking for additional honey and teas meant she was becoming the liability he had referenced when talking with Bernice. Rumors of a cruise to Alaska becoming a killing ship attracted attention he did not want. If she did not complete her goal with this batch, she had to consume her purchase, and he would see that it happened.

CHAPTER

18

Olivia studied the pattern of movement left by Marcus before Delinda lost contact with him. All timelines pointed to a peaceful departure with an Asian or Indian woman with whom he left willingly. No report of a missing person would prompt local officials to act, except for Tiberius. As an officer of the law in Seattle, he would act.

A description of a car produced a slim lead. He had entered the car without trauma according to the witness. Was he victim or changing his mind about Delinda? Had he been coerced by some information of a negative nature or simply found another female appealing?

Olivia gave little credence to his willing activity with the woman. His behavior with Delinda offered strong evidence that something bad happened. She called Tiberius to relay the events and timeline. He asked if Marc and Joan knew, to which she responded in the positive.

"I think I'll call Jerry and bring the reinforcements," Tiberius said. "We can't wait for missing persons to act. They'll say he found someone he likes better." Olivia agreed.

Delinda entered the room as Olivia spoke with Tiberius. She held her phone in her hand as if waiting for Marcus to call. Liv clicked off her call. "Have you heard from him?" she asked.

"No, but Dad just called. He's taking a red-eye and will be here in the morning."

"Did you tell him about Marcus?"

"Yes, he acted less concerned about the situation and more interested in explaining what was happening in Minnesota. Why does he do that? Just ignore what I want?"

"His mind is occupied. What he's doing is a major change for him." Dee tilted her head and raised an eyebrow. She frowned

"I guess. But if anything happens to Marcus, I'll just die."

Olivia reached out arms and enveloped the young lady. Tears drained from swollen orbs. A buzzing interrupted the venting of emotions. Delinda's phone vibrated her hand. She broke away to discover Marcus number on the screen. Delight shone forth as she answered. "Marcus, where are you? I've worried."

An unfamiliar voice spoke to her. "He is safe for now. I need you to do something, so he remains safe."

"Who is this? Are you the girl who enticed him to leave class early?" Not quite a scream, her voice timbre pushed through the speaker.

"Yes, he came with me without effort. Please contact his father and mother and inform them he is safe. I suspect you have connected with them about his missing dinner with you."

"They know. Do you know who you're dealing with? You'll never get away with this."

"Contact them. Or forget about seeing him again. Ever." The threat sounded real. Dee softened her tone.

"I will. Can I speak to him? To know he's okay? Please?"

Marcus spoke, "Dee, follow the driver. I'm okay for now. They want my Dad in exchange for me. Let them know. Follow the driver." The call ended.

"He's okay. They want Marc. They'll exchange him for his father. He told me to follow the driver." Olivia smiled.

"That boy is brilliant." Delinda scrunched her face. "He sent a message to us. Somehow the car has a designation or a camera which has caught it. We need to follow Marcus's tracks. Give me everything you know about where he was at any given time. We then trace any of the cameras in the area to see if the car license can be seen."

"Why does this lady want his dad?"

"I think she may be attached to the people on the ship. They were not successful in eliminating Detective Jefferson. This is an attempt to isolate him and finish what was started on the cruise." Tears rolled from her eyes as Delinda heard the words. She collapsed onto a chair, curling into a ball as the tears became a full weeping. Olivia knelt on the floor next to her and stroked her brunette locks. The action changed nothing, but she continued. Delinda had no understanding of the depth of deception which ruled the world in which they lived.

Marcus sat on a chair next to a small, yellow, kitchen table. His cuffed hands were behind his back. The metal, digging into his wrists, cut circulation to his fingers and cut the skin underneath. He smelled the blood pooling on the chair. "These are too tight. My hands hurt and I'm bleeding. Can't you loosen them? Please?" The woman ignored the pleas for easing the discomfort. Her phone sat on the table far enough away from him that he only could see part of the wallpaper screen.

He adjusted his seating but produced no comfort change. As he writhed, Mai Ling looked at him and spoke, "I do apologize for the rough treatment. My instructions were clear. Get Marcus by any means possible and be sure he does not get any advantage."

"How are you involved in this? Are you related to the twins? Or Pepper? What reason do you have?"

"That's none of your business. Besides, I won't be involved long enough for you to care what happens." She watched him for a moment. "You should have died in Skagway. Along with that girl. Your father should have died, as well." Marcus detected a hint of remorse in her words. Her eyes traced to the floor as she spoke.

"My Dad can help you get out of this mess. What do they have on you?" Another idea thrust forward from deep inside his head. "My brother and sister are safe from any harm, aren't they? You only said they were in trouble to get me in your car. I guess I'm the fool for believing you." Her eyes connected to his eyes. A hint of deception melted away. He finished his monologue. "Let me free, so I can help you escape this insanity. The only outcome for you is harm. Or even your death. If those twins are directing this ploy, they don't care about you. You will be a liability. They won't let you live. Liabilities have a way of going missing without a trace and not because of any new identity and a wad of money to run and hide."

Her eyes narrowed. She leaned forward, almost within a distance Marcus could use his head to batter her and knock her out. "I am not listening to your rantings and ravings. No one will hurt me. I am important to the scheme." Marcus scooted on his chair to be closer.

"No one is that important, but I know my father. He will eliminate you and those evil twins. Death will be a welcome conclusion." She leaned closer. He continued, "You should be making decisions which favor your survival.

"I think my survival is fine. Yours is not as secure." As she spoke his mind calculated the amount of force needed to crush her skull and not disable his brain. Concussions had a negative effect which he did not want. He changed tactics. A quick movement brought his lips to hers. She retreated, a gush of air intaking her lungs.

"I have wanted to do that since you enticed me to come with you. I figured there was more to this kidnapping than my sister and brother being in imminent danger. I'm sorry if I scared you." Her heart pounded in her chest as breasts rose and fell. His plan to transfer fear to palliative thoughts in her seemed a plausible result.

"Don't do that again." Her words carried little danger for him. Her breathing, shallow and short, deviated from earlier coarse actions.

"I didn't mean to scare you. I just wanted to kiss you. I find you exciting. If we were to become more intimate, my girlfriend needn't know. Then you can release me. You and I can run from your cohorts, and you can be free of their wrath."

"What do you know of their wrath?" She placed her hands across his ears and pressed her lips to his mouth. Releasing him she sat back. "Is that what you want? To make me believe you want me and will not hurt me?" Marcus smiled.

"I don't want to hurt you. And I do understand the wrath of those girls. Whether you know it or not, one of them forced me to have sex with her while I was strapped naked to a bed. She mistreated my girlfriend and forced me to have sex with her. She then tried to kill us. I do know the wrath from which you will not survive." A flicker of remorse escaped her gaze.

"Release me and let me help, or you will be dead right after my father. They aren't likely to want you around to mess with their freedom."

She stood and walked to the kitchen sink. Turning on the water, she filled a glass and drank. She returned with the glass and offered it. Marcus opened his mouth and waited for the rim to touch his lips. As the glass came near, he sipped down liquid and swallowed. As she turned to place the glass on the counter, he rushed at her.

CHAPTER

19

The announcement of the arrival at SeaTac International Airport awakened Randolph Middlebury from a fitful sleep. The early morning flight from Minneapolis on the Boeing 737-800 did nothing to alleviate his angst about changing living arrangements and starting a new medical practice without any security as to where he might begin it.

As the passengers retrieved duffel bags and small carry-on luggage from the overhead bins, he sat, thinking about the position in which he placed himself. The aisle in front of him cleared, so he stood and grabbed the small bag he carried with him. He checked his larger case.

While walking to the baggage carousel, his phone buzzed. The screen was a welcomed name. "Olivia, my plane just landed. I'm getting my suitcase." She interrupted.

"Marcus has been kidnapped and is being held in exchange for his father."

"What? When did this happen?" He forgot about the black bag which passed by him. "Does Dee know?"

"She was to have dinner with him last night. He didn't show. After a few hours, someone called and explained she had him and was to exchange him for Marc. Randolph, I think those girls are here."

"Is my daughter okay?"

"Yes, she's holding up well, considering."

"I'll get my bag and catch the train into Seattle. I'll get a ride from University station to you."

"No. I'll be there to pick you up. I'll bring Dee with me. She needs you right now."

The call ended. Middlebury grabbed his bag as it returned from its journey around the moving belt. He walked across the overhead walkway and rode the elevator to the level with the ramp to the light rail station. Each stop along the way raised his anxiety. Marcus was a levelheaded kid whom he had come to admire. Not wishing Delinda to fall for a shipboard romance, his mind cleared to the understanding that she and Marcus were a couple. They endured far more than any two people did in a lifetime and neither was yet nineteen. Life threw curveballs in the baseball game of living.

As the train approached the University station, his mental condition rose to a fever pitch. Disembarking the car in which he rode, he found two beautiful women awaiting his return. Each embraced him. His mind relaxed. "I am so glad to see both of you. Delinda, I am so sorry about Marcus. I went to your mother's gravesite and realized my love for her was now reflected in what you have with him."

"Thanks, Dad. We need to find him." He nodded.

"Olivia, I also realized what I want from you. Are you willing to put up with a mangled old man for the rest of your life?"

"Are you asking me to marry you?" Her jaw opened with a grin superimposed on her face.

"If you'll have me, yes."

"You have no idea what you're getting into with me." She spoke with a hint of doubt. After a pause, she finished, "Yes." They hugged again.

Arriving at the house, they discovered Tiberius and Jeremais waiting for them in the living room. Alanna sat with them, silent. Ti stood and spoke, "Welcome back, Randolph." As they shook hands, he then directed his conversation to Olivia. "What do you know about Marcus? Have you heard any more?"

Olivia said, "His captor called last night, and we heard his voice, as I explained to you when I called. We've heard nothing more. And you. Did you find any cameras which gave you the car?" Delinda clasped her father's arm.

"I found three possible angles which produced several automobiles. One camera on the campus has Marcus leaving a building with a young lady, but we have no other shots yet of them together."

Jerry added, "If they want Marc in exchange, I don't see how we can allow my nephew to do that. We need to find Marcus and prevent putting anyone in a perilous place," A knock on the front door halted any further conversation. Olivia went to see who was at her house. She wasn't expecting any guests.

As she opened the door, Marcus pushed a woman in and grinned. "Place this person under arrest for kidnapping, torture, and false imprisonment. She noticed the damage of his hands.

"Marcus, I am so happy to see you." Delinda heard the voice, came to the foyer, and jumped at her man and held him tight as she kissed him and hugged him.

"What happened? I was afraid you were dead." Tears welled up in her eyes. He returned her kiss and led her into the kitchen where others waited.

Tiberius grasped his grandson and then asked, "What happened?" Olivia entered with a rather disheveled woman bound up with duct tape. Tiberius released him and smiled. "So, your captor discovered your intelligence and abilities." Olivia sat the woman in a chair. Blood stained her face and shoulders. An eye was swollen, as were her lips and chin.

"This lady told me Sarah and James were in trouble, and I was to go with her, so nothing happened to them. She led me to a location in Fremont and handcuffed me." His hand was deep-purple around the same thumb, dislocated in Skagway. "She turned her back on me, so I attacked her. Because my thumb was not fully healed, I slipped one of the cuffs and used it to disable her. I need to see a doctor about my hand."

Jerry cut the bindings of the woman and placed wrist restraints on her with hands behind her back. "You need to come clean with us about what reason you had for kidnapping my nephew."

The young woman looked away from Jerry. Her eyes engaged Marcus and Delinda. "They want revenge for what happened on the cruise."

Jerry kept pressing for answers. "Why you? What connection do you have with Andrew Pepper? You're Asian. They're Hispanic."

"I worked for Helene Paulukaitis. When the operation collapsed because you and your brother and nephew took down Pepper, I had nowhere to turn. I freelanced my services and was hired by the twins to finish off your nephew. Nothing went as planned aboard the ship, so they improvised."

Tiberius approached, as did Olivia. Alanna, Delinda, and Marcus vacated the room, so that an interrogation could continue. Jerry asked, "What do you mean, improvised?"

"I don't have to say anymore. Are you arresting me?"

"I might just let Marcus complete his work. You underestimated him, and he isn't pleased with the twins. He might make your pretty face into an ugly mess. You turned tricks for a person who turned evidence and is out of your reach. Your freelance days are done." Jerry turned away and signaled Tiberius.

"What has she given you?" Ti asked.

"Nothing more than she worked in Pepper's organization and knows the two ladies who attacked your grandson in Skagway."

"Let me have a crack at her."

Olivia placed a hand on his shoulder. "Hold a minute. She wants to delay us for some reason. Call Marc and get him over here as soon as possible."

Tiberius opened his phone and clicked the numbers. It went to message. He left details about the situation and clicked off. He turned to the stranger in the chair.

"My son is safe and away from the twins. Why don't you come clean with who you are, and where they may be?" He paused to let her start talking. She remained mute. "Unless you like honey and tea. We could give you some of the evidence we brought with us from Alaska. I'm guessing you have to be physically fit enough to survive the side effects." Her eyes stared at him. The cold darkness emanating from them explained her position.

"I have nothing more to say. Let me go, and I won't press charges for unlawful imprisonment." Olivia sat in a chair opposite.

"You are under arrest for the kidnapping and illegal imprisonment of another human being. Threatening his sister and brother brings charges of assault. Prostitution is also illegal and will cost you another ten years. I figure you'll be an old lady before anyone sees you running the streets." She recited Miranda Rights and directed the Jeffersons to let her be, for the moment.

Marcus entered the room and spoke with his grandfather and uncle. "She wants Dad. I called him when I freed myself from her control." He pulled a phone from his pocket. "This is hers. I think it might be of help in working out what she's up to."

Olivia said, "I don't think we should open the apps without a proper warrant."

Marcus smiled. "I figured that was the case, so I opened it and wrote down some of the numbers. I was going to call them until I got Kerrine. I wanted her to know I was still alive and waiting for her."

Tiberius asked, "Did you call? Any of the numbers?"

Marcus smirked and handed him a piece of paper with a phone number on it. "Call it. They don't know you, and I already talked with Kaliana. She wants to meet."

CHAPTER

20

Jerry signaled Tiberius to follow him outside. Standing on the patio in the backyard, he said to his older brother, "I called JJ. I wanted him to understand our enemies still operate. He said he heard from Marc. The twins bugged their house, and Marc spoke with Kerrine. She threatened the kids unless he cooperated with her about finishing what started on the ship."

"But that means Marc dying." Tiberius bit his lower lip.

"JJ says they formulated a plan to upset that goal of hers. It's dangerous, but Regina is coming down from Vancouver to help. By the way, she told JJ the RCMP rounded up the remaining members of the cartel and stopped the smuggling."

"When can they get here?" Ti said.

"He indicated they would be here by ten tonight. I gave him the address to Olivia's house."

"We better get back." They reentered the house passing their prisoner. They stopped to ask a question. She looked at one and then the other. She spoke with them before they could say anything.

"I want a deal. I want the same deal you gave Laila and Helene Paulukaitis. I know where your adversaries are, and I can point you in the correct direction regarding the honey."

Tiberius sent Jerry to get Olivia. "We already have leads to them. The only thing you can offer is the honey. Tell us what you know. We'll work to make you the deal you want."

Olivia returned with Jerry. Tiberius repeated what their prisoner said. Olivia offered a reason for her to cooperate. "We have given you an opening. I suggest you accept fate and surrender your information. The Federal charges against you will not be plea bargained. All you can do is lessen the extent of the years you will forgo freedom."

"Then I choose to remain silent."

"May we know with whom we are speaking, or is that, too, part of any deal you want?" Olivia sat in a chair next to the exotic but altered beauty before her. An icy stare answered her inquiry. "Then I guess I will ask Marcus to interrogate you." A quick widening of eyes flashed and returned to ice. Olivia grinned. She stood and departed to get him.

Tiberius said, "Oh, I am sorry for you. My grandson is young, but he has learned from one of the best detectives in the area." Marcus came in, and his uncle and grandfather left.

In the living room, they sat with Olivia, Randolph, and Delinda talking about the frightful night and delightful day which had passed. As time ticked off the hours of evening, ten o'clock approached. Lights shone in a front window when a car turned into the drive. Jeremais Jefferson Jr. and Regina McDonald opened car doors, got out carrying small duffel bags. They walked to the front door and were greeted by Jerry who hugged his son with relish at his being safe and in the care of a talented Mountie. He then hugged Regina and whispered in her ear.

"What did you say, Dad?" JJ asked.

"I told her to marry you because we need a daughter in our family. I also said I would adopt her if you didn't." They laughed, but JJ and Regina had decided their future already.

"Where's my cousin, Marcus? He's the one who should make an honest woman out of Delinda." She blushed. Jerry pulled his son aside.

"What have you and Marc theorized as a way to entrap those menacing twins?" Tiberius joined them, as did Olivia. He explained the plan and the proper execution of it. Since he had not been part of the Alaska adventure which came close to killing his cousin, his actions would not be suspected until too late. Regina knew of the twins but had little interaction with them. She was to decoy them when Marc met with Kerrine and Kaliana.

"I don't like sacrificing my son to them. This better work." Tiberius planted a fist in his other hand. Marcus joined the throng of family and friends.

Olivia cocked her head. Jerry leaned forward. Delinda placed an arm in her father's arm. Tiberius, with fist in hand, stared. Randolph place a free hand on his daughter's arm. Only JJ and Regina remained animated and lively.

"Marcus, you look like hell." JJ clasped him before he could speak. Regina locked hands behind her back.

"When are you two going to decide a future?" Marcus asked.

"About the same time, you and your lady decide," JJ answered. "Now tell us what you've been doing in there?" He pointed to the kitchen.

"Her name is Mai Ling. She's from Hong Kong and started working the trade as a teenager. Andrew Pepper brought her to Vancouver and then Everett. He kept her as a concubine and lent her to clients when they requested a companion. She was under the guidance of Helene Paulukaitis until your raid curtailed any more business. She says the twins are in Wendlesburg. As for the toxic honey, she knows the twins have access to it, but she is not aware of the source." Faces just stared.

Tiberius broke the silence. "That's my grandson. How did you get all of that out of her?"

"Trade secret. Isn't that what you taught Dad? Never give up your methods?"

Fearing the worst, Jerry and Olivia entered the kitchen. Mai Ling remained as she had been. JJ followed. "So, this is the culprit who underestimated my cousin." He approached, observing the bruising and swollen eye and jaw. "Mai Ling? My cousin has an ability few can match. He will wrest any remaining knowledge from you before the night is over. You shouldn't have kidnapped him. I imagine his next move will be to let his girlfriend have a crack at you. Neither of them is very happy about the circumstances in Skagway." A whimper echoed from the walls as she sat, "wrapped up like a deuce in the middle of the night."

Olivia offered the next options. "Let's get some sleep. I'll keep Mai company for a time. Tiberius, you relieve me after a couple of hours, then Jerry. We'll cycle through to be sure our guest arrives in the morning as secure as she is now." All agreed, and two people were left to sort through hours of lonely co-existence. She heated water for tea to stimulate her mind in the early morning. Mai begged for some. Olivia ignored the plea.

"You can listen to me since I'm positive you'll cry foul when you retain a lawyer. I think what happened in Everett and aboard the Salish Sea were despicable acts of cowardice. Several people died because of inappropriate behavior on the part of Andrew Pepper, Jarina Camacho, and Captain Lars Dalgaard. They're all part of the history of life. Each has suffered a miserable dishonor and disgraced end. You are heading to the same fate." The kettle on the stove whistled its plaint song of boiling rage.

After fixing a pot to share with the next person in line to care for Mai Ling, she again sat opposite her adversary. Neither attempted to gin up a conversation. Olivia reminded Ling of the consequences and after checking her security removed her own body to the couch in the family area.

After a couple of hours, Tiberius entered to find coffee and a sleepy Mai Ling. With a book by Robert Dugoni in hand and a mug of fresh brew, he sat in a chair and read. She peered at her jailer without a word of exchange. The plastic ties cut into her wrists, but she whimpered not. Wriggling her arms against the metal part of her belt, she manipulated the straps until they snapped apart. The iron esthesis of her blood dribbling to the seat cushion and the floor left a tell of her attempt for freedom. She remained still. The book absorbed Tiberius's attention.

Another hour passed, and sleep overcame her guardian. She slipped the strap off and as quiet as a mime, sneaked to the patio door. Opening it without much of a sound, she departed the house to find safety in another place.

The cool breeze from outside alerted Tiberius to a change of atmosphere. Awareness of his surrounding cleared the fog in his brain. He saw the blood, strap, and open door. "Shit." His whisper was meant to keep others unaware of his lapse. He followed her out to the backyard and through the gate in the fence which led to the drive and front of the house. In the glow of a street lamp, he watched for any movement and listened for any odd night noises. Nothing.

Walking the street from one end to the other gained nothing. Mai Ling had eluded his guardianship and evaporated into the late-night mist. Explaining her escape to his colleagues was not an exercise to which he looked forward. He had made a mistake which could ruin any plans Marc and JJ had concocted.

CHAPTER

21

Joan paced the bedroom of her parent's house where she had gone with Sarah and James. Marc enlightened her to the conversation with Kerrine. He did not enlighten her as to the plan of which she would most likely disapprove. He had departed for the sheriff's office and a meeting with Glenmore Fellington, his boss.

A knock on the door startled her. She opened it to find James rubbing his eyes. Sarah remained in the spare bedroom used as a storage room most of the time. "Mom," he asked, "is Dad here?"

"No, he's gone to the office." She rubbed an arm. "Did you need him for something?"

"Just wondering if we are going to be here long, I need to get to school." Joan understood routine and the desire for her children to maintain a semblance of it. Life since returning home had been far from normal. Classes at the middle school and high school had begun earlier in the month, and neither child had missed any classes until yesterday. She called with a concocted excuse.

"I know. We must be here for a little while longer. Stay home today. We'll see about tomorrow, later." James trudged back to the other bedroom, used as a hobby room.

Her phone buzzed. The name on the screen surprised her. "Uncle Jerry, What's up?"

"I can't raise Marc on his phone. Is he with you?"

"No, he said he was headed to the sheriff's office to speak with Fellington."

A gruff noise crossed the airwaves. "I called his office, but he's not there. No one had seen him." Joan's heart skipped a beat. She realized what he was doing, and neither sister was going to be kind about meeting him. She feared for the loss of her husband.

"He had a call from Kerrine last night. Do you think he is meeting with her?"

"That's why I called. Marcus interrogated his kidnapper and discovered her connection with the sisters. She escaped last night. I fear she's heading your way. If you're at home, please leave your house."

"We did already. I'm at my parents with our children. Marc left about an hour ago."

"Good, we're on our way to you. JJ and Regina are with us, as well." The called ended, and Joan fought to keep from spilling tears. Another incident involving lies and deceit. She had been patient when he investigated cases. Her idle threats to leave meant nothing more than for her to vent.

Another incident threatened to leave her without a husband because he charged into the line of fire to rescue others and to correct the wrongs perpetrated by indecent individuals. She had enough of worrying.

What was Marc planning? She had married into a family of cops. Another knock shook her from the doldrums her brain sailed. She opened the door to find Sarah.

"Are we staying here again, tonight?" She invited Sarah into the room.

"Have a seat on the bed. You father has left for the office. Uncle Jerry and your grandfather are coming here. JJ is coming, also."

Sarah wriggled her toes which were unshod. "He's going after those girls, isn't he?" Recognition of the serious nature of life since Uncle Jerry's faux suicide made her grow to adulthood far sooner than needed. She witnessed much of the seamy side of human behavior because her father was a detective. Her desire for the end of the reign of terror saddened her. It eluded any sense of accomplishment. As one event concluded, another popped in to take its place.

Joan sat with her. "Yes, dear. I fear he has." They sat together, apart and yet welded together by a common bond to the one man they both loved.

⋈ ⋈ ⋈

The directions for the meeting place were simple. He sent a text of them to JJ with instructions to leave their fathers uninformed. Regina received a copy of the message. As his car reached the appointed place, earlier than planned, he scanned the waterfront for others. If he arrived early, so could they. Nothing seemed unusual. The park had a few children playing on the equipment with parents sitting nearby oblivious to imminent danger.

The boat launch parking lot was empty of cars. He figured he had arrived before them. He saw the Seattle ferry moving past Washington Narrows toward the dock. JJ and Regina were supposedly aboard. They knew to come to the park and back him up. When Kerrine and Kaliana arrived, they would step out from hiding and arrest them. The end of their reign of terror complete.

A tap on his passenger-side window brought attention to his not being alone. Kaliana smiled and signaled for him to unlock the door. He clicked the button by him on the door rest. She opened the door and sat down. "It's so good to see you again." Her salacious tone reminded him of Kerrine's attempt to seduce him on the Salish Sea.

"I'm not sure I share the same sentiments. Where's your sister?" The back driver-side door opened and Kerrine pointed a pistol at his head.

"Good morning, Mr. Jefferson. Shall we depart before any of your family arrives to save you from a fate you deserve?" She sat and closed the door.

"What is it about you that you that makes you so dramatic?" He turned the car key and revved the engine. "Where to?"

"Drive until I tell you to stop. We have sent people to pick up your children at school, so I suggest you keep following my directions." He kept quiet regarding his children's absence from education. He hoped they didn't know of Joan's parents' residence. A bluff, he figured, to keep him on track. The tracking device he attached to the car activated when the engine switched on. After stopping, the device would remain on for an hour and send a message to JJ. He had no way of checking its operation but accepted that it worked when he tested it the previous night, and JJ had called to confirm before he arrived at Olivia's.

With the operation started, he played his part as best he could to convince them they had the upper hand and control of their intended victim. He knew nothing of Mai Ling or her escape. Marcus had called to say he was safe and had captured his captor. A father's pride boosted by a son's ability to remain calm and thinking. Worry was a wasted emotion, so he concentrated on the situation presented by his being the guest of these lethal women.

"Are you taking me to a place where we can finish with your intention to engage in a sexual union with me? Or am I to die and that's the end of it."

"Now it's your turn to be less dramatic. If you want to participate, your change of mind is not acceptable. I want you to beg for me to release you from the torture I intend to inflict."

"Sex usually doesn't have to be sadistic, and I am not a masochist." He drove along Kitsap Way until they approached Highway 3.

Kerrine said, "Turn north on the highway." He signaled his intent to switch lanes and headed to the divided road.

Increasing speed to match the traffic, he said, "I thought it clever of you to bug my house. Did you get enough satisfaction watching Joan and I engage in our play? Did you get enough recording of my children to force me to comply with your plans?"

"Shut up and drive. When you get to Newberry Hill, get off and head toward Seabeck." He hoped the range of the tracker was not beyond JJ and Regina. The ferry had landed after he was ordered to drive. Depending on the time needed to vacate the boat, distance became critical. Waiting for the line of cars to move when the light at the exit turned green, he slowed the progress hoping he'd miss a turn and would have to wait for the next cycle.

"Don't miss that light," Kerrine scolded.

"I have no control of the cars in front of me."

"But you do have control of the speed at which you follow. Stay close and go through that light even if it is a late yellow. Understood?"

He pressed the pedal to give the engine more gas. The last car preceded them through the intersection as the light cycled to yellow. He wanted to stop and figured they wouldn't harm him in such a public place. He applied the brakes and waited as the light changed to red. A minute can be a long time to wait and patience in impatient people can bring pain. He waited for her to reprimand him for halting progress. Noting the silence from the back seat, he asked, "Where are we heading?"

The silence remained. Kaliana pointed another gun at him and spoke, "Kerrine is not happy and wants to harm you. Drive when the light turns green." He checked the rear-view mirror but saw nothing. Had she simply disappeared? He had not heard the car door open or felt a change of atmosphere. He figured she was crouching to hide from something or someone. What had spooked her?

CHAPTER

22

The light cycled to green again, and Marc drove up Newberry Hill to the Seabeck Highway. Kerrine had reappeared by the top of the grade at El Dorado Blvd. Marc's curiosity prompted a question. "What compulsion impels you to this action? I was just doing my job."

Kerrine placed a cold barrel to his neck. "We had an assignment. So, I guess you could say we are just doing our job."

Kaliana added, "We like to be sure to complete what we start."

"It makes little sense to me," Marc said, "to complete this assignment when nothing remains of the cartel which made the assignment." He emphasized the word assignment to strike a chord of common sense for them.

Kerrine removed the barrel. "True enough, so now we have a reputation to uphold." He laughed. "It's not funny. We are cold-blooded killers, or haven't you noticed." Her sneer diverged from the obvious. They had killed others, but more than that, Marc detected a moment of reality. Kerrine was colder than Kaliana.

"Kaliana, I think your sister is right. She is a cold-blooded killer."

She responded, "Why aren't you afraid? We're taking you to a remote place to eliminate you and bury you, so no one knows where you are. And yet, you act like this is another drive in the country to see grandma."

He had sparked the flint to drive a wedge between them. "Who wants the play to end, when the main act has yet to be played? You want some acting on my part. Am I not correct?"

Kaliana asked, "What acting? What are you talking about?"

"Kerrine made it clear I was to entertain you before the final scene. We are to engage in the age-old play of relational interplay." He waited for a response. None came. "Kerrine, you were not satisfied with my failure to succumb to your seductiveness when naked before me on the ship. Aren't we to reproduce the situation and have me melt with desire for you?" He focused on the road as Seabeck came into view.

Kerrine's gruffness waned as he spoke. "I do want to taste the skin of a cop. I've never been one to pass on a pig buffet." Kaliana stared at her sister awed by words she had heard about other victims, but not so deeply expressed about Marc. She realized a new profound emotion in her sister. Love. More than lust, she realized Kerrine admired the one man who stood against her and showed no fear.

"Take a right on Scenic Beach Drive," Kerrine ordered. Marc turned and slowed the car a bit. He figured the GPS unit was out of range for JJ and Regina. As they drove, he had not seen any other car familiar to him.

"How far? There isn't much more road before the State Park, and few houses are past the park. I assume that's why were here. Do you have a safe-house nearby?" Marc planned a different scenario with JJ. Now he would grace the stage as a solo act. Divide and conquer, he thought. Divide and conquer.

⋈ ⋈ ⋈

Regina checked the screen. The blip was nearly out of range. "Where are they heading?" She asked. JJ slipped a glance at the screen.

"It looks like they are going out to Hood Canal." He sped through the Newberry Hill light as it changed to yellow. A red light halted progress at the train tracks which supplied Bangor Submarine Base with munitions and other supplies. "Damn." The blip edged toward oblivion. He had to arrive as planned. He was not going to lose his cousin to a couple of insane sisters.

The light cycled back to green. Three cars in front of him dragged their passengers with the speed of a northwest slug. When the two-lane road came, he raced past. "It's gone," Regina said, calm and resolute. He pushed past the top of the rise and down the other hill. As he picked up speed, blue lights flashed behind him.

"Shit. I don't need this." He pulled to the side of the road. The deputy sat a moment, probably running the plate number before confronting another careless driver. He then got out and walked to JJ.

As the window descended, JJ heard, "License and registration, please." Instead of complying, he showed his Snohomish badge and said, "I'm in pursuit of a pair of felons who are holding my cousin hostage."

"A little out of your jurisdiction, aren't you?" The deputy seemed unimpressed.

"Yes, but my cousin is Detective Marcus Jefferson of your department." The deputy's attitude changed when he heard Marc's name.

"Marc is your cousin?" JJ nodded. "And he's being held hostage?" JJ nodded again. "How can I be of help?"

JJ said, "We're tracking his car, and he seems headed toward Hood Canal. What's out there?"

"From this road? Probably Seabeck or Scenic Beach State Park. Holly is out there, as well as Lake Symington."

"Alright. Follow us so we can pick up the radar blip."

"I can lead you with lights."

"No. Better we find him without warning his captors. We will need your assistance when we get to wherever he is being held." The deputy nodded and returned to his car. JJ raised his window and started off to the intersection at Seabeck Highway. The sheriff followed.

Regina asked, "Do you think he'll call for others to help."

"I hope not as they may be monitoring scanners." JJ pushed the brakes and pulled to the side of the road again. He got out of the car as the deputy pulled in behind him. He approached the car and announced that no report should be sent, just in case of monitoring of police channels by the felons.

"I already called it in." His face fell into a state of remorse.

"Well then, let's find my cousin as soon as possible." The hunt resumed.

Regina's eyes widened, "I have the blip again. They are on Scenic Beach Road." He raced the engine and pressed for more speed. The sheriff increased his speed to keep pace. Passing Seabeck

Conference Center and the marina, speed was above that posted but not in any dangerous manner which would cause harm to the pedestrians alongside the road.

"Turn here," she said. At the entrance to the park, she indicated the car was inside. They drove through the gate and followed the screen into a parking area where Marc's car was parked. JJ parked nearby and got out. He pointed at the sheriff to park away from the car and stay in his car. He then checked the engine hood which was warm. The car had not been parked for long.

Regina got out and joined him. "Are they here?" JJ shrugged.

Another sheriff arrived and pulled in beside his colleague. He stepped from his car and approached his fellow officer who pointed at JJ and Regina. He came to them; his authority pronounced by the stripes on his shoulders.

"What is going on here? And please identify who you are." They pulled their identifications from pockets and showed him.

"My cousin is Marcus Jefferson, one of your detectives. He and I are trying to outwit a pair of young women suspected of assaulting several individuals and probably effecting the death of at least three."

The sergeant folded his arms across his chest. "What was your plan?"

"We were to follow him. As they took him to some unidentified place, we were to arrive and neutralize them. His car is here, but we have not yet searched for him on the grounds."

The deputy joined the three people talking about the plan. The sergeant looked around the grounds. "If he's here we should be able to locate him quickly. If they had a car waiting for them, the search is going to take somewhat longer. What are they capable of doing? What do they want from him?"

JJ answered, "I'm not sure, but Marc indicated they wanted to finish the business from their encounter aboard a cruise ship named the Salish Sea when he and his family were on vacation. He thought they wanted to kill him."

"Well, then let's clear this area of any possibility they're here. And let's get forensics out here to check this car." The deputy made the arranegments. The others walked through the park from the pavilion areas and picnic tables to the shoreline of Hood Canal. The deputies found no trace of Marc or the twins. A couple was present, but when asked about a man and two women, they did not give any positive information.

Back at the parking area, a search of the area showed no indication of any other car being in the lot, including any car for the young couple. Had they been part of the conspiracy by providing an alternate way to leave the park? The deputy was sent to find the couple and bring them to the lot.

"If an alternate automobile was here, we are not going to find them soon enough." The sergeant shook his head. JJ pounded his fist in his hand. The plan had failed.

CHAPTER

23

Bernice crawled down the ladder to the storage room under the greenhouse used by Eden to pollinate rhododendrons and azaleas. Bumblebees transformed the pollen to make honey. Mad Honey. The coolness of the room was a natural refrigerator to keep the raw honey fresh until pasteurization.

She filled a small box with twelve vials and sealed the lid. As she climbed from the hidden room, her brain recalled the first time, over a decade ago, her bumblebees made the toxic honey. Several customers became regulars, and she didn't want to know the use. She suspected Chris knew since he researched potential buyers before completing any contract.

The young man who came from Edmonds, Washington, was her last contact. His death was ruled naturally occurring but unusual. Fear of discovery drove her to act alone and provide an avenue for ending the activity. Chris had made the enterprise lucrative, and her retirement fund was large and offshore, as well as, tax-free.

She needed a way to escape with her plan intact and no way of discovering her whereabouts. Sending some of the honey to certain places could be dangerous but helpful. Eden's questions about the bees and her desire to incorporate a daily routine of apiary knowledge scared her. The time had come to separate from the Montague Wholesale Nursery.

In the greenhouse, she buried the box which she would remove later. Dressed in her netting, she checked her beehives for any anomalies. The production of honey included fall blooms of a variety of plants. These were to be mixed with the 'Mad Honey' using a ratio of four to one. No one died or became sick from Montague Honey varieties.

After satisfying her mind that the bees were healthy and productive, she removed her netting and left the greenhouse. Walking the grounds and avoiding speaking with others, she cut across to the area of the offices, stopping at the supervisor office to speak with Chris. He was not present. At that moment she realized she should not let him know her plans. He was not a happy person if crossed, and this action would be a cross.

Entering her own office, she sat a moment before pulling a folder from the bottom drawer of her desk. She needed to extricate the folder containing the list of customers she sold 'Mad Honey' from any records which legal officials could use to convict. She placed the folder in a manila envelope and addressed it to a post office box she maintained away from her residence. "Insurance," she thought.

Checking her watch, the time for another lesson for Eden about bees was soon. She pulled two books for her to read. The next step was to have her boss work a box. The anxiety about what reasons Eden had for learning to work the hives, rose in her. Could she last long enough? She had to.

A knock awakened her to the proximity of another person. She looked up to see her student. "Good morning, Eden. Let's get started." Eden sat in a chair and leaned forward. "I have a couple of books I want you to read. Then we will be practicing with one of the beehives until you are proficient."

Eden said, "I do appreciate your teaching me. I'm worried about the future of Montague, Inc. My father's death before his time and Malcolm's heart failure shook my world. I've hidden long enough from my responsibilities to your future and Chris and his expectations. We have a great place here, and I want it to continue."

Bernice handed the books to her and said, "These are not difficult or elaborate, but they contain the basics of apiary work. Then we can use what you find in these to practice with me. Let me know when you are ready." Eden accepted the two readings and left for the main house. Bernice sat down again. A sigh escaped. She picked up the envelope and placed it in her valise. She would mail it to herself as soon as she was near a post office away from the destination.

The day was approaching mid-afternoon, so she decided to call it an early departure. As a salaried employee, no time card kept a record of the length of her workday. If the work was done, she was paid. Grabbing her coat and hat, she walked from her office.

Before she got to the door, Chris called to her from his office. He had returned without her hearing him. Eden's presence probably interrupted her usual hearing of the squeak of his chair. She turned and entered the room. "Leaving early?"

"Yes, I checked all the hives and gave Eden a couple of books to read. Soon as she is ready, I'll work with her to practice on a box."

"Are you worried she's losing her mind?"

Bernice shrugged, "I don't think so, but one never knows." She leaned against the door jam. A hint of fertilizer wafted through her nose.

"Her wanting to work the soil with me is as odd as what she wants from you. I don't want any interference with our arrangement. I would hate for an illness to disable such a beautiful person." His stare was meaningful. No one should get in his way.

"Do you think her husband, Malcolm, died as a result of our honey?"

"Do you?"

"I've never wanted to think he ingested the honey by mistake. The other possibility was that he was deliberately given the honey and died as a result. Since neither you nor I would do such a thing, I've wondered if Eden knew and wanted to get him out of the way."

"You suspect her?"

"I don't know what to believe. I wanted nothing from our escapade except financial security. I believe you want the same. Anything more jeopardizes our operations." Straightening her body and shifting her case, she turned to leave. Looking back, she said, "Don't underestimate Eden." She left the building.

As she drove from the grounds, her doubts about Christopher Colella and his desired relationship with Eden Montague haunted her. She knew about the short and sordid affair after Malcolm died of heart failure. The meticulous records of honey production worked against him. She knew how much was available and how the amount needed for general manufacture. The remaining amounts were a rich trade in illicit activities by people who wanted to eliminate their enemies. Some honey had gone missing without a trace and Eden became a widow.

At a post office away from her zip code, she paid the required postage and left the envelope with an agent. The package would arrive within the week, and her security would be in a safety deposit box just afterward. The additional step of mailing the package was to assure the timeliness of a postmark for proof of her complicity and subsequent assistance in stopping the trade.

Eden hadn't killed her husband, but there was no proof Chris had. The strange note Eden referenced necessitated caution and cessation of the production of mad honey. She decided to do nothing about making any more until the spring flowering of rhodies and azaleas. By then she would be a ghost of her own making.

Bernice collapsed on the couch in her house without removing her coat. She sat a moment and then decided to have a drink before making a simple meal for her dinner. With a sunset within an hour the day turned into twilight. The equinox was a mere week away. Night would become longer and days shorter. She wanted the warmth and sun of a Caribbean island to live out the remainder of her life.

Another complication she had to eliminate was the possibility of the twins coming to her for more of their preferred weapon, the luteum honey. There was no more except for the 12 vials buried at the farm. She would label them and place them in the shipment scheduled for the end of the week. She had two days to prepare proper brand name tags for delivery to various places.

With the death of a couple of people and the testing of blood samples, Bernice hoped for a clue to lead them to the farm and the arrest of the culprits who supplied killers with a natural weapon. Regardless of any possible outcome, she had to contact Kerrine and Kaliana to inform them of the end of their careers as nature's killers. Informing the others on her list by other means had to be untraceable to her.

After eating and drinking far too much, she prepared for a long night's sleep. Lying on her bed awaiting the arms of Morpheus to claim her, thoughts swirled in her brain. Was she safe from any harm? Would Chris figure out her plans and come after her? Could she be gone from the farm by the time authorities arrested everyone? A fitful sleep answered her questions.

CHAPTER

24

Kerrine pointed the gun at Marc and directed him to get out of the truck. Kaliana had driven it to the small cabin down a dirt road at the end of Scenic Beach Drive. The switch of vehicles at the state park had gone off without any hitches. The isolation of the building raised a bit of angst in Marc. Disarmed as they started the journey, he hoped his cousin would figure out the hint left at the abandoned car. He had little time to make sure something would guide them. Taking a second tracker with him, he turned it on as they switched vehicles.

"Open the door," Kerrine said. Marc complied and entered a small room with a kitchen area in the corner. Two other doors probably led to a bedroom and a bathroom.

"I need a bathroom," he said. Kaliana opened one of the doors. He walked in it and started to close the door.

"Leave it open," he heard Kerrine say. She trained the gun on him as he finished his bladder evacuation. These girls had no scruples. He returned to the main center of the house.

"What now?" he asked?

"Now you die," Kerrine answered. Splaying out hands, he shrugged his shoulders.

"I thought you wanted to play before I had to die. I was looking forward to being with both of you. Then, I'm guessing; I get to dig my own grave."

Kaliana said, "See, I told you he would cooperate." She opened the door to a room which had a four-poster bed, a dresser, and a side table. He walked in and took off his jacket and hung it on a post.

"I think I should dig first. I might not have enough energy after our romp. If I dig, we can allow for me to get some rest and then we can play. I'm in no hurry to die."

Kerrine smiled, "Delaying the inevitable. Smart. However, no one is coming to rescue you. We can do it your way." Kaliana stroked his cheek with the back of her hand and licked her lips. He pulled her to him and whispered in her ear. Kerrine's smile faded. "What did you say to her?"

Kaliana answered, "He said you thought he had ice in his veins." He kissed her and squeezed her bottom. "I don't think he does."

"He's trying to drive a wedge between us. He doesn't care about you."

"I do care, though." Marc released his hold. "I want to be sure no one kills before you have a chance for behavior modification. I'm also curious as to the source of the honey. Grant me that last wish. To know where you got it."

Kaliana watched her sister's eyes change from dark to a lighter brown. She pointed the gun at the floor. Marc was not near and remained at the end of the bed. "I guess we can grant you that wish, but only after we play. I don't want you to lose interest and try something stupid."

"See," Marc said to Kerrine, "your sister has a generous heart. I think you do as well. You want your victims to die with a smile on their face. Let me know the source, and I will dig a deep trench in which to lie for eternity."

"Fuck you." Kerrine pointed the gun at him again and waved it toward the door. "Outside, mister ice in your veins. You can't halt the inevitable. I might change my mind and kill you right after you make your grave."

Marc opened the door and stepped out into the sunshine. His mind thought of the tracker in his pocket. He wanted to place it where the girls would not discover it on him. Kerrine directed him to a shed behind the house. He retrieved a shovel and pick, leaving the tracking device on a shelf behind a can of oil. He observed a chainsaw, ax, wedges, and sledge hammer.

The trio walked into a clearing about a hundred feet from the shed. The soil had been disturbed as if other graves had been dug. Marc pointed at one place which looked to be a recent dig. He said, "Looks like I'm not going to be alone. Who's the person in that hole?"

Kerrine waved the gun at him to begin his work. Kaliana answered his query. "I don't know if a body is in there. We just needed a place for you."

"Shut up. He's delaying in a wasted hope for his rescue. Or a chance to overpower us." Kerrine looked at Marc, "Now dig."

The ground was not as easy as he first suspected and use of the pickax was needed to churn up rocks and cut through tree roots. He rolled up sleeves and kept working. His meticulousness slowed progress. The hole became deeper and wider as time passed. Finally, Kerrine directed him to stop.

"That's good enough. You can shower and prepare for our playtime. Once we have sated our desires, we'll come back out here, and you can lie down in the hole."

"You're going to bury me alive?"

"Shooting a gun out here won't be noticed." Kerrine grinned.

Marc climbed from his digging. He dropped the tools by the hole. "I guess you'll need these later." His pants and shirt were dirty, his face smeared with sweat. "I do need a cleansing. Either of you care to share the shower with me? I need my back washed." He heard a slight gasp from Kaliana. Kerrine remained stoic.

Inside the house, he altered the conversation. "How did you become such, I hate to use the term, bitchy young women. You're beautiful, smart, educated, and talented in the most negative of ways. Why? What happened in your past which infused this deadly activity?"

Kerrine winced. Marc seemed to have hit a nerve. She stuck the barrel of the gun into his chest and said, "You're too nosy. But since you have little left of your miserable life, I will tell you." Kalaina turned toward the door, hearing a noise outside. "Go see what animal is trying to get in."

Before she could explore, the door burst open and JJ entered the house. With the distraction Marc grabbed the gun, twisting Kerrine's hand and wresting the weapon from her. Kaliana dropped to her knees and raised her arms. Regina followed JJ into the house. Mark dropped Kerrine to the floor and placed a foot on her left shoulder.

"Glad to see you made it to the party." Marc's comment drew smiles from his cousin and his Mountie friend.

"Nice of you to leave a clue about the second tracker. By the way, you look like shit." As he spoke Regina placed plastic wrist ties on Kaliana. She then did the same to Kerrine.

Sitting them on the chairs around a small kitchen table, Marc asked, "Anyone wish to be the first to spill their guts about the remaining members of your army. I'm a bit tired of finding more of them every so often." Neither twin responded. "Okay, I guess we'll do this the old-fashioned way."

JJ said, "Marc, we have a couple of your department's deputies outside. They're securing the perimeter."

Regina offered, "Since neither of your girlfriends is willing to talk, might I suggest a trip down memory lane."

"What?" Marc and JJ stared at her.

"I do believe these items belong to them." She held two small containers which she placed on the table. "Let's see what materials they carried here for your enjoyment." She opened the first of the containers and removed several tea bags.

Marc's mouth closed and straightened as he stared at the material which contributed to the death of author James Blackthorne aboard the Salish Sea and the assault of Marcus and Delinda in Skagway. Regina opened the other container and removed several unmarked bottles of a yellow fluid which Marc suspected to be the 'Mad Honey' which was used to create muscular paralysis, a contributor to the heart failure noted by the Alaska forensic scientist.

Picking up one of the vials, Marc faced the twins. "Which one of you wants to explain where you get this substance?" He pushed the bottle under the nose of each one of the women and repeated his question. "Which one of you? No answer? Maybe you need to sample your weapon of choice. Maybe I'll let one of you live and watch the other die from the effects of the tea and honey. What is it called? Oh yeah, grayanotoxin. I suppose one of you will help with my investigation when the other is suffering from the effects of the toxins."

Regina added, "I'll heat some water. For tea." She entered the kitchen area of the room and searched cupboards for mugs and a kettle for the water.

JJ left the house to speak with the deputies outside. He wanted the deputies occupied with other chores. They reported the hole in a clearing in the woods, and what to them seemed to be other areas disturbed by digging. JJ returned to the house and spoke with his cousin. Marc turned again to the twins.

"What's outside beside my grave?"

CHAPTER

25

Olivia and Randolph sat in the bedroom they now shared. Shared by them in her house. They were alone for the first time since his return from Minnesota. Delinda and Marcus had departed for the dinner, missed when he was coerced and confined by Mai Ling. Tiberius and Jeremais had returned to their families and official police duties. JJ and Regina were off to find out how to help Marc capture the elusive twins. A message for his eyes only explained a need for father and uncle to not involve themselves in the plot he was undertaking. So, they were alone.

"I am making some serious changes in my life by moving here to Seattle." Randolph reached for a hand. She watched him. Unsure of his thinking, his focus was on the carpeting by the bed on which they sat. His life was cruelly upended when his wife received diagnosis of a rapid action cancer. Her death wrenched away any calm future.

"I love you the more for doing it. Delinda needs you here, and I'm pretty sure she wasn't leaving Minnesota because she hated the weather." He grinned. A funny noise escaped his throat.

"I never wanted anything more from life than I had. The death of my wife caused a major rift in my life. Nothing made much sense to me until I met you. I fell for a nurse and got an FBI special agent. Go figure."

She stood up, still holding his hand, and pulled him to a standing position. "I want you to understand why I was willing to accept your friendship and love. My daughter Alanna is the result of a tragedy in my life. I was attending nursing school. A guy I was seeing became more aggressive and controlling than I wanted. I broke off the relationship and finished school. I started a career in Atlanta and was happy." She grabbed his other hand and faced him. "This is the part which I haven't told anyone for many years. He found me there and forced me to be with him. He wanted sex with me, but I resisted. He raped me, and I got pregnant. After a month of his abuse, I left. I had no money, no future, and little hope." She released hands and walked away.

Turning to Randolph, she continued, "I found a clinic in Virginia which hired me. I explained my situation and the female manager empathized. I was back on my feet. I gave birth to my daughter and thought all was well. He found me again, but this time I was ready. My manager's husband worked for the FBI and made sure I was not assaulted or abused. He then offered to help me become an agent. They watched Alanna so I could attend Quantico. I was sent to the Portland office and began a career investigating illegal drug smuggling. When the opportunity for the undercover work in Seattle came about, I accepted. Alanna was a teenager and attended a private residential school in Portland. I arranged for her care and began working with Pepper. The rest of the story you know." She turned and stared out the window.

Randolph stood beside her. "I guess you want me to say something, but I don't have any words." He wrapped fingers in hers. "I love you."

"Those are good words to hear."

They remained at the window without any exchange for another minute. Finally, Olivia asked a question which shocked him. "Do you want more children?" She watched him.

Scrunching his face, he said, "I haven't thought about it. I figured Delinda was the only child for me. Her mother and I wanted another, but complications at birth ended any future offspring. And you? Do you want more children?"

"I didn't until I met you. If we're doing this get married thing, and don't get me wrong, here, I want to, then I was wondering about it. That's all. I know we're not young, but ..."

"We'd be really old kindergarten parents. And if we did want this, I think we should get married right away and start the family." Silence grabbed the conversation as the reality of telling Alanna and Delinda welded their words.

Randolph broke the status. "Delinda wanted to have a sister when she was younger. We thought about adopting and decided to focus on her. She might not want a sister now."

Olivia responded, "Alanna grew up in a hectic world of crazy schedules and time with other people watching her. Although I have been in other relationships, nothing made sense until you. She will be surprised, but I don't know if she will accept a younger sibling."

"Delinda likes her."

"Alanna thinks your daughter is solid."

"I'm losing control of my life as if I thought I had any before."

"I have focus for the first time in a long time." They stared at the backyard.

Birds chirped. A dog barked. The light of the day was fading with the onset of twilight. A light breeze swayed leaves, now turning gold by the advent of fall. Several fell in a swirl to the grass below.

Randolph added to the conversation of nature. "They will just have to understand." She squeezed his hand. A journey of a thousand steps begins with just one.

Delinda and Marcus finished dinner as the evening wandered along with them. After paying for their meal, they walked into the room rented for the night. Each day together built a stronger union for them. They wanted to share every moment they could regardless of the challenges thrown at them. A bond, forged in the hell of their experience in Skagway, united their lives as no marriage could. Together, life was safe. Apart, remembering hell was a torture Satan proffered, and they rejected.

After a satisfying congress of love, Marcus said, "I don't want to wait much longer before we get to live together. I miss you when I'm at the frat and can't see you. I want to come home to you and study with you. I want to know we are one."

Delinda cuddled closer to him. The warmth of his body melted into her. His body exuded a hint of their activity. "When Dad finds a place to live, I will know more. I want us together, also."

"Do you think he'll marry Olivia?" Marcus asked.

"Probably. He might stay with her instead of finding us a place. I don't want to share a room with Alanna. I need a place of my own."

"Then let's talk with our parents and let them know what we're thinking." He stroked her hair and wanted more of their activity. She purred and kissed him. They made love a second time.

Afterward, Marcus arose from the bed and showered. Delinda joined him in the cramped tub. They dried each other and went to bed for a night of sleep intertwined in love.

His kidnapping by Mai Ling had interrupted the plan for this moment, but nothing was to interfere with a future together. For this moment thoughts of the ordeals his father endured in Alaska receded to the depths of his mind where he had hidden the ordeals, he and Delinda had survived. The hunt for any remaining enemies of a secure and safe life could wait. All that mattered was this moment feeling the soft flesh of a girl he had met only a few weeks ago. A girl who was now the woman he wanted for the rest of his life. As he slept, dreams of mayhem stalked his sleep.

Delinda fared no better. She had filled her life with one piece of living stolen from her when her mother died. Although she didn't question her father's love, she desired to share with someone that which she experienced with her mother - a sharing of ideas, plans, and futures. Her father loved her, but his grief displaced her wants. She blamed no one for the emptiness in her heart when she accepted a trip aboard the Salish Sea with her father who acted as the medical director.

Each of them came into a world of intrigue without the proper defenses. They changed the world together with better defenses as a family.

Morning came with restless bodies wanting another few minutes of intimacy. After dressing, Marcus said, "Dee, if your dad stays at Olivia's house, will you want to move out? Find that place of your own?"

"I think so." She finished buttoning her blouse. "Will you live with me?" His smile and nodded. They packed the few items they brought with them and left the hotel. As they drove to the frat house, she remained quiet. He kissed her when they arrived, and she left.

His mind conjured up unusual scenes of them tied to bedposts and assaulted. He shook his head to dismiss the images. What future annoyances might invade their lives? What tragedies could befall their wanting peace and serenity?

CHAPTER

26

Eden reread the note from Vanessa Christine. Something was to happen soon, so she decided to connect with her sister and uncover the reasoning. Her farm was her life and nothing she did caused anyone any harm. She strolled across the main yard of her home to survey the expanse of plants and greenhouses which comprised the farm.

Her life included several tragic moments, her father dying and leaving her and Malcolm to continue running things. Then a sudden, unexpected heart attack ended Malcolm's life. She was alone.

Chris Colella and Bernice Harapat kept operations working during a period of mourning. Nearly two years passed before Eden started overseeing the nursery. Her short and ill-advised affair with Chris was the last tragic moment for her. She abandoned any further interruptions and made sure she knew the financial aspects.

Now her mind was bent on learning more about the operations. Nothing was to interfere again. The note from Christine was a distraction she would clarify. Picking up one of the books Bernice gave her to read about bees, she skimmed the table of contents and tossed it aside. Another book provided more interest. She sat and read.

A chapter about mutating the abilities of bumblebees intrigued her. Had Bernice created a species more resistant to toxins in certain plants? If so, did Chris modify plants to increase the toxicity of those plants? The note referenced an investigation. What was the investigation indicating? A trip to Seattle could answer the questions.

She finished reading the chapter and placed the book on top of the other book about bees. "Find Bernice," she thought. "Find her and ask about mutating bees." She departed her house and walked to the office building. Bernice sat at her desk, writing in a log book. She looked up as Eden entered.

"Oh, hi," she said. "How are you doing today?" Her demeanor appeared calm, but Eden sensed a tension when she closed the booklet. "What can I do for you?" She placed the book in a top drawer of her desk.

"I was reading one of the books about bees. One chapter explained the process for increasing the strength of hive members so to survive any adverse toxicity in some plants." Eden watched Bernice roll back into the chair and fold arms. "Have you been experimenting with mutating hives?"

Bernice leaned forward and planted her elbows on the desk. "As you know, we have a process for creating honey which is called Mad Honey in many parts of the world. We need to be sure the bees are not negatively affected by the pollen they collect."

"You are creating super bees."

"I wouldn't call them super bees. They are better suited to the conditions we have established." Her eyes rose to the right and returned. "Are you questioning my methods?" Her tone deepened, as a frown laced her eyebrows.

"Should I be questioning your actions, I would have called you to my house for an explanation. You needn't be defensive. I merely asked a question based on one the of the books you handed me to read."

Bernice relaxed, "I'm sorry. I don't want you to worry. Nothing is wrong with our processes." Eden nodded. She turned to leave when Bernice asked, "Are you troubled because of the note you told me about?"

Eden turned back. "Why do you ask? Should I be worried about an investigation?"

Bernice hesitated. "I want nothing more than success for you and this nursery." She stood and walked around her desk. "Eden, I am not a problem to you."

"Are you indicating there may be a problem I should be aware of?" Bernice didn't answer. Eden left to find Chris and ask him similar questions.

She changed her mind and decided to contact her police friend and sister, Vanessa Christine. In her garage, she picked her smallest vehicle and left the property.

As she drove south to Seattle, she punched the phone button on her steering wheel. When the list of recent calls from her cell phone displayed, she touched the screen for the personal number of her friend.

"Eden, what's up? You in trouble?"

"No, Nessi, but I want to discuss with you the problems you indicated in your note to me. I'm on my way to Seattle."

Vanessa said, "Do you think it wise to meet here? Let me come out to our regular place. I can be there in an hour."

"Okay, I'll see you there." Eden clicked the steering wheel icon to end the call.

As she drove to the small restaurant in Edmonds, ideas mixed with fears. Vanessa did not contact her about investigations without reason. Something was happening, and she was the target. She had to uncover what it was.

As she sat in a booth to wait, Eden contemplated her thinking about the powerful honey she mixed with other types to create the unique blend. The inventory of Mad Honey was never large. It was used by Bernice to create the brand. She couldn't imagine any other use. The records were clear. Every bit of honey was mixed and diluted to become harmless.

Vanessa entered and sat opposite her. "What's up?" she said.

Eden asked, "Am I in trouble?"

"No. Why do you ask?"

Eden leaned in and put her arms on the table. "You sent a note indicating an investigation may come to my farm and ask me questions about my products. It sounded ominous."

Vanessa reached across and held her hands. "One of my sergeants returned from Alaska where he and his son were involved in a life-threatening attempt to silence his son. The main weapon used was a lethal type of honey made with rhododendrons. The report he handed me said it was made with rhododendrons. Their written report read that grayanotoxin was intensified and deadly. At least two people aboard the cruise ship died from consuming the honey made from rhodies. Tea was laced with rhodie leaves."

Tears formed in Eden's eyes. "You know we produce a honey from rhodies. Is this why you contacted me? Am I to be arrested for supplying the attackers?"

"I don't know. We haven't started an official investigation."

"Who has?"

"Started an investigation? Probably Marcus Jefferson of the Kitsap Sheriff's office. He's the son of my sergeant. Someone on the cruise ship targeted his family. He nearly died."

Sitting back after freeing her hands, she said, "I don't need this. Nessi, what if I am arrested for something I haven't done? What if there is another reason? It has to be another nursery, but I don't know who would do this."

"Eden, don't cause yourself any angst. I will lead it away from you if needed."

A waitress approached them. They ordered coffees and pastries. She departed to get their fare. "I have another concern which is outside of your domain." Vanessa interlaced her fingers and waited. Eden scanned the room as if intruders were present and spying. "When Malcolm died, I didn't think much about his death other than a heart attack was surprising. Heart attacks happen for many reasons. But with these deaths aboard the cruise ship because of toxic honey, I began to wonder if he was dead because of our honey. It may have been an accident, but I can't reject the idea that he was deliberately poisoned."

"We can re-check his autopsy and test for grayanotoxin. I can't guarantee any results because the tissues may not indicate anything other than his heart failed."

"Would such a request point at me?"

"Probably, but I'll keep it under wraps."

"I don't want you getting into trouble trying to help me."

"You needn't worry. This is an important issue and if Malcolm was murdered, we need to find out who did it. Being in Snohomish County, you are under the jurisdiction of their sheriff. Jeremais Jefferson would be involved. He's my sergeant's brother and uncle to Detective Jefferson. He's been in the mix of all of the problems in Everett because they destroyed a drug cartel a few months ago."

Eden rested her head in her hands as elbows sat on the table. The waitress returned with coffee and pastries. Vanessa observed a breath catch as a jaw dropped and eyes blinked. Had she heard? Vanessa grimaced at her and set lips in a straight line cowering her into forgetting what she may have seen or heard.

"Let's get out of here," Vanessa said. Leaving a twenty on the table, she guided a sullen Eden from the building. They walked to the waterfront, near the ferry to Kingston. "Something is bothering you more than what you said inside."

Eden stared at the fishing boats and pleasure craft bobbing on Puget Sound. A ferry horn sounded its arrival from across the waters. Without altering her view, she asked the question burning in her heart and soul. "Vanessa, what's bothering me is the idea that I am responsible for Malcolm's death." She faced Vanessa. "Have I created a commodity which is misused by some and therefore lethal? Did I kill my father? My husband? And not understand what I did?"

CHAPTER

27

The Asian beauty entered the offices of Montague Wholesale Nursery and wandered until finding the correct door. She read the placard next to the opening, Chris Colella, Supervisor. Staring into the room, she turned away to hunt for the person whose name emblazoned the sign. "May I help you?" She gasped.

"I'm looking for Chris. Is he here?" The small Hispanic woman studied the foreigner to her domain. Turning she pointed outside to the greenhouses.

"He's in number two house with the roses." Mai scooted past her and hurried across the yard to the doorway. Opening it, she entered.

"Close that door," a voice boomed. It clicked shut. Chris faced the intruder. "What do you want?" he blared before recognizing his mistress. "Mai Ling, what are you doing? You shouldn't be here."

"I did as I was asked and kept him prisoner. I did what they wanted, but he overpowered me and took me to her house."

"Slow down. What are you talking about?" Chris caressed her hair, noticing the bruising around her eye. He kissed her forehead.

"They asked me to coerce that Jefferson kid into going with me, and he did. I handcuffed him and kept him at the house in Fremont. He escaped and attacked me. He hit me and hurt me."

"Be calm. He'll suffer for what he did to you. More than in Skagway." He hugged her. "How did you get here?" He looked around the building. They were alone.

"I caught a bus to Snohomish and then an Uber. They had me tied up at that FBI woman's house, but I cut the ties and escaped when his father fell asleep. I need your help."

Chris thought of ridding himself of this albatross but changed his mind. Hiding her alive was easier than as a dead body. "Okay, let's get you out of here and to my place in town. Stay there until we can move you to safety."

"Can you come with me?" He nodded. Day was close to twilight, and the transient workers were most likely finished and in their trailers. The permanent staff would not question a woman accompanying him to his office and then off the property. He enjoyed her companionship most of the time. She satisfied animal instincts with an ability not experienced with other females. Paulukaitis taught her well.

As they drove down the length of the road leading to the highway, he instigated an argument to have an excuse for what he wanted to do. His stash of honey and tea was at his house. He would fix some for her as a way of asking forgiveness for his attitude. She would comply.

As they approached the house, he apologized for his gruffness, explaining the harsh day he had as a reason for being mean. She respected his explanation and forgave him. Inside they went to the bathroom for cleansing and bandaging.

"I need a shower," she said.

"As do I." They washed each other's stench and guilt from their bodies. He dismissed his plan. He wanted her. Her graceful curves enticed as much as any Siren of Greek lore. He placed clean clothes on his body as she dressed in fresh jeans and a t-shirt he kept for her. She watched as he prepared a small meal.

"Explain what happened." They were sitting at his dining table.

She related the tale of convincing Marcus that his sister and brother were in serious trouble and he needed to go with her. He acquiesced. When she cuffed him and led him into the house, he sat where he was told. "I turned away after offering a sip of water to him. He attacked me. I hit my head on the counter. He kicked me in the ribs and struck my face with a foot."

Chris responded with a grunt. "He shouldn't have done that to you."

As they cleaned the table and kitchen of dinner, they teased each other. Chris wanted Mai Ling relaxed and open to discussing her future, compromised by her failure.

One last session using her ability to sate a man's lust forced his actions for comforting her. He had to tie up this loose end and dispose of any remaining detail which pointed to him. They went to the bedroom and stripped clothes from bodies. They climbed into the bed and pleased each other. Sleep captured the last of their energies.

In the morning, Chris awoke to the aroma of bacon and eggs. He robed his naked body, shuffling in slippers to the kitchen. His loose end had made breakfast. He did not think of himself as a heartless person. Maintaining safety remained paramount, but no threat executed against the life he lived. They ate a quiet meal. She served him coffee with cream and honey as options. He declined both and drank it black. The yellow fluid in a marked bottled caused no concern.

"I have to go to the nursery and work my job. Stay here and out of sight. No one should be disturbing you."

"I have nowhere to run. I can hide here as well as anywhere. When you return, we can plot my escape. I do not want any other interaction with any of them. I do not have a hatred for the Jeffersons as do Kerrine and Kaliana." Extracting a promise from her to stay in the house, he departed for Montague Nursery.

His concern now rested with Bernice. She acted strangely of late, and he did not want any interference. She was complicit with the plan to create lethal honey. Any hesitation from her and his focus for loose ends would change. Mai Ling didn't intimidate him as much as Bernice. The beekeeper had all the records and information which would convict him. She played a game with him as a cohort, but a strain on the relationship could flip the allegiance forged over several years and many mutations of plants and bees.

His other difficulty was Eden Montague. She now engrossed herself in his soil work and plant hybrids. Was she concerned with the business or questioning his integrity? She knew nothing of the side business Bernice, and he had constructed while she and Malcolm ran the financial side.

When questions arose about the use of honey made from rhododendrons and azaleas, Chris instilled a plan which cleared the way for an expansion of the lethal business run by them. Malcolm had to die. Using the only weapon which would not be questioned or suspected, he switched out the honey in their kitchen with the honey from their secret supply. Eden did not use honey as a sweetener. She drank coffee straight. Malcolm drank tea and sweetened it with honey. The result was a massive failure of his heart.

Eden sank into a remorseful period of mourning. He was home free. Now the situation changed. She interfered with his pattern of work, asking questions, seeking information, watching operations. Was she suspecting more than her actions exposed? His affair with her was an attempt to become an equal partner and then take over running the business. When that failed, he upped the ante with an increase in illicit honey which sold with huge profits.

Three women. All talented, smart, and cagey. Life was at a crossroads, and he didn't need or want distractions or encumbrances. He had to plot a course to extricate himself from them. One had information which implicated him. One had serviced him well and now could ruin him. His greatest problem was his boss.

Standing in one of the tree fields, he thought of the way a tree manufactures the nutrients it requires for survival. All it needed existed in the air, water, and soil. Photosynthesis provided the operation. Was there a way to extract meaning as to his requirements for survival? The workers tended the saplings which would be uprooted, carefully balling those roots, and transported to stores across the northwest.

If parts of human remains went along for the ride, the trees would have one of the requirements supplied. If parts were small enough, no detection would happen. An experiment centered on testing the theory grew in scope in his brain. The mess of vivisection needed containment. His first trial would be a small sample. An animal of a size large enough for results to be determined, but not hinting of nefarious future actions. Mai Ling was the least problematic as she would not be missed. Bernice's disappearance could be attributed to her moving away for other work.

His greatest challenge was how to rid the world of Eden Montague without any suspicion of wrongdoing by another human being. He watched the trees as they swayed in the light breeze, their leaves turning golden and dropping. He then spotted something which convinced him he could accomplish his aim and be free to run this company without any interference. All he needed was one change. Eliminating Eden.

CHAPTER

28

After the two forensic investigators finished the conference and were in the hotel packing, their deal with Donovan MacAvoy to stay and investigate required clearing a leave of absence from the Portland office. Ryan Wittingham and Jeremy Caldwell called and extended their stay in King County, Washington. The evidence of two young women having an alleged connection to the death of two deliverymen in Seattle had raised the interest of the Washington State Patrol Forensic Laboratory director.

"It would help us greatly if we could find those girls," Ryan said. He folded three shirts and placed them in his suitcase. "We should connect with the detective from Seattle."

"He wasn't so friendly last time we talked with him." Jeremy closed his bag, zipping it shut.

"Yeah, but he has the lead."

A knock on the door interrupted the conversation. Ryan flipped the flap of his bag and answered the door. The detective stood before him. "You gonna let me in?" Ryan stepped to one side. Detective Sergeant Manny Espinoza walked in.

"You two seem to have some kinda pull. I received what amounted to an order from the forensic director to contact you. I don't like infusing amateurs into my work."

Jeremy spoke, "We apologize for any inconvenience. We were called up by Director McAvoy to explain our answer to a question he asked during the conference."

"Oh, so you're now hot shots. I bow down before you." He plunked himself on the chair in the room. "What is it you have? Those ladies of mystery? Did you find them?"

Jeremy answered him, "We haven't found them, but they are the connection to what happened to those two guys in Seattle. I'm sure of that."

Espinoza spoke, "Let me get this straight. You're both forensic scientists or doctors or whatever. I'm the detective who brings in the evidence which you boys are supposed to sort through and then tell me what I already know. How are you of any help to me?"

Ryan said, "Any evidence you have that needs any testing for results you cannot obtain on your own, we can do. We had a team scour this room yesterday for prints and DNA. We should have some answers by the end of the week."

Espinoza popped up from the chair. "I have all the evidence I need. We tracked the van they stole to the cruise pier in Elliot Bay and then found it abandoned in a lot in Ballard. No prints or other evidence was found. These ladies are very careful."

Jeremy responded, "I understand all of that. The thing that gets me is they stole a flower delivery van and made the delivery for the guys they offed. Why?"

Espinoza shrugged his shoulders. "Maybe they felt bad about wasting all those flowers."

"And maybe they wanted to get something on the cruise ship," Ryan said.

"We assumed that was the reason, so we are looking into it. The ship sailed to Alaska." Espinoza sneered.

"How long ago did all of this occur?" Jeremy folded his arms.

"A couple of weeks ago. Why? Wanna take a cruise?"

"Yeah, but that's not the point. Where's the ship now?" Jeremy asked

"Anchorage. It was scheduled to return this week."

Ryan interjected, "When does it dock?"

Espinoza said, "It's detained in Anchorage. The return trip was canceled."

Ryan asked, "Why? What happened aboard the ship that authorities would interrupt a scheduled cruise and disrupt a couple thousand peoples' lives?"

"I don't know, yet."

"Maybe we should find out."

"We?" Manny Espinoza sneered at Ryan, then Jeremy. "We is

not how this works. I'll check with the cruise office. You stay out of my business. Go find your girlfriends." He turned to leave but stopped. "McAvoy may think you have some wisdom to impart. I don't need it." He opened the door and left.

"He's still not friendly," Jeremy quipped.

"I wonder what cruise line it was?" Ryan zipped his bag. "He indicated there was an office in Seattle. Maybe we should talk with them about the reasons for a cruise to be interrupted. The only one I can think of is a suspicious death during the sailing."

Jeremy placed his bag on the floor and pulled the handle. "You mean like the story I read of the man beating his wife to death and then asking crew for help to dump her overboard? That would stop a cruise for him, but not necessarily for all of the passengers."

"I agree. That detective is not going to like us probing into his case, but I don't care. Like he said, we need to find those girls and uncover what we can about the death of those deliverymen." They departed the room only to move to another in the same hotel. Their special leave was being picked up by Washington State Patrol. McAvoy wanted them on the hunt.

After settling into the second-floor room, they drove the rental car with an extended agreement to the Seattle office of police. "Might as well start at the source," Jeremy said. He had called to make an appointment with the head of detectives and was directed to Assistant Chief Vanessa Christine. He spoke with her office manager and set a time. They were early, but both men were interested in exploring the large metropolitan building.

"Think this person will be cooperative with our involvement?" Ryan asked as they approached the parking area and the gate attendant. They flashed badges as the man checked a clipboard. He then clicked a button and raised the bar.

Jeremy drove in. "Only way to find out is to talk with her." He parked the car in a visitor designated space. Riding the elevator to the main floor and reception, they didn't speak. This building housed the Seattle offices of law enforcement as did the building in Portland, but it was bigger. And taller. At reception, they indicated their business and were asked to sit until called. No inspection of the place for now.

"That detective, Espinoza, is going to throw a tizzy when he finds out we came here," Jeremy said. "And I don't care. We have been asked to follow through with our evidence, and this is as good a place as any to begin."

Ryan smiled. Before he could speak the receptionist called them to the desk. After receiving appropriate identification badges, they were directed to proceed up to the fifth floor.

As the elevator doors opened, they scanned the large room with cubicles and people milling about. They asked a person near them for Chief Christine's office and were directed to the end room. As they approached the door with a placard which indicated her room, another person stopped them. Espinoza snarled, "What are you doing here?"

"Hello again, Detective. We have an appointment with the chief." Ryan halted at the door. "Care to join us?" He turned the handle, and three men entered the outer office of the chief.

"May I help you? Oh, hello, Manny. Are they with you?" He shook his head.

"I'm Ryan Wittingham. This is Jeremy Caldwell. We have an appointment with Chief Christine." She picked up a receiver and spoke into it. Standing up the woman directed them through the inner door. Manny followed.

"Good afternoon, gentlemen. Manny. How may I be of service?" She directed them to chairs and sat on the side of her desk.

"We have been asked by State Patrol Forensic Lab Director Donovan McAvoy to follow up on a lead we have for a case which Detective Manny Espinoza is the lead. We wanted to be forthcoming about our involvement."

"Ma'am, I don't need these Oregon interlopers messing around my case." Espinoza flopped back into the chair.

"Relax, Manny." Turning her attention to the forensic scientists, she asked, "What do you want from this office?"

"We have a lead about the ladies in the security video feed. We want to know about the cruise ship. They stole the van and delivered the flowers. Why? What was it they wanted to get on the ship? Why is the ship detained in Anchorage? Are there any leads as to the location of the two women?"

"Slow down, cowboy. I had a chat with Donovan about the two of you. He thinks you can aid our investigation. Detective Espinoza will fill you in on the particulars."

"Pardon my intrusion, chief, but I don't need these yokels messing in my case."

"Manny, they are correct in asking about the cruise. Sergeant Tiberius Jefferson was enlisted by his son, Kitsap Detective Marcus Jefferson, to aid in an investigation aboard the ship. An author died under mysterious circumstances, and the ensuing inquiry nearly got Detective Jefferson killed." She plopped a folder in front of Manny. "Tiberius gave this to me. It's from the Crime Lab in Alaska. I want you three to read through it and tell me what you think."

Ryan reached for it, but Espinoza retrieved it, first. He opened it and began reading. His eyes widened as he swallowed. He gave the folder to Ryan and asked, "Can this happen?"

Chief Christine answered, "Apparently, so."

Ryan acknowledged the disbelief, "I've run across cases of 'Mad Honey' causing problems in Oregon. Mostly, it's farm animals and pets which eat the rhodies that vets most worry about. Could that be what they wanted aboard the ship? 'Mad Honey'? Who were they after? Who was the author who died?"

"Manny, include this report in your case file and keep these two informed," Christine said.

"Yes, Ma'am." Scowling eyes scanned Ryan and Jeremy.

Jeremy joined the conversation. "Was the FBI contacted?"

"An agent was undercover. Security included Detective Jefferson who was the original target." Manny started to speak but stopped. "We had a drug cartel operating in Everett, Washington, which a multi-unit team destroyed. Kitsap, Snohomish, Seattle, and Everett all participated. There was even a Canadian Mountie."

Ryan guffawed, "Wow, that was some team. How did that happen?"

Manny interjected, "Jefferson's uncle is a Snohomish County deputy and was involved in an undercover sting. It didn't go well. He was released from service and pretended to commit suicide. That was over two years ago." He crossed a leg over a knee.

Expressions on Ryan and Jeremy told of their surprise. Jeremy asked the obvious. "How does one pretend to commit suicide?"

Ryan asked the other obvious question. "Undercover sting? What was he trying to do?"

Vanessa entered the fray. "One of my sergeants has a son in the Kitsap Sheriff's Department. He's also the brother of Jeremais Jefferson, the Snohomish sergeant who worked with his sheriff to squash the illegal drug running business which came out of a legitimate import/export business. Because of corruption in the department, the operation failed. He plotted a two-year long scenario of revenge. He left a letter for his nephew, and the play began."

Ryan finished the story. "I suppose it ended with the cruise."

29

Kerrine wriggled on the floor of the cabin. Kaliana sat in a chair. Shoes and socks sat on a counter with a deputy on guard. "Why are we being treated as common criminals?" Kerrine asked.

Marc laughed, "I suppose you're right. There is nothing common about either of you." He turned to his cousin. "JJ, thanks for being smart enough to figure out what I meant by scratching t2 in the dirt."

He smiled, "Actually, Ginnie saw it and checked the computer. The second blip showed as clear as could be. We followed. Parking away from sight lines, I asked your deputies to stop any traffic from coming up this road. Didn't think the girls needed reinforcements. We also detained two people at the park. They may have brought the truck so the switch could be made."

"Digging my grave staved off any desire they may have had to accomplish their goal. You showed at the right time."

Regina said, "We saw you enter the cabin with them." She faced the twins. "I guess you will never have a personal encounter with Mr. Jefferson. Anyone willing to speak, yet?" She turned to Marc. "Maybe the hole shouldn't be wasted. Which one do you want to occupy it?"

"You can't do that," Kaliana screamed, "You can't just kill us and bury us."

"Shut up," Kerrine said, "she's baiting you. We have rights, and these are upstanding police officers. They want to convict us, so we rot in some jail cell." She looked up at Regina. "Isn't that right, Mountie. Just let us rot in some scumbag prison."

"You're so smart. I don't believe rot will happen. You will, however, explain the source of the honey or sit in a muddy grave. I leave the choice to you."

The deputy sergeant entered the room. "I had the other couple transported to lockup."

"Thanks, Max," Marc said. Directing attention to the twins, he added, "If they speak first, you two are done. I won't miss either of you. We do need information about the honey and tea. If we canvass every grower in the state, we'll find the source. Time is on our side. You don't have any."

Regina offered another suggestion. "Maybe we could strip off the rest of their clothing and leave them outside while we arrange for pickup and the forensic team. We need their clothing as evidence."

A smirk crossed the sergeant's face. JJ smiled. Marc nodded. "They are much happier without any clothing on. I've seen Kerrine naked. I suppose her sister looks the same."

Kerrine growled, "I'm going to file a complaint with your sheriff. You are not allowing us our Constitutional rights to a lawyer. And. You're mistreating us, which is a violation of the amendment regarding unusual search and seizure."

Sergeant Max laughed, "Beautiful and educated. Too bad. Marc, I can see why you want them cooperating. They have assets which can help finish the investigation you and your uncle started. I am sorry I missed it." Regina grasped Kaliana, standing her next to the wall.

She unbuttoned the blouse as Kaliana wriggled to make her stop. Regina pulled the blouse off her shoulders and down the back. "I will defend myself if you stop me from removing your pants. I will unfasten them and pull them down, so you can step out of them." Kaliana halted any further protest. After removing the pants, Regina approached Kerrine, lifting her from the floor by her hair. Regina removed her clothing without a fight. Each item was placed in a bag and tagged. To remove the blouses, Regina unlock the cuff on one hand of each twin, removed the sleeve and then cuffed it again to the sister. When finished, they stood back to back, right hand secured to left hand.

"Now what," Kerrine asked, "we get to sit in the hole out back?"

"You wanted me to spend eternity there. I'm only asking for a few answers. Miss McDonald is not worried about our United

States protocols regarding due process. I'm sure you will have an attorney as soon as we return to headquarters. In the meantime, any information you wish to volunteer will be greatly appreciated. We have a forensic team coming and your clothing is evidence."

Regina guided them to the door, opened it, and hesitated. A glance at Marc, who nodded, gave her the guidance she needed. Kerrine and Kaliana struggled to stay inside, but the force applied pushed them into the late afternoon coolness. A large truck with Kitsap Sheriff emblazoned on the sides arrived as they were led to the back of the cabin. A canine and its handler vacated the side door as another pair of deputies exited the back.

Sheriff Glenmore Fellington got out of the front of the truck along with the driver. "Jefferson, you better have something out here. I brought the body dog and a sonar scanner."

"My cousin, JJ, thinks there may be more bodies out back. Our girls are sitting in the hole I dug for my body. We've collected their clothing for evidence, but they would be more comfortable in county jumpsuits."

Fellington directed the driver to get two outfits. "Team, go to work." The dog and handler moved around the cabin. The forensics team entered it. JJ, Marc, and Sergeant Max followed the dog. At the hole, the semi-clad women were given clothing, freed of restraints, and told to dress. Shoes were not part of the ensemble. Barking alerted them to a find by the dog. The deputy planted a stake and moved on. Another bark and another stake.

When finished with the survey, the deputy had planted six stakes. Marc approached the twins, "Attorney or not, one of you needs to explain the body count. The other will be an old lady before she gets out of prison." He waited as the deputy returned with the scan machine.

As the deputy scanned over the staked areas, the screen showed outlines of what appeared to be human remains. Flora had grown over some of the sites. Digging would be a challenge.

Marc turned to Fellington. "We're going to need more people out here." Glen made the call. Approaching the twins, he said, "I'm not sure of your involvement with the body count, but any of these can be connected to either of you, it will sink any future freedom gained by good behavior in prison. Remain silent and take your chances with the courts."

Kerrine muttered, but Kaliana moaned, "I'm getting cold."

Two deputies had begun digging one of the less overgrown sites. As they progressed with clearing a ring around the target area, another was clearing the dirt from above the body. After several minutes, he declared, "We have a skull."

Marc, JJ, and Sheriff Fellington watched as the team cleared earth away from the remains of a person, still clothed. As more of the body was exhumed, the identity of male or female became apparent. The clothing remains appeared to be an expensive suit. A white shirt and tie, dark jacket and pants, along with leather shoes hinted at a business deal gone bad.

"Any identification still with the body?" Marc asked. One of the deputies checked the coat pockets and removed a wallet. He handed it to Marc. Searching through the remnants of the folders and pockets of a three-fold wallet, he found a driver's license which identified the corpse as a man missing from his family in Port Orchard.

"Glen, we seem to have solved the disappearance of William Dumont." Another detective in the south division of the sheriff's office had worked with local police to find him, missing almost eight months.

Marc faced his nemesis. "Kerrine, if you know anything about these bodies, life will be better for you, if you cooperate." Her sneer answered any question he might ask her.

"Kaliana, do you have anything to say?" Eyes met eyes. Tears puddled and cascaded soiled cheeks.

The smell of freshly turned soils mixed with decaying material. Neither woman spoke. Marc figured they had little or no knowledge of the other bodies. His was to be the only one contributed to them. A stretcher was placed by the exposed remains, pictures were taken, soil samples gathered, and a tarp laid out on which to place the evidence.

Marc walked around the yard surveying the placement of stakes. As he observed the graves, another person joined the growing number of people. Although many counties had no forensic experts, Kitsap hired one from the crime lab in Olympia. "Marc, I see you have work for me."

"As if you didn't have enough to do."

They laughed. "What do we have here?" He surveyed the scene and began observing the first body. He took bug samples, as well as flora. "These will tell a story."

CHAPTER

30

Tiberius glanced at his watch. Where had time flown? Returning home to share a lunch with Gabriella, his shift was about to begin for the afternoon. Although his captain was acquiescent to his finding the toxic honey source, the parameters of the search were limited to only a few days. "Sweetheart, I've got to get back to work." He cleared his spot of the kitchen table, kissed her, and left to connect with his brother, Jeremais.

Their rendezvous place near the Seattle's Colman Dock held a special place in his heart since he proposed to Gabriella at Ivar's Acres of Clams nearly forty-five years ago. Jerry waited for his brother at the outside Ivar's Fish Bar.

"You eaten anything?" Jerry asked. Tiberius nodded and observed the bag.

"What did you get?" he smiled and licked his lips.

"Nothing for you. You don't like oysters." Jerry consumed a breaded, fried piece of his meal, offering a French fry. "Why are we meeting here?"

"I wanted a place away from the squad room and other distractions. We'll have a guest joining us." The mystery person arrived as he spoke. "Jerry, I'd like you to meet my chief, Vanessa Christine. She has information for us about our investigation of Andrew Pepper and his gang."

They sat in the enclosed area near the food ordering area after asking if she wanted to order any food. Addressing Jerry, she said, "Sergeant Jefferson, you and your brother have found a complex and confounding criminal enterprise which does not want to die a peaceful death."

Jerry responded, "It was not my intention to shake loose a menace in King or Snohomish Counties. Then to have my nephew assaulted aboard a cruise ship while on vacation raised the level of criminal infestation to a new high."

"That's as I understand. Tiberius has informed me of the encounters you and he had in Alaska. I know about the near death of your nephew and two of his children. I also think a connection exists to a case I have one of my detectives working."

Tiberius entered the conversation. "Detective Manny Espinoza is working the case of two men found dead in an Aurora Avenue motel just before the cruise ship left for Alaska. They were the scheduled drivers for the floral delivery service used by American Pacific Cruises. The people who delivered the flowers and baskets were two females. I suspect we met them in Alaska. Two forensic scientists attending a seminar in Bellevue may have encountered them, also."

Vanessa continued, "I am asking both of you to work with Detective Espinoza and the two forensic scientists to close this case and find any other members of this cartel you confronted and destroyed." She crossed arms over each other and glared at Tiberius. "Do not forget to include your son. He is the one who has the most to gain, and the most to lose."

"I agree," Tiberius said. "He has been attacked in a way none of us can understand."

They sat for several moments before Jerry broke through the loudness of the silence. An alarm next door at the waterfront fire station interrupted his conversation. They watched as a truck and EMT vehicle departed to an emergency somewhere in downtown.

"As I was saying before the clanging from the station, I spent two years pretending to be dead. I promised myself and my wife that nothing would halt my working to end the malicious group in Everett. If this case in Seattle has any connection to Everett, I want to uncover who is involved and end their rampage."

"Chief, is Espinoza okay with our involvement?" Tiberius asked.

"He's accepting it." She paused. "At least he's not complaining more than usual." She opened a satchel she brought with her and pulled a folder out. Handing it to Tiberius, she continued, "This is what we have on the Aurora motel case. I'll connect you with

Jeremy Caldwell and Ryan Wittingham from the Oregon Forensic Lab."

As he scanned the material of the folder, he handed a picture to Jerry. "Do these two girls look familiar?" Jerry studied the blow-up, squinted, and tilted his head. Tiberius pulled another document and handed it to his brother. Jerry took it but kept eyes on the photo. Vanessa grinned as her eyes flitted from one to the other. She remained attentive to the need for quiet.

Jerry spoke first, "It's hard to tell from this picture if these females are the same ones in Alaska. However, the resemblance is very close." He flipped the picture so Tiberius could see it again.

"Do you think the report from the detective is missing anything?" Tiberius asked. Jerry looked at the document. The silence returned for a moment.

"I don't know, but we should speak with him." Jerry handed the paper to his brother. Vanessa rose from her seat, pulled her cell from a jacket pocket and clicked a preset number. Walking away from the policemen, she turned her back to them. After a minute she ended the call and turned.

"Espinoza will meet with you at the Aurora Avenue motel. He's contacting the two Portland boys to join you. Play nice." She gathered the folder from them and departed the enclosure. A ferry horn sounded the arrival of a boat from Kitsap County.

"Yes, ma'am," Tiberius answered in a hushed tone. She disappeared around the corner passing the fire station. Turning to Jerry, he said, "Let's get there and find out what they know. We can keep silent about where the girls are now. I heard from Marc. They have the twins in custody in Kitsap. He said something about bodies buried on a property near Hood Canal." Jerry nodded.

"I'll drive," Jerry said. As they wound through the waterfront neighborhood of Alaska Way and Western Avenue, Tiberius stared out the window of the car. He seemed lost as Jerry glanced at him. "What's on your mind?" Ti looked at his younger brother, frowning.

"Marc's been through so much at the tentacles of this octopus. I hope we can help end any further assaults on him and his family. We need to find the source of the honey."

Jerry stared forward as he drove and said, "My department is putting together a list of honey producers in Snohomish County.

We should expand to other counties."

"Yes, I'll compile a list from King County. Maybe Thurston, Pierce, and Skagit Counties will comply."

"Can't forget about Kitsap, Mason, Jefferson, and Clallam Counties," Jerry echoed.

"We're going to end up with hundreds, if not thousands of possibilities." He pulled out his cell phone and called his son. After a short conversation, a set of pictures arrived on the screen.

Jerry crossed the Ballard Bridge and turned east on Market passing the Safeway store and construction site. After a few minutes, they arrived at Aurora Avenue and headed north to the motel. Parking near the office area, they vacated the car and entered to speak with the desk person or the manager. Espinoza and the other two men were not present.

"Good afternoon, gentlemen. May I help you?" the young man behind the counter asked.

"Yes, were you on duty here when the two men were found dead in one the rooms?"

"Who are you?" Tiberius and Jerry showed their badges. The man acknowledged their occupations and answered the query. "No, I heard about it when I came to work later that morning." He licked his lips and swirled fingers through his lengthy hair.

Tiberius said, "We'd like to see the room. I understand it's been released for use, but we want access to it."

Searching reservations on the computer, the kid wiped his brow, looked up and then back at the screen. "No one is in it right now." He picked up a phone and called for assistance. "One of the maids will meet you at the room." He gave them the number and directions.

"Was he shaking while we were there?" Jerry asked.

"Yeah, we might want to visit him again and find out what he really knows." Tiberius grinned. "There seems to be a connection which no one has mentioned."

As they entered the room, Espinoza and another car arrived. Two young men got out and followed Manny to the room.

"Sergeant Jefferson, Chief Christine says I'm to work with you. These two pups are to tag along. What do you want to know?" He placed hands on hips and snarled. The younger men glanced at each other and the Jefferson brothers.

Tiberius extended a hand. "Name is Tiberius. This my brother Jerry."

Ryan spoke first. "Nice to meet you. I'm Ryan Wittingham. My fellow forensic scientist is Jeremy Caldwell. Chief said you were involved in the Alaska cruise incident." He shook hands with Tiberius as he communicated. They exchanged more hands.

Jerry interjected with his cell phone and the images sent by Marc. "Do either of you recognize these ladies?"

Ryan's jaw fell open as his eyes widened. Jeremy had a similar reaction. Tiberius reflected with a simple, "I guess you do."

Manny stared at the picture and asked, "Where'd you get that?"

"My son, Marc, apprehended them in Kitsap County and has detained them as witnesses and as suspects in the death of your two drivers for the floral company. He will also press charges against them for the attempted murder of himself and two other people aboard the Salish Sea."

Jeremy said, "We had dinner with them a couple of nights ago. We met them at the airport. That one invited us to meet them at our hotel in Bellevue." He pointed at Kerrine.

Tiberius asked, "Have you seen the crime scene photo of the suspects at this crime scene?"

Ryan answered, "Yes and I think they are the same females. We could try a facial recognition comparison to see if they are. We have a picture which we can compare."

Espinoza snorted. Folding his hands, he asked, "Why are we here? What are you looking to find?" Ryan and Jeremy entered the room and scanned it.

"Has anybody been in here since the bodies were discovered?" Jeremy asked. He moved toward the bed to check under the ruffles around the mattress. Ryan put latex gloves on and searched drawers.

Manny Espinoza flung arms in the air and uttered, "These two are idiots. Of course, we released the room to management after CSI swept it clean for clues."

"Then they should get some more training." Jeremy held a small bag which contained what appeared to be tea.

Espinoza stared as Tiberius and Jerry smiled. Could this be the tie-in to the twins?

CHAPTER

31

Chris placed the small package in the soil of the fruit tree burying it under the root ball. Calculating the decomposition rate, he figured his experiment should last about three to four weeks. Any added time was not a problem, but the need to be rid of his immediate impediment remained. Mai Ling was a possible hazard to his freedom and satisfaction. He hadn't tired of her either mentally or physically. The problem remained with her knowledge and liability of her spilling her guts to another person or persons who would be interested in the honey business he ran.

He returned the sapling to the row of other small apple trees and left the greenhouse. Outside he scanned the area, observing anyone who could be a potential witness. No one was nearby. He rounded the corner of the building and headed to another greenhouse. Inside he marveled at the restraint he felt about what he planned. The business had grown to a size which produced a small dedicated clientele who paid extreme amounts of cash for small amounts of the honey and tea, by-products of the Montague Wholesale Nursery.

He found Bernice working a hive of honeybees which gathered pollen from the asters and marigolds growing in neat rows on the tables nearby. He placed a netted pith helmet on his head as a precaution. The bees were a docile breed, but his body had not enjoyed his one encounter with another, more aggressive breed of bees. He watched her as she gathered honey from the rack, drawn out of the boxlike hive.

He walked to her side, making a slight noise to alert her to his presence. "Hi, Chris." Her words were calm and relaxed, a condition he knew she maintained while working a hive. Riled bees were not a healthy condition for a handler. He nodded acknowledgment and waited for her to finish. She placed the board in the hive box and walked to the table and clothing rack. After removing her protective clothing, she turned to him as he put the helmet on a shelf.

"What do you want?" she asked. Her tone hinted anger and her eyes showed it.

"Nothing much. Just checking on our business." He calmed his growing tension which of late, manifested with any contact between them. The clash of personalities festered. The emotions did not help with civility. He knew she was bothered by something outside of his understanding and he wanted answers without asking questions.

"Business is fine if you mean what we grow and produce for Eden. If you mean our other products, there is a problem with inventory." He flinched at her words.

"What problem? I thought we had enough to satisfy our clients through the winter."

"We have either miscounted, or someone has pilfered our special supplies." Christopher didn't say any response. "What have you hidden from us?"

His festering emotions boiled inside as he answered. "Are you thinking I am stupid enough to steal from our stash? I have no need for anything other than the money generated by your bees and my plants."

"Someone has removed four vials of honey and a small packet of tea." Bernice squared her shoulders and folded arms across her chest. Lips closed across clenched teeth.

"I promise you. I didn't take any. Which means one of our crew has betrayed us or Eden knows more than she is letting on." Chris turned away, smacked a fist into a hand and faced her. "You are not an idiot, so I cannot believe you would do such a thing. Blaming me, though, is a mistake."

Uncrossing her arms, she flailed them in disgust at his calm demeanor. "Colella, you are such a boob. Eden must know something is wrong. That's why she wants to become a hands-on owner. She wants to uncover what is happening here, which has undermined her security regarding the business."

His roiling state of mind exploded as she finished. "I want you to stop snooping about like some scared rabbit trying to find a way out of the stew pot. If Eden is suspecting we are running an illicit business, she can't say anything." His face wrinkled with a snarl. "We left her name on every scrap of paper which contains any record. She's the monster the cops will find, if they get a warrant for searching the grounds. She's the one who authorized our production of Mad Honey. So, get your act together and stop acting as if Christmas is over and the next destination is a prison."

"Go to Hell." Her words echoed in the building. Two workers at the far end of a row of plants looked up from their tasks. Seeing them, she lowered to a whisper as she continued, "Those papers also contain our names. We signed off on inventory and supplies. My signature is on the inventory lists of honey production. Your name appears on plant purchases and schedules for workers."

He sneered as he responded, "My name is on legitimate documents which can withstand a serious audit. You have a challenge if such an audit shows the lost City of Atlantis is a lack of Mad Honey for Eden, as documented." Bernice stomped from the building. The door slammed shut and the two men approached Chris.

"Is Miss Bernice upset with our work?" One of the farmhands asked.

Chris smiled and calmed his turmoiled head. "No, she and I had a disagreement. Keep up the good work." He left the building and decided Mai Ling needed to help him soothe rabid thoughts. Regretting the profligate manner of his actions, he decided Bernice was a more serious liability for the moment. Since honey was an improper weapon, another way had to be devised and placed into operation. What kind of accident could be formulated and executed without raising suspicions? Careful consideration might take more time than he thought he had. Still, suspicion had to rest with her.

As he approached the office building, his mind considered suicide as a viable way for her to die. But what kind of suicide? What manner of demise? What type of note expressed regrets and sorrows for providing people with the deadly sweetener and teas? Before he entered the door to his office, he notice Eden with Bernice. What were they plotting?

"No," he uttered aloud but with soft tones. "I must not become paranoid." He continued entry to his office. Gathering a few financial records to review at home, he packed his valise and left for his car. Surveying the grounds for anyone who would interrupt his departure and finding no one, he started for the parking lot. Opening his door, the heat of the day which had accumulated escaped like a blast from a fire. He winced.

"Car rather warm for you?" The voice startled him. He turned to find Eden. Her face reflected the maddening argument with Bernice. She had squealed on him.

"Yeah, a bit. Not as big a surprise as you, sneaking up behind me, though."

Eden smiled, "Didn't mean to frighten you. Are you sneaking away from work?" Her smile faded as arms crossed her chest.

"What? No. I'm not sneaking. Just finished what I could. I'm taking the financial records with me to study them at home. I'll report to you tomorrow." He smiled to assuage her temper.

"You and Bernice have worked with me for a long time. Whatever is between you had better be resolved. Soon. I don't need any adversity." He noticed a bead of sweat forming along her hairline but attributed it to the car's escaping air. He nodded to her and sat on the hot leather upholstery.

Starting the engine to engage the air conditioning, he looked out at Eden who remained affixed to her spot. He hadn't thought a response was required, but her demeanor demanded one.

"Bernice and I are not adversaries. We will fix it. I care about you and the farm too much to inject enmity into our operations." She turned and walked away. He closed the door of the car and put it in reverse. A quick thought of backing into her raced through his brain and was quashed before he could affect such a consequence on Eden. He drove to the entrance of the farm and turned onto the road leading to the highway home. The situation with Bernice was unraveling, and the fiber of his thinking was to reweave the fabric and hide the strife among the three of them, at least until he had a plan for extrication and alteration of the management of the property.

Eden's only heir was her daughter. Her son had died in Iraq. Another death in the family would necessitate a change of the will. Who would she trust to continue the legacy her family had developed? Once before he knew how to woo her. He had to figure a way to repeat the action and create the desire to make a proper change. Then he would execute a second action to remove her impediment from his coup.

CHAPTER

32

At the Central Kitsap office of the Sheriff, Marc completed his report of the escapade with the twins. Kerrine and Kaliana sat in separate interrogation rooms, cooling off from the spate of epithets expressed at their recently acquired handlers. He saved the entry and ran a physical copy for Fellington's desk. Free to interrogate his irritants, he stepped into the room with Kerrine.

"Had enough time to contemplate life without parole?" Sarcasm drooled across the table to the cuffed and manacled beauty whose sole aim in life seemed bent on ending his.

She looked at him and smiled. "Too bad we didn't get to hook up. I would have fucked you until you died." Eyes narrowed as a sneer coursed her lips. Marc sat in the chair across from her. He interlaced fingers, placing the hands on the table. "I hate you."

"I know. It doesn't change anything. I don't hate you." His mind conjured severe and painful ways of exacting revenge, but he sacrificed nothing until she cracked and told everything she knew about Pepper, the remnants of the octopus-like cartel, the source of the poisonous honey, and the names of other victims of her and her sister.

He continued, "All I want from you is the name of the person who supplies you with honey and the doctored tea." He leaned forward as did Kerrine. "Well?"

"You're a shithead."

"I am to you, but your sister thinks I'm just fine."

"She's going to surprise you about her feelings."

Marc stood and turned back to face Kerrine. "I guess we'll know after I speak with her and she opens up to answer a few questions.

She'll be getting a better deal with the prosecutor." He opened the door and left without listening to her pleading.

As he opened the next door, he hesitated, hoping a voice might beckon him to enter. He was not disappointed. "Marc, is that you?" He walked around the door and shut it behind him. "Marc, I'm sorry for my behavior. I did what my sister asked." He thought of reminding Kaliana of her right to remain silent but remained silent himself. He sat in the chair across from her and waited. "I should be happy my life will improve."

Marc cocked his head to the right and pointed. "How do you think your life will be better?" He folded his arms across his chest and leaned against the back of the chair. Her eyes watered and droplets rappelled her cheeks. She rattled the chains of the restraints hobbling her movements.

"Don't you care about me? I still care about you." She attempted to dry her face with her upper arm. The chains refused to budge. "Are these necessary? I won't be any trouble to you."

He retrieved a tissue and handed it to her. She dabbed her eyes and clutched the wet paper. "The restraints are required for all alleged felons." He stood and walked to the mirrored window acknowledging the people on the other side of the glass.

"I didn't want to be like Kerrine. She has a mean streak. I wanted to enjoy our ability to mess with boys' lives. She wanted to mess them up." Marc turned and faced her.

"Whose idea was it to use toxic honey?"

"I guess it was hers. Kerrine wanted to be a killer for hire. The honey just became the agent of choice. And the tea mixture. Everything went so well. Until you messed up the game."

He sat down. "Who are the bodies out at the cabin?"

"I don't know. Kerrine was told to lure you there and have you die and disappear."

"Who ordered the hit on me?"

"Which time?"

He thought about the improbability of her question. She was right. More than two times his life was targeted. Pepper kidnapped him from his home before dying in the warehouse in King County. Someone ordered Jarina Camacho, the cruise director on the Salish Sea, to oversee the second attempt. Kerrine and Kaliana were brought to the ship to execute a try after James Blackthorne died using materials meant for the Jefferson family. It had to end. He bore too many scars from fighting this criminal entity.

"Fair question." He leaned toward to her "The ship. Was Camacho in charge or following orders?"

"I don't know for sure. Jarina contacted us and we came to Juneau. You were supposed to have died eating the food in the basket. How did it end up with that author guy?"

He contemplated explaining the circumstances and dismissed it. "A mistake," was his answer. "If Camacho was not in charge, could it have been Captain Dalgaard?"

"Jarina gave us the plans. She didn't say who gave them to her."

"Was it necessary to kidnap my son and Dr. Middlebury's daughter?"

"Kerrine wanted to have some fun with them and lure you into a compromising snare. I wasn't part of her assault on your son."

"You helped lure them to the house. As I understand it, you were to take them there and administer the sedatives."

Her chains clanged as she tried for more comfort. "I'm sorry, Marc. I know an apology will not rectify my bad behavior, but please remember I care for you."

An idea crept into Marc's head. He stood and left the room as a bewildered Kaliana rattled her surprise. Her demeanor soured as the door closed.

Outside he smiled at his cousin JJ and at Regina. "What if she isn't given an opportunity to confess her complicity but has to hear that her sister is singing like a canary." He entered the other interrogation room to speak with Kerrine.

"What now, you here to tell me my sister has written the next best selling tale of criminals and their victims?"

"Something like that." He approached the table but remained standing. "Which one of you wanted me dead?"

He waited for her response. She simply stared. He turned to leave, but Kerrine spoke. "It was just business."

"Like going to the store and buying milk?"

"Yeah, something like that."

"Who ordered the hit?"

"What did my sister tell you?"

"I'm asking you. Who ordered the hit?"

Kerrine looked at Marc like a long lost friend. He assumed she was not answering. He reached for the door and grasped the knob. A hesitation for effect produced nothing. He left.

Returning to Kaliana, he sat in the chair and watched the pouty face morph into the same long lost friend countenance of her sister.

"What did Kerrine tell you? I'm guessing nothing. She hates you, but I love you. When you resisted my sister's charms, I knew you were the type of man I wanted in my life."

Marc decided to play her game. "Better circumstances would have been more productive for your aspirations. Would it have mattered that I am married?"

She cooed, "I could be your mistress. We could share time. I wouldn't say anything to her. I'd please you in ways she thinks are nasty."

"Then I need from you the source of the honey. We can see about getting you out of here and settled somewhere before the trial."

"A trial? Why? Can't you drop all charges? I think we have a deal for immunity if I tell you everything." Marc nodded.

"I can't promise, but I'll talk with the prosecutor. Maybe something can be worked out." Marc decided to play his trump card. "Kerrine explained the relationship you had with Pepper. His death must have been a huge shock."

"Did he have to die?"

"He was cornered and refused to surrender. You made the right decision when you complied with the deputies and me. We can talk as friends and settle all of this nasty business."

She lowered her head and pursed her lips. "And get on with the other nasty." Marc's face remained stoic.

"Well, then who is the supplier?"

Kaliana raised her head, smiled, and said, "Kerrine took care of obtaining our material, but I think it is some farm out in east King or Snohomish County."

Marc reached across the table and placed his hands atop her manacled ones. "Thank you. I'll see what I can do about your request." He stood and departed.

JJ smiled and said, "Ooh, cousin, you have a girlfriend." Marc chortled.

"At least until she discovers her time with me is limited to this interview."

Regina entered the conversation. "How many growers are there in east King or Snohomish County?"

Marc nodded, "I'll contact my father and see what he knows." They turned to stare through the glass at the two sisters in separate rooms. Each had a personality as if they were different parts of one person. A cold, calculating killer. And a demure, conniving accomplice. Marc gave instructions to a deputy to transfer them to separate cells away from possible contact.

The three officers of the law left the interrogation rooms and made their way to Marc's desk. "I'll write up these notes and call Dad." Had he received enough from his adversaries? He knew several beekeepers in Kitsap County, but the number of possibilities in King had to be much larger. Could Seattle Police detail a list?

CHAPTER

33

Jerry and Tiberius glanced about the motel room for any other missed evidence. The teabag, secured in a bag and marked, promised a lead to the source of the honey. Manny clocked in the additional information and left the room. Ryan and Jeremy followed.

"Those three don't play well together," Tiberius quipped. He and Jerry left the room and secured it. Manny Espinoza planted another do not enter sign on the frame and doorway. A low growl emanated from deep in his throat.

Ryan removed his latex and placed them in an evidence bag. Jerry asked, "Are you saving those for something?"

"Habit acquired in school." He marked the bag. "We were taught that anything we use to gather evidence could become potential evidence, as well. Something might cling to the glove and could be tested." Sealing the bag, he gave it to Jeremy who had the tea sample.

Tiberius entered the conversation. "Let us know as soon as you gain anything from this. I'm contacting my son and heading to Wendlesburg with Jerry. We want to meet these twin assassins again and wrench out of them what we can about the honey source."

Manny sneered. "Don't trust your son to do a credible job?" He turned and headed to his car with his shadows in tow.

Jerry asked, "Is he always so kind and loving?"

Tiberius grunted. "You mean Manny. I only really know him by reputation. We don't have much interaction. That is until now. His demeanor is rough, but he has a street cred of solving crimes. His rate of arrest and supporting convictions is pretty good." They sat in his car and watched the other men depart. Clicking open his cell phone, he punched a preset and waited for Marc to answer.

"Hi, Dad. I'm glad you called." Tiberius smiled.

"Jerry and I are coming to Wendlesburg to meet with your young ladies."

"They're in the Central Kitsap branch of our offices. When you get to Silverdale, I'll meet you."

He clicked off the phone and updated Jerry. The ride to the waterfront was not complicated except for the major construction of the retaining seawall and the upcoming destruction of the Highway 99 Viaduct.

Waiting on the Colman dock for the next ferry, they said very little. Cars and trucks lined the dock, indicating a full boat.

"Do you think we can get anything from these girls?" Jerry spoke with doubt in his voice. "They have an advantage. We want something, and I'm sure they would be willing to part with it for a sizable consideration of a lesser jail term."

"We'll see." Tiberius didn't open his eyes as he basked in the warmth of the afternoon heat. Idling a car engine was not acceptable. Air conditioning was obtained by windows down, but the marine air moving around the docks offered little relief.

"I never met them when I was undercover." Jerry's comment stirred no interest from his brother. He continued. "I would've remembered either of them had I run across them. They're not the type to slip from memory." He stared at Tiberius. Nothingness was the only response.

A boat whistle sounded the arrival of a ferry. Jerry looked at the nameplate emblazoned below the pilothouse. Chimacum. One of the newest of the ferry fleet's many boats. He smiled for no apparent reason. As the cavalcade of bicyclists and motorcyclists vacated the lower ramp, he glanced at the parade of walk-on passengers on the upper walkway, marveling at the number of people.

"How many of those people have committed a serious offense?" Tiberius stared at his brother. "Well, the number of individuals means the odds are someone has done something."

"Your brain was warped by you playing dead for two years." The 'now loading' announcement interrupted them. Each row of vehicles followed the directions of the ferry workers.

When situated on the boat, they decided to exit the car and go up to the passenger deck. They found a couple of seats near the cafe and watched the crowd. "Which one of these fine people thinks of doing something nefarious?"

A low growl emanated from Tiberius. "Maybe no one's thinking of anything at all. Everyone's so wrapped up just living."

Jerry rocked his head side to side. They sat in silence for the remainder of the crossing. Passengers minded their own business, and no nefarious activity occurred.

As the ferry entered the mooring in Wendlesburg, Tiberius and Jeremais sat patient and bored. Cars ahead of them began moving. Tiberius followed the parade off the boat and to the main streets. Separating from the other drivers, they headed to the sheriff's office in Central Kitsap and their visit with the latest residents of the jail cells.

Entering the building and stopping at the information desk, they introduced themselves and waited for Marc to be contacted. Jerry said, "I figured we'd be afforded some professional courtesy." He sat in a seat. Tiberius joined him.

"Patience, little brother, patience." Marc appeared behind the desk and signaled them to follow him. In a small office Marc used when in this precinct, he offered chairs for them to sit.

"Dad, Uncle Jerry, I'm glad you're here. As you know, we have the girls in lock-up. They'll be transferred to County later. I interrogated them, but neither is willing to advance the case."

Tiberius spoke, "Marc, we came here to assist you any way we can. Let us have a chance at them." Marc agreed.

In the hallway outside of the cell area, they waited for Kerrine and Kaliana to be escorted back to separate rooms for questioning. They watched as the women were placed at the table in each room and secured by manacles. Tiberius and Jerry entered the room containing Kerrine.

"Well, if it isn't mommy and daddy coming to the rescue." Her sneer met steely stares from the two men. "What's the matter? Marc can't play anymore?" They sat in the chairs opposite from her.

Tiberius asked, "Do you care about anything other than you?" She stared at the mirror-window and stuck out her tongue.

Jerry asked, "What if I told you we know how you procured the honey and tea used in your desperate attempt to kill my nephew? What if I pointed out how we have the needed evidence from a motel in Seattle where you killed two van drivers and stole their truck? What if I explained how your future might be shorter than you might want?"

"What are you talking about?" she asked. "You don't have anything on us. And you have no idea about any sources of honey or tea."

Tiberius smiled. "Oh, but we do. You see, you and your sister made a mistake when you hooked up with those two men at the airport."

She sat against the back of the chair, rattling the her restrain chains in the process. "I don't know what you're talking about."

"Sure you do. See, those boys you had dinner with and then went to their room for dessert, are from the Portland office of the Oregon State Crime Investigation Lab. They're forensic scientists."

"So?"

"So, they made you. They identified you as the two women at the motel where those men died from your toxic compounds." He waited for the information to seep through her veneer and into her brain.

Without a response, the two lawmen stood, hesitated a moment and left the room. On the hall side of the door Marc asked, "Are you serious about those guys from Portland?"

Jerry answered, "Nothing definitive, but she doesn't know that."

Tiberius said, "Let's regale her sister with the same tale. We might get different results." The three men entered the second room. Two sat in the chairs across from Kaliana. Marc leaned against the wall by the glass.

Jerry started the conversation. "Your sister had some interesting things to say about the two men you hooked up with in Bellevue. Care to elaborate?"

"What two men?" Her eyes focused and brows scrunched. She breathed deep and quick. "You mean those guys who asked us to dinner?"

"Yes, those guys who asked you to dinner. And dessert? Who did you get for dessert?"

"What?" She leaned forward clanging chains. "What did Kerrine say? That we had sex with them? So what? They wanted it as much as we did."

"Did you know who they were when you met them at the airport?"

"No. They said they were attending some conference. We met them, had dinner, and went to their room. We did order dessert."

Tiberius entered the exchange. "Their conference was a police conference."

"They're cops?"

"No. They're scientists. They have placed you and Kerrine at the motel where you killed two flower delivery drivers and stole their vehicle. You left evidence behind."

"No, we didn't. I mean. We couldn't have left anything since we weren't there."

"We have pictures of you," he said. "Pictures of you entering with them and pictures of only you and Kerrine leaving."

"So what? They were alive when we left. We had fun and they had to make deliveries or something."

Jerry asked, "Where do you get the honey and tea used in your assaults on people? You're implicated in three mysterious deaths in King and Snohomish Counties. You are guilty of kidnapping, assault, false imprisonment, and attempted murder of my nephew and his sons."

Tiberius continued, "Help us with this or face a needle along with your sister."

Kaliana cried as she spoke, "I can't help you. We have a pact. Sisterhood. Bonding. Being twins is important. I can't say anything." Streaks ran down cheeks as her hands cupped her head. "I can't." Marc straightened his stance.

Tapping his father and uncle, he said, "We have what we need." To Kaliana he smiled as he spoke. "Thanks. You have clarified everything." The three men left her with her misery.

CHAPTER

34

As they sat awaiting a Kingston ferry to Edmonds, JJ and Regina chatted about the process his Uncle Marc used to ensnare the twins.

"Thanks for coming to help my uncle." She reached for his hand. He smiled.

"I've come to love your entire family. Well, not as much as I love you, but they are such nice people and so hard working."

"Flattery will get you anything you want." He raised her hand to his lips. A blare of the incoming ferry announced its arrival. "Saved by the whistle." He released her hand and watched the boat approach the mooring.

"Do you love me?" Her quip meant nothing but starled JJ.

"You know I do." He stared at her. She smiled.

"I think we're an odd couple. However, I wouldn't want it any other way."

JJ recalled his first sighting of her and decided he needed to ask something. Not the situation he planned but still needed. "Why do you care about me so much?" He watched the boat again.

"Sometimes I think you're a bonehead." He looked at her. "I mean it. If we are serious, I'll give up my standing in the Royal Mounties for you."

"I know. I would do the same for you and head to Vancouver." He started his car as the last of the vehicles exited from the MS Spokane. He reached for her hand. They intertwined fingers. He smiled. Cars began moving.

After parking on the outside rows of the lower deck, they walked up the stairs to the passenger deck and found a table and bench seats. "Do you think Marc will break those girls and find the source?" Regina cuddled next to JJ as she spoke.

"If he can't, my Dad and Uncle Ti will." Eyes met and then lips. The horn sounded and the boat moved from the dock, interrupting them. They watched the pilings pass by as the boat cleared the moorage. Happiness exuded from the young police officers.

"Do you want anything to eat or drink?" JJ asked. He turned to leave for the cafe but stopped. An envelope sat on the bench beside him. "Ginnie, is this yours?" He pointed at it but did not touch it. She glanced across his shoulder.

"It has some writing on it." She shifted for a better look. "Can you read it?" A scribble of letters appeared to be 'Your eyes only.'

Pulling out a pen, JJ moved the object, so the letters faced them. Three words. Your eyes only. "I didn't see anyone drop this," he said. "Do you have any gloves?" She shook her head.

Regina said, "I'll get some from the cafeteria." She climbed from the bench and left him.

JJ scanned for people around him. No one paid attention to the odd behavior of two passengers dressed like the others. A couple across from their table glanced away from him. He approached them and asked, "Excuse me." He showed them his sheriff's badge. "Did either of you see anyone place an envelope on that bench while we were looking out the window?" They stared at each other and at JJ. "Well?"

The man answered, "A woman."

"What did she look like? What was she wearing?"

"I don't know. She looked like everyone on this boat."

"Black? White? What?" JJ looked back at the bench. "What clothing?"

The man stood up. "Why? What's going on?"

"Would you recognize her, if you saw her?" Regina returned with latex gloves. "Would you be able to identify the woman?"

"I don't know. I didn't get a good look at her." He glanced at Regina and back at JJ. "She was Hispanic. I know that. About 40ish. Kind of tall." He sat down as JJ and Regina returned to the table.

She pulled gloves on to handle the envelope. She picked it up and examined it. The flap was not glued, so she opened it and extracted a piece of paper. Unfolding it, she read the short message. JJ placed a pair of gloves on his hands and took the note. He read it.

"What do you make of this?" JJ asked. He waved the paper.

"I think someone's afraid we got too close."

"She's still aboard." He folded the note and returned it to the envelope. He guessed no fingerprints were on it, but it was evidence and needed investigating. "Did you ask for a storage bag." Regina opened one as he spoke. After sealing it, he wrote time and date and type of object on it and signed his name.

Regina said, "Let's walk around and see if we can find her." JJ nodded, but his hopes of discovering the mysterious woman were minimal.

"We're not going to find her. She's probably already in a car downstairs."

Ginnie placed the evidence in her backpack and locked her arm in his. "Let's try. We might get lucky."

As they walked, no one matched the scant description of the only witness. In the aft, they curled around the seats and headed forward. No person stood out from the crowd. The ferry approached Edmonds. They found the stairs to the car deck and descended.

Regina suggested they walk through the cars and search. Little time remained for a complete search and halting the progress of the ferry into Edmonds with flimsy information was not happening. They walked until the announcement for passengers and drivers to return to their vehicles. They headed for the car.

Sitting and waiting for the vacating of the middle section of the boat, JJ asked, "Why would anyone connected to Pepper want to leave such a note? It makes no sense to me."

"The note is meant to scare you into doing what we all know won't happen. Nothing is going to happen to any of your family."

"Marc should know as soon as possible."

"What's the number for the office where we left him?" He gave her the number and turned the ignition key.

Another car came parallel to them as they crossed to the ramp into Edmonds, Washington. The driver did not look at either of them, but JJ glanced at a female of Hispanic background about the correct age. "Ginnie, write that license plate." He pointed at the gray Honda inching ahead. She pointed her cell at it and clicked.

"Anyone we might know?" she asked.

"Can't be sure. Looked like the lady that guy described."

"Should we follow?" JJ nodded. "If she is the same person, she might want us to follow."

He changed lanes to proceed behind the suspect vehicle as it coursed through the city toward downtown. As they continued up the hill past the stores, the Honda slowed at an intersection near 9th Avenue South and turned into a residential area. At Walnut Street she turned east.

The car parked in a driveway. The lady got out and watched as they following her. JJ continued past the house and Regina recorded the address on her phone. They drove on to the original destination at the Everett locale of the Snohomish County Sheriff's office.

Regina handed the information regarding the unknown person to the desk sergeant. JJ met with another deputy who compiled fingerprint evidence and asked for an examination of the envelope and note. As they headed to his desk, another deputy intercepted them and directed them to Captain Kopinski's office. They looked at each other, shrugged and trailed along after the officer.

"Jefferson, you and your RMP have been quite busy lately." He directed them to sit in chairs next to his desk. He remained standing. "A request from you and your father for a listing of potential honey producers in the county has hit a snag. Navigating through the list of producers has terminated at nearly 200 operations." He reached for a manila folder and handed it to JJ. "Take this and sift through it. If anything crops up, let me know." JJ nodded and stood, as did Regina.

"Thank you, sir. I hope this has what we need." They started to leave when the Captain stopped them.

"When you see your father, have him contact me."

"Yes, sir." JJ and Regina returned to his desk, sat and opened the folder. He handed several papers to her and gathered the rest for himself.

Ginnie asked, "What are we looking for in these papers? Legitimate businesses with too much money? Shoestring operations making a tidy profit? Those don't mean the company is fraudulent."

JJ answered, "I don't know. Something will stand out like a tell in a poker game. Subtle and hard to read. But observable nevertheless."

As the reading of pages progressed, they whittled down the

obvious detractors and created a potentials list. A pattern emerged of growers who worked with rhododendrons and azaleas almost exclusively. Several of the companies were honey only producers and contracted with wholesalers for the raw combs. Three were large growers of retail stock and were sellers of honey products and related items. The folder held no more names.

"Do you think we have a possible culprit?" Ginnie asked.

JJ sat and stared at the three names of the large growers. He didn't need anything more. He had worked for one of the names on the list.

CHAPTER

35

Workers moved luteum azaleas into the small greenhouse and placed them in neat rows. Space between rows had tables on which the bumblebee hives would be set up. Each bush was about two feet in circumference and three feet high. Buds of the yellow flowers had formed and would blossom within the next two months.

Chris guided the arrangement while Bernice directed the apiary workers who constructed the bumble hive boxes. "Do you have enough space for the hives?" he asked. She nodded. He still suspected she was not as enthusiastic about the honey production as she was in the early years of their collaboration.

Her lack of conversation irritated him, but he let it go for the moment. "How much are we making?" He held a clipboard poised for writing.

"You know as well as I do, it depends on the bees." Her tone raised his hackles. "If we have as many plants as last year, I anticipate about 30 pounds." He wrote on the paper. "How much did you put down?"

He glared at her. "20 pounds. For Eden. The rest can be ours." Bernice folded her arms.

"Eden is expecting 25 pounds." Her arms dropped. "Why do you want to hold back more? She already suspects something's wrong."

"She won't find out."

"Eden's a smart person. Don't act so cavalier." She turned and directed a trustworthy member of their illicit business about the placement of a box. "This has to be the last year. The deaths on that cruise ship are going to lead to our discovery."

"You're so paranoid. If you don't want this, get out and let me run the operation." He placed the clipboard on a table.

"You do not know about bees." She turned to leave with the two men who worked the hives with her. All was ready, and she wanted away from the one person she feared the most.

"I can learn." He watched as the three people vacated the building. As sunlight filtered through the panes in the ceiling creating a warm environment for the bushes, thoughts infused within him about eliminating his competition.

He observed the installing of a sprinkler system to water each plant on a regular cycle. Plant food was added and again in three months to promote the growth of flowers. Bees would be added to the boxes when blossoms opened.

Eden entered. His eyes closed and a grunt hinted at frustration. "Chris, when will we be collecting in here?" A blank stare greeted her question. She repeated it.

"Ah, we have to wait until the blooms are coming. Then the bees will fill the boxes and spend their time creating the honey for us."

"How much is expected?"

"You should ask Bernice. She knows more about it than I do."

Eden glared, "I'm asking you. How much?"

"Bernice said about 20 pounds."

"The number seems less than previous years." The air cooled as the sprinklers came on and increased the humidity of the greenhouse. She pulled her jacket around her body. "I'll talk with Bernice. Tomorrow." Eden left before any comment from Chris.

Muttering a quiet curse, he found the remaining workers and dismissed them from the greenhouse. Nothing more was going to be accomplished this day. He closed and locked the doors after he vacated the room. He spotted Bernice entering the office area, surprised she remained on the property.

Could he effectuate two goals in one evening? He dismissed the idea of destroying his adversaries. Eden and Bernice would live for a while longer until a master plan could be instituted. Mai Ling remained at his residence, another of the obstacles to his future success. For now, she remained a person for physical satisfaction. She was not as much a problem.

As he watched, Bernice entered her car and drove away. He

figured Eden had entered her house. He went to his car and drove off the property at a distance behind Bernice. She entered the highway as he continued into Everett.

At home he found his lady watching a television talk show. He kissed her on her right cheek and headed to his bedroom for a shower and change of clothes. He turned to see Mai Ling in the doorway. "What do you want?" he asked as gentle as possible.

"Are you going to shower?" He nodded and cocked his head for her to follow. In the bathroom they stripped off clothing and entered the shower, bathing each other and beginning a satisfactory massaging of all parts. They finished in the bedroom after drying each other.

Lying in quiet embraces, Chris decided he wanted his China doll with him more than to be alone. He would deal with her later. First, he needed a plan for ridding himself of two women in Snohomish County who would be missed if they simply disappeared.

Implicating one as the perpetrator of the death of the other would deflect from involving him. What was the best way to get it done? He needed a plan. And one was forming, slow and deliberate. Eyes closed and sleep intercepted planning.

Morning arrived with Mai Ling still sleeping. He extricated from the intertwining of their arms and legs. In his office, he contemplated how to remove obstacles to running the business Eden's father had begun. The attempt to woo her heart after the death of her husband had failed. Now she wanted involvement in the actual day to day operations. He had to prevent her intrusion.

Bernice's cowardliness about continuing the honey operation irked him. If she killed Eden and was caught, both problems were gone. All he needed to do was push her to act. To act without knowing he wanted it. To act for her own gain. Then he would implicate her.

He wrote a few notes on a pad of yellow paper, but a noise alerted him to another person approaching. He shoved the pad into a drawer before Mai entered. "Here you are," she said.

"Good morning, sweetheart. Did you sleep well?" A hint of jasmine wandered in with her. "What are you wearing?" She looked down at her sleep shirt and panties. "No. The perfume."

"It's something the twins gave me a little while ago. Do you like it?" He smiled. An idea crept into his head.

"Can you contact them?" His eyes glistened. He stood from the desk and came around to her, taking her hands in his.

She winced when he applied a pressure. "I guess. I have a number of the person with whom they are staying." His pressure increased. "You're hurting my hands." He released her and leaned against the desk. No apology happened.

"They may be able to help us escape so we can be together and away from the mayhem Pepper's group caused."

Rubbing her fingers, Mai Ling answered, "Andrew Pepper and his band are gone." She turned to leave, still rubbing fingers and hands.

"Where're you going?" The gruffness stopped her. "I'm sorry. I didn't mean to be harsh. I want to leave the company, and they can help." He reached for her, but she flinched. He abandoned any idea of touching her, trying to control the building rage. She hurried from the room. He closed the door to isolate himself from any more intrusions. At his desk, he removed the yellow pad and continued notating a plan of action for extrication from the impending doom sensed by Eden's sudden interest in day to day operations.

Checking the time, he decided to fix a quick breakfast, dress, and attend to the business of growing azaleas. Work beckoned. In the kitchen he watched Mai Ling construct a meal fit for a king. He leaned against the wall not wanting to interrupt. Admiration for certain skills learned at the feet of a master madam quenched the rage and lit another fire. Strolling behind her, he wrapped arms around her waist with hands cupping her breasts.

"Can breakfast wait?" he cooed into her left ear. She reached for a paper towel to clean her hands, and then she covered his hands.

"Here is fine with me." Her body pressed against his rising desire. She reached down with one hand to remove her silk underwear. He released his grip and lowered his pants and boxers, sliding his unit between her cheeks. She spread slightly to accept him.

As he completed his part of the action, Mai Ling clung to his hands moving in a rhythmic motion until a quiver shivered through her. He caressed her neck and tugged her hair when she clasped the counter for stability. His body demanded another session. They enjoined their desires for a few minutes before they climaxed again, together.

Chris asked, "What have you concocted for our breakfast?" She explained her egg dish and fruit. They ate in silence without clothing their intimacy. He wondered if forgoing such delights was worth the effort of disengaging from her by force. His plan for his employer and his colleague tempered in his mind as he imagined capture and incarceration away from such a morning. He apologized for his voice in the office and decided Mai Ling's talents could aid his plans, an unknown asset to confound any discovery of his involvement.

CHAPTER

36

Ryan and Jeremy forged through the evidence gathered from several suspicious deaths not suspected to be homicides. A pattern of mysterious heart stoppages convinced them several people were targets of perpetrators and the twins were not the only ones engaging honey as a weapon.

"I don't think we have enough in some of these cases to convict," Ryan said as he closed a folder. "Using this method of paralytic heart dysfunction is quite clever and hard to unravel."

Jeremy answered is statement, "But we do have enough to squeeze our two young ladies. They may also be involved in some of these other mysteries." He stacked several folders into a carton marked with the words, 'Unresolved Deaths.'

Ryan continued, "Let's contact the Jeffersons and tell them what we know from these files. Maybe they have an idea of where to search. Can't be that many flower-growers and honey producers in the western part of the state."

"When are the results from the crime lab due back?" Jeremy placed a lid on the box.

"Should be tomorrow or the next day. A rush is on the order, although if this lab is like ours in Portland, that may be ignored." Chuckles followed.

Manny Espinoza entered the room. "You two uncover anything I don't already know?" The scoff in his voice masked the sarcasm of his words.

Ignoring the caustic tone, Ryan answered him, "I don't think so, but we agree a pattern of unrelated deaths have a certain commonality, and we think several people have procured the mystery honey from our unknown source. We need to trace the bank account of relatives and business partners and seek a pattern of withdrawals conforming to the same timeline of the deaths."

Espinoza's eyes rolled up and left in their sockets. A guttural noise accompanied the roll. "You think I haven't checked?" He held out a hand for the folder containing their notes. "Show me what you uncovered."

Ryan placed the folder in Manny's hand. As he opened it Ryan said, "We agree with you about the need for additional information. What do you suggest we do?" A shaking head answered the question.

"Go back to Oregon and leave me to do my job."

Jeremy asked, "What's the matter with you? We're not the enemy. Let's find a common path and accomplish the goal we all have."

As he read the assessment of their review, Manny's mouth curled into a smile. "You are thorough. I'll give you that. Nothing here points to anything new for me. However, since I'm required to play nice with you, I have an idea which we could pursue." He pulled a folded paper from his jacket pocket and laid out the sheet on the top of the other papers in the manila file. He handed it to Ryan and pointed at the list of names.

"These are the businesses which grow plants and are honey producers." Ryan gave the folder to Jeremy. "I'm surprised the list isn't longer."

Jeremy closed it and gave it to Manny. "It's long enough for me. We should be able to eliminate half the companies before today is over."

"Don't get hasty, boy scout." Manny snarled again. "These are some of the biggest suppliers to the public marketplace. If we go in with guns blazing, we'll lose any surprise and more than likely the perps will melt away."

"What do you suggest?" Ryan asked.

"Let me contact Sergeant Jefferson and see what he and his brother have uncovered. We can coordinate with them and narrow the list to the most likely suspects."

Jeremy said, "We should contact the Sheriff in Kitsap and see what they have for us."

"We need to interrogate those ladies," Ryan said. "They'll be surprised to see us."

"You two do that. Meanwhile, I'm connecting with Sergeant Jefferson."

The forensic scientists left for a ferry ride to Kitsap County and a reconnection with their dates from a few days ago. Nothing ventured nothing gained was their collective motto. Driving through the construction rampant in downtown Seattle and along the waterfront slowed their progress.

"We're going to miss the ferry. According to the schedule it leaves in 15 minutes." Jeremy said. The frantic squeak in his voice raised a smile on Ryan's face.

"Don't worry. We'll make it. The route is all downhill." At the waterfront signs guided ferry traffic to a southern entry point which led to a parking area filled with cars. Two signs alerted them to the proper lane for Wendlesburg and their destination.

Ryan lowered his window and hailed a woman dressed in green, wearing a yellow life vest. "Can you please point me to how I get on a ferry?"

She asked, "Where're you heading?"

"Wendlesburg."

"Stay in the lane to the left. It's marked. These other cars are headed to Bainbridge Island."

"Thank you." He followed her directions passing the waiting cars and trucks going to another destination. "I don't think those people are very happy with us."

Jeremy stared at the throng of vehicles. At the ticket booth, he gave the proper fare. Driving onto the waiting area, another man directed them to park behind a beat-up truck filled with cord wood. A loud whistle announced the arrival of one of the two ferries which shuttled cars and people across Puget Sound to the west side. The ride to the island was a half hour. Wendlesburg was an hour away.

After the unloading ended, cars and trucks began the methodical trek onto the decks of the boat. Ryan watched the people walk across the upper gangway to the passenger level and remarked about the number of people commuting from the city to suburbia. He wondered about the number who lived in the county across Puget Sound.

"Do you suppose they enjoy traveling across the sound every day to work?" Jeremy looked at the people and then Ryan.

"I don't know. I read somewhere that Seattle is one of the fastest rising housing markets in the country. Maybe they live where they find affordable housing and commute to jobs to pay for it."

Ryan said, "Well, they can't all be workers. Some are probably just visiting for the day. We should play tourist while we're here. I want to see the Pike Place Market and ride the elevator up the Space Needle."

"First, let's reacquaint ourselves with our girlfriends. They'll love seeing us again." Jeremy looked at the line of cars ahead and beside them. Ryan snaked his way onto the upper deck on the south side of the ferry. "I'm heading up to the passenger deck. I need to pee."

Ryan nodded and vacated the car with his partner. The stairs were nearby, and they found the bathroom next to the top step. "I'll sit over here." He pointed at an empty table and benches. Jeremy bobbed. As Ryan turned another couple sat on one side of his target. He sat across from them. Neither person acknowledged his presence.

The ride lasted the required hour and an announcement alerted all drivers to return to their vehicles. Ryan hadn't noticed the number of people who wore bicycle or motorcycle outfits when they first arrived on the passenger level. Now, many of the people, male and female, descended the stairs ahead of him to the main vehicle deck. He thought of the hill of Seattle and what fitness must be required for people to pedal up from the waterfront to streets with higher elevations. Most of the tallest buildings were on Third, Fourth, and Fifth Avenues.

They entered the car and waited as the bicycles disembarked. The roar of motorcycles was next as they departed. Drivers were given the signal after the two-wheeled transportation had cleared the ramp. The drive through the downtown was slow but steady. Unlike Seattle, little construction hindered progress.

Directions to the Central Kitsap regional office of the sheriff delineated on Jeremy's smartphone GPS map. As they parked the car in the lot, a sheriff's car rounded the building and disappeared behind it.

They entered the building and asked for Detective Jefferson, displaying badges. As they awaited him, Ryan and Jeremy scanned the room. Nothing denoted any outlandish misuse of public funds. The Spartan walls hid secrets. Marc entered from the secured door and introduced himself.

"I understand you two had a night with our guests. I hope they're receptive to your coming for another meeting."

At his desk, he signaled for the scientists to sit in chairs. "I'm finishing a report regarding our interrogation of them. After you're done with them, I'll add what you get out of them to the report. You can have a copy."

Ryan responded, "Thank you, Mr. Jefferson."

"Marc, please. We're in the same business."

"Yes sir," he answered.

"And sir isn't necessary." Ryan smiled. Marc picked up his desk phone, punched a button, and asked for the girls to be placed in the interrogation rooms for another round of we ask, they ignore.

"You think they might refuse to see us?" Jeremy asked Marc.

"They have no idea you're here. It might be helpful for each of you to question one of them and then switch. They aren't willing to help me since I keep surviving their attempts to elimination of me."

A deputy informed Marc the girls were in place. The three men entered the viewing area and watched for a moment. Ryan spoke after a moment of observing the beauties he and Jeremy had shared for an evening. "Time to surprise them."

Jeremy said, "Let's go in together and see Kaliana first. It might have an impact on her, seeing us again." Ryan agreed. Marc remained behind to observe.

As the door opened, they noticed the quick inhaled breath and widening eyes. "What are you two doing here?" she uttered.

Jeremy answered, "We've come to take you away from all this. All you have to do is agree to be dessert again." She glared, heat rising in her face.

"Who are you? How do you get to be here?"

"Did we forget to tell you about our conference?" Ryan sat as he spoke. Jeremy leaned against the wall. "We're forensic scientists and are now helping solve some mysterious deaths in Seattle and Edmonds. Know anything about them? Because we do."

Jeremy straightened as he said, "Once we determined who you

were, we gathered a few pieces of evidence left with us because of our escapades after we had dinner. You left a few DNA markers for us. Results are coming soon. If we connect you to the unsolved deaths, we won't be dating anymore."

Kaliana remained silent. Tears welled up and slipped down her cheeks. Ryan and Jeremy approached the door to leave. Opening the door, Jeremy waited as Ryan left. "Last chance, love. Last chance."

"Okay," she said. Jeremy returned to the chair and sat. Placing a recording device on the table, he waited.

Outside the room, Marc and Ryan watched the conversation. "I'm going to visit my girlfriend in the other room," Ryan said. He opened the door and watched a similar reaction from Kerrine.

Marc shook his head. These young men and women interacted as long lost lovers rekindled. But the singing of songs of intrigue and death warmed his heart. These Portland scientists had clicked with the girls. Now, a possible trail to the source of deadly honey and tea entertained an anxious audience of one.

CHAPTER

37

Marc rocked his head as he watched the interplay between these four individuals. One night of pleasure for the twins begat one glorious interrogation with the two forensic scientists. They gathered information with suggestive language and lustful words which bore fruitful discovery.

As the three men sat and assessed the knowledge gained, Ryan said, "Kerrine may not have wanted to cooperate, but realizing the gravity of her situation and the possibility of lesser charges kicked her to our side."

Jeremy said, "I don't think Kaliana was as ingrained with the murder for hire as her sister. She indicated a mixed emotional connection with you, Marc. What happened aboard the cruise ship?"

"Nothing." He jotted notes on a yellow legal pad. Jeremy dropped any further inquiry. "I'll get a hold of my father and uncle and see if we can meet in Edmonds. Hopefully, JJ and Regina are available, as well." He walked away from the desk for some privacy.

Ryan followed his movement but said, "Whatever happened on that cruise affected him deeply."

Jeremy felt the buzz of his cell and retrieved it from his left breast pocket of his jacket. He read the message which had initiated the reaction. "That teabag we found at the motel contained rhododendron leaves along with regular black tea. Nothing else, though."

"Any idea about the source of the bag or the tea itself?" Jeremy shook his head. Marc returned.

To the two young scientists, he said, "My father and uncle are meeting with us in Lake Forest Park at the intersection of Ballinger

Way and Bothell Way. We'll meet them at the Bar and Grill. If you want to go with me, we can take one car. Or you can follow me."

After a short discussion, they decided to ride with Marc. Upon returning, they wanted one more crack at the twins.

Marc said, "How did you two get so cozy with those vipers?" The journey to Kingston and a ferry ride had begun.

Ryan answered his question with one of his own. "What happened aboard that cruise ship?"

"I'll answer that after you explain your close connection."

Ryan and Jeremy glanced at each other and then at Marc. Ryan was sitting in the front seat. He began relating the saga of the flight to Seattle from Portland and the conference which generated excitement. "We had planned on being diligent about learning as much as possible." He stopped talking and stared at Marc for a second or two. "I guess an opportunity arose at the elevator which was not expected or planned. We were not looking to hook up with them."

Jeremy cut in, "Yeah, but they're so attractive, who would turn down a dinner opportunity?"

Ryan said, "Kerrine asked if we had transportation. I said we were heading to the rental agency. I asked if they had a ride. She responded in the affirmative." He blushed as he continued. "One thing led to another, and we had a promise of a dinner with them. They left us to go up the elevator to get their car."

Jeremy said, "We never anticipated they would follow through. We laughed at the idea of them showing up and blew it off."

Marc interjected, "But they didn't blow it off. They arrived and asked for your room."

"No," Ryan said, "they were at the bar in the hotel as planned. Surprised us as we figured they were just playing us. Anyway, we had a nice dinner. They wanted to go to our room and have dessert. We ordered some and had it sent up."

"Did you find them amenable to be your dessert? Or was it more their idea?" Marc approached the intersection which led to Hansville. The light was red, and a line of cars waited for it the change. He looked at Ryan. Disbelief had created a somber expression.

Ryan looked at Jeremy, then said, "I guess it was their idea. We did ask the waiter to have our actual desserts sent to our room. We ate them before we, well you can guess."

"Yes, I can guess." The light changed to green, and the intrepid trio continued to Kingston in silence and a trip across Puget Sound to Edmonds. At the terminal, a line of cars waited to pay the crossing toll for auto and driver. The parking lot seemed about half full of vehicles waiting for the next ferry to dock and disgorge its population of travelers and commuters.

Curious about the escapades of the two men and the twins, Marc parked in one of the lanes and asked, "When you finished your sexual exploits with them, were you offered any tea with honey?"

Jeremy answered, "No. We asked them to stay the night with us. They declined and left."

Marc said, "At the conference a case was presented which included two female suspects identified as Hispanic twins, and you became intrigued by the knowledge of having spent an evening with two women who fit the descriptions of the suspects."

"That's pretty much the situation." Ryan cocked his head a grinned.

"You do understand, you're fortunate to be still alive. These girls are lethal. They don't leave evidence and they don't leave witnesses."

Jeremy and Ryan nodded and stared at each other. A whistle announced the arrival of the ferry. Noting the time, Marc called his father's cell to apprise them of the timeline for arriving at the restaurant. He learned about JJ and Regina arriving as well.

"Do we have any leads as to which wholesaler might be our target?" he asked. The answer created a smile. He clicked off the call. "Seattle supplied a list of potential growers. It's lengthy. With the list from Snohomish County which my cousin obtained, we'll have our work cut out for us."

The line of cars exiting the boat slacked as the last of them departed. A delay of a few minutes for the inspection required by Homeland Security to clear the boat of passengers and baggage frustrated Marc. He growled a comment, "Hurry up and start loading." His comment was aimed at no one.

Ryan said, "Patience, Marc. I know you're tired of fighting this octopus. We'll finish off the body soon enough." A stare was an unexpected answer. Car engines whirred to life as the lines began a methodical progression to the ferry. Nothing more was said while

Marc maneuvered the car to fit the lanes on the south side of the first deck, leaving enough room to allow for extraction and a trip to the bathroom at the top of the stairs.

Seats in the passenger area filled quickly as most people claimed benches with tables. Several seats remained open, and Ryan and Jeremy sat awaiting Marc's return.

"Just spoke with my father," Marc said as he returned from the bathroom. "He and my uncle are at the restaurant awaiting our arrival. My cousin JJ and RCM McDonald have been contacted and will be there."

The rest of the trip had little interplay between the officers of law enforcement and investigations. The trip was thirty minutes across from Kingston to Edmonds. The day was bright with Mt. Rainier to the south and Mt. Baker to the north extolling the virtues of living in the northwest. Snow still covered the highest peaks in Washington.

As the ferry approached the dock, the predictable announcement for drivers and their passengers to return to their vehicles blared from speakers. Marc, Ryan, and Jeremy descended the stairs to the lowest deck and occupied the car awaiting the opportunity to disembark.

Ryan asked, "How far is this restaurant from here?"

"About twenty minutes," Marc answered. "Mostly because of the traffic." Ryan nodded. Jeremy slumped into the seat and closed his eyes for a power nap.

The volume of cars slowed the progress as traffic signals seemed to play a delaying game with them. Arrival at the Lake Forest Park Bar and Grill ran a bit longer than the prediction. Marc didn't recognize any of the automobiles, but he figured maybe they were driving cars from a motor pool.

Inside they found four officers dressed as civilians. Joining them, Tiberius asked the forensic boys, "How was your date with your girlfriends?"

Jeremy spoke first, "Very enlightening. We surprised them."

Ryan added, "They didn't expect to ever see us again. But we have a lead, I think."

"Alright, then let's order some food. I'm hungry," Tiberius said. "Then we can share what we have and narrow the possibilities."

A waitress arrived to take orders. No alcohol was part of the order since all considered themselves to be on duty.

As they waited for their food to arrive, JJ pulled out the list he received from the office. "Not many names on this list, but one of them is familiar to me. Dad, remember the summer I worked on that wholesale farm in eastern Snohomish near Monroe?" Jerry acknowledged the information with a nod. "The Montague Farm is on the list as a producer of honey products. I remember the problems between Mr. Varian and Chris Colella, the foreman about how to run the farm. After I left for school, I heard Mr. Varian died of an apparent heart attack."

Jerry said, "That sounds suspicious, in light of what we now know. Do you think the foreman had something to do with the death?" He aimed the question at no one in particular.

CHAPTER

38

Eden departed her front porch after stopping and scanning the view. Row after row of trees, late summer flowers, bushes, and workers attending to them. Serenity, she thought. However, the noise of silence masked the turmoil apparent in her conversations of late with Chris Colella, the foreman, and Bernice Harapat, her apiary specialist.

The walk across the yard to the offices of the wholesale plantation was not long. A mild increase in the air's temperature from the previous couple of days hinted that summer was not yet ready to yield to fall. Business was booming and trucks made daily deliveries of fall and winter plantings to the retail businesses around Snohomish and King County. Other buyers waited in Kitsap and Pierce for deliveries in the next week. On the surface, all was well.

Opening the outer entry, she walked to her isolated space, unlocked the door, and after observing the emptiness of the hallway, moved to her desk and sat. She logged into the computer to work the previous day's reports which had been sent by a software program used by the managers and workers. Everything seemed as it should be. The financial records accounted for the sales and payments of the last few days. Payroll was next. Her workers were loyal and compensated at a rate above other farms. Migrants provided proper identification of their legal status as did the permanent immigrant families.

Yes, all was well. A noise in the hall alerted her to another person. A knock on her door prompted an 'Enter' response. Chris Colella came in.

"Good morning, Eden. If I may have a word with you?" She

pointed at a chair. He remained standing.

"What is it?" Her voice was curt and concise, maybe more than she meant for it to sound.

"Deliveries have gone out for today. Financial transfers will happen as soon as drivers have completed their drops."

"Thank you. Anything else?" She clicked on a program to open it.

"No," Chris said. "Just wanted you to know. Are you coming out to the fields?"

She looked at him. A murmur escaped from her which sounded like a yes.

"Are you alright? Is something bothering you?" His demeanor was friendly, a contrast to other interactions. Her stare remained as a downward curl formed on her mouth.

"I'm fine. I do wonder about you and Bernice. Are you having differences of opinions about our fall production of honey? I'm sensing tension between you two." Chris rocked from one foot to the other. His head stayed steady, but his eyes lowered.

"Nothing serious. I want to produce less this year and Bernice thinks we should keep production at our usual rate."

Eden stood and moved around the desk to the door. "Let's go see what she has to say." She opened the door and moved to the hallway. Still holding the door, she asked, "Are you coming?"

He followed her to the greenhouse area of the farm and the building housing the rhododendrons and azaleas. Neatly ordered rows of pots with rhodies and Luteum Azaleas sat awaiting the late fall blooming mastered by convincing plants that it was the right time. Bumblebees buzzed about the boxes housing them; not their usual setup, but one which suited the temperamental insect.

Bernice dressed in her net-wear attending to one of the boxes. She looked up but ignored the wave of a hand by Eden, who did admire the way her apiary expert coaxed work out of the pesky flying tanks. After a few minutes of attention to detail, Bernice came to them.

"Good morning, Eden. Chris. To what do I owe this visit?"

Eden smiled and said, "I understand you and Chris have a disagreement about the final outcome of your little pets' hard work."

"Nothing we won't fix by the end of the season."

"How much produce will your bees create?" Eden's tone was

less collegial than her usual conversations with Bernice.

"What did Chris say?"

"I'm asking you." Bernice glanced at Chris.

"I think we can get about twenty pounds." Heartbeats pounded in her throat. Breathing thinned.

"Isn't that down from previous years?" Eden eyed her apiarist with a suspicion about what was happening on her farm. Vanessa Christine had warned her. An investigation by police in Seattle regarding the suspicious deaths of two men by a natural substance. A true production accounting was more probable in this latest collection. She had to know the exact amount these super bumbles could produce.

"A little, maybe. Nothing to worry about, though. We'll have enough for mixing with the other collections. You'll have your products."

Eden turned to Chris. "I heard nothing which indicated a problem between you two. Make it work." He nodded, a tiny grimace marked his mouth. Eden departed.

As she walked back to her office her cell buzzed. The name on the screen sent a shiver through her. "Hello, Vanessa, what can I do for you?" She inhaled a heavy amount and waited for the drop of bad news.

"My detective just informed me you are on a list obtained by the Snohomish sheriff's office. It's now in the hands of my sergeant and his family. They are going to visit each place and ascertain viability. Please assure me you are not guilty of supplying the honey."

Eden paused. "I'm not the one who is doing anything illegal." Tears dripped down her cheeks. "I'm just not sure I'm innocent in their eyes. Something is going on here which worries me."

"Eden, meet me at our place and explain what you mean. I don't want to hear it over the phone." The call ended with an agreement to interact about what could transpire. She walked into her office with a foreboding in her heart.

Bernice scowled at Chris, "What was that about?"

His answer was less than acceptable. "Nothing. Stop worrying.

I'll fix it."

"Chris, she thinks we're not honest with her. If what we're doing is uncovered, I not sure I can handle it."

Chris frowned and set his jaw. "Be careful what you say to me."

"Or what? You'll kill me with my honey? You think this is safe from discovery? You may be a bigger fool than I am."

"Do what needs doing and will cut our losses. Get a hold of the twins and inform them this will be our last batch. They can have the entire lot. I'll contact the others and see if we can get them to outbid for it."

"Greed killed the Golden Goose, moron. Or didn't you ever read any fairy tales."

Chris waved his hands in the air. "Stop worrying. We'll get out of this what we can and disappear." At least, one of us, he thought to himself.

He left the greenhouse to oversee the trucks still in the yard. He observed Eden leaving the grounds. "Where is she going?" he wondered.

Each of the trees on the last truck contained the small parts of animals which were unwitting accomplices in his experiment to dispose of a body or two.

Bernice was a thorn to be plucked from his rose of an ideal life. She would grace the root bundles of the next bunch of trees and bushes. All he needed was time alone with her to make it happen. He had it planned to the last detail. How to kill her. Where to hide her body. When to dismember her. Creating the proper root balls and placing her parts in them.

He figured he would need nearly a hundred plants for her to neatly disappear and not be found. After all, instructions stated to plant the entire ball with the burlap wrap into the ground. No fuss, no bother.

As the last truck rolled out for delivery, he turned to see Bernice leaving the greenhouse. He ran to catch her and apologize.

"What now, Chris? Come to tell me how stupid I am?"

"Bernice, I came to apologize. We need to be together on this. I was out of line. Please accept." He held out a hand.

She glanced at it and without taking it said, "I accept. But this is the last batch which has any extra for us. Next spring the rhodies will be for Eden entirely." She turned away to leave him before any other words exploded from her mouth. She did not believe the sincerity of his words. After all, she thought, sincerity begins with sin. And she felt she had enough for one lifetime.

Chris let her go. As he watched, his mind filed through the ideas for her demise. Honey was not going to do it. Another non-bloody method would be up close and personal. His brain coursed through his daily activities and reminded him of Eden's departure. What was she up to that she had to leave in the middle of the day? Was she meeting someone? And who would she need to meet while business needed conducting? He decided to check her office.

CHAPTER

39

Tiberius organized the group of hunters, asking for the lists to be displayed for all to see. JJ placed his list on the table. Jerry pulled the pages from the folder retrieved from King County. As they viewed the names, a count of more than thirty halted further work.

"This is too many," Marc said. "We need to narrow the list by whatever means we can."

Ryan interjected his information from speaking with Kerrine in Central Kitsap lockup. "When I interviewed Kerrine, she hinted at a Snohomish location and dropped the name Bernice as her contact."

JJ responded to the name with a gasp. "That's the name of a person at the nursery where I worked during the summers when I was at Wazzu." He pointed at the Snohomish list and continued. "This is the nursery."

Jerry spoke next, "I remember an investigation of the death of the owner. We were called out because a man died under unusual circumstances, but the death ultimately was classified as heart failure."

JJ said, "Yeah, and Dad thought it would be a good place for me to get a job." He pointed at the name. "Eden. Eden Montague. Yeah, she ran the place."

Marc answered, "Well, it's as good a place as any to start. Jerry, get the particulars on the guy who died."

"Are you thinking we might have another honey death?" Jerry asked.

"It's worth a look."

Tiberius interrupted, "If someone died by honey out there, we might want to be cautious about how we approach the people. One of them may not want us to investigate."

"Dad, you're always the smart one. You're right, of course."

"I'll get the name of the man who died and the autopsy. If any tissue samples still exist and can be tested, maybe new info will result."

Ryan said, "Jeremy and I can review the report and see if anything seems out of place."

Marc said, "Good, are there other growers we should speak with about their honey products?" Three other names in King County were deemed possible. The audacious band divided tasks and planned another gathering at the same location for the following day.

They departed for their various duties. Marc sent Ryan and Jeremy with his Uncle Jerry to review the death of the mystery man at Montague Farms. Tiberius was to contact the King growers identified and determine any value of pursuit. JJ and Regina were driving to Eden Montague's as a young couple wanting to purchase plants for a garden at their home. Marc headed back to Wendlesburg but wanted to speak with his girls in lockup before going home. The day was nearing evening.

JJ and Regina arrived at the farm as dusk was creating orange and purple hues in the sky to the west and east. He scanned the main entry for the offices, which he hoped had remained as he remembered. Regina pointed at a large structure, resembling a house.

"Is that home of Eden Montague?" she asked.

"I think so," JJ answered. "I don't remember much about it as I was a field hand and we worked away from this area. I recall coming through another gate to get to work."

He parked the car in a round-about in front of the home. They vacated his vehicle and approached the house. No one seemed to be home. Looking around, they discovered the customers' store and decided to inquire there about the owner. The sign on the side wall by the door indicated the hours of operation. It was still open.

JJ opened the door and held it as Ginny went in. He followed.

Inside two women were behind the counter, one was completing a transaction. The other person looked at them, smiled, and asked, "May I help you?" She stopped sorting through stock items on shelves behind the counter.

JJ said, "Yes, I was wondering if Eden is available. I used to work summers in her fields when I was going to college. I'm back in the area now and was hoping to see her." He clasped his hands behind his back. Ginny wandered the aisles as if looking over the merchandise. She stopped at a display of various honey products.

The woman thought a moment. "Let me contact her office and see if she is available." Picking up the receiver of the phone on the back counter, she punched a couple of numbers and waited for an answer. After a moment she placed the receiver on its cradle. "I'm sorry; she's not in her office."

"Might she be at her house?"

"Possibly, but we do not contact her there. She left instructions that only an emergency should prompt a call to the house. I can contact our foreman, Chris, and let him know you're here."

JJ's eyes widened. "Yes, he was my supervisor, as was a man named Jorge."

"Let me try his office." Before she tried, JJ interrupted her.

"Does the beekeeper still work here? I think her name was Bernice or something like that."

The woman held the receiver in her hand. "Did you want me to try and contact her, instead?" JJ nodded.

"That would be splendid. Thanks." Ginny brought three jars of honey to the counter.

"Let's get these. They are most interesting." JJ wagged his head and whispered.

"Eden's not in her office. We'll try the house after here."

The woman turned her attention to the couple. "Bernice is coming over. I didn't get your name."

Jeremais. JJ for short. This is my wife, Regina." He figured the small tale was not too far from the truth.

The woman asked, "Did you want these?" She indicated the jars.

Ginny answered her, "Yes, please. The various flowers listed on the label are most intriguing."

"Yes," the woman said, "we pride ourselves as the best honey in the county." The door opened, and another woman entered. She was dressed for work and not for shopping. "Ah, here's Miss Bernice." JJ stuck out a hand.

"I don't know if you remember me. I used to work summers here when I was in college. My name is Jeremais Jefferson. This is my wife, Ginny." Bernice shook their proffered hands.

"I don't necessarily recall. We have so many part-timers. When were you here?"

"I venture to say about five or six years ago. I worked three summers between semesters at Washington State."

"Very nice to see you. Did you want to tour the grounds before it's too dark to see anything?" JJ determined he needed a more direct action but waited.

"Thank you. That would be nice. We're looking for plants for our new home in Sultan." Bernice turned and waved for them to follow.

Ginny said to the lady behind the counter. "Hold these for me. I'll return to purchase them." She was not going to leave potential evidence behind.

Outside the temperature had dropped a few degrees. Fall was swinging into action. "We are finishing our deliveries this week and next, so there may not be much from which to choose, depending on what you want." Bernice did not indicate any nervousness or recognition of him. He did recognize her, though.

"Is Chris still here?" His inquiry halted her movement. She turned and faced him.

"Did you want to see him, instead?" He detected a tone of anger or maybe disappointment.

"No, I was just asking. He was my supervisor."

Ginny stopped and said, "I'm going to purchase my honey. I don't want to be a third wheel on your memory lane walk." JJ understood her plan.

"Can you show me the hives you work? I've always had a fascination with bees. They work so hard to pollinate and provide food for the hive. We humans come along and take their product for our own selfish wants."

Bernice scowled, "My bees are not abused. They make enough for all of us. After all, your wife is buying some right now, I suspect."

JJ nodded, and they continued to the greenhouses. The daylight had waned into a twilight shading the view of plants on the grounds. She opened a door and led him into a large room with rows of small trees and bushes. She flipped a switch illuminating the plantings.

"You might find what you want in here. You mainly want trees and shrubs to begin your landscaping. Establish flower beds after the areas are decided."

"Yes, this is fine. We'll come back tomorrow or the next day. I'll bring a plat map so we can plan correctly." JJ turned to leave and stopped. Chris Colella entered.

"Bernice," he said and stopped. "Oh, I didn't know you had customers."

"I was just leaving." JJ brushed past and departed for the store and Ginny. He waited outside the door and listened.

Chris asked, "Who was that?"

"He claims to have worked here a few years ago."

"Why do you look like you've seen a ghost?"

"His name is Jeremais Jefferson. That was the name of the sheriff who came out here when Malcolm died." JJ heard the panic in her voice. He left before being detected.

CHAPTER

40

Eden entered the restaurant and scanned for Vanessa. Without a uniform, she blended into the crowd of customers. A quick wave indicated her location.

"What's the alarm I heard in your voice?" Eden asked.

"Not alarm. Concern. I have a detective working a case about two men who died curiously. It's thought the material causing the deaths was a form of honey with lethal toxins." Vanessa reached for her sister's hands. "Please, be careful what you say or do. I can't stop this investigation."

"Nessi, you're scaring me. Does this guy think I'm guilty of providing the honey?"

"He doesn't know about you or your farm. Yet. Another group of officers from Snohomish and Kitsap Counties are heavily involved. Also, two forensic scientists from Portland have wrangled their way into the case."

Eden sat with her mouth open and her hands squeezing Vanessa's hands. "Do these other people suspect I had something to do with the deaths?"

Vanessa released her grip. "That's the problem for you. I think so." Glancing around the room, she then said, "I can delay them for a while, but sooner or later, they will be coming."

Eden leaned forward across the table. Her whisper was audible to Vanessa. "I think something is wrong on my farm."

"Like what?"

"That's another problem I have. I don't know. Chris and Bernice act like I'm an intrusion because I want to learn all aspects of the workload the crews have. I want to learn about bees. I want to know the soils on the farm."

"Ever since Malcolm's death, you've let them run the place. Now you want to know what they do?" Vanessa sat back. "Seems to me they are correct to be suspicious."

"Speaking of Malcolm. I know the coroner filed that he died of heart failure. What if someone wanted him dead and poisoned his food?"

"Why do you say things like that? He died of a heart attack." Vanessa's eyes widened, and her voice winced a sound of discovery. "The honey on the farm, can any of it cause problems with circulation?"

Food arrived as Eden readied her answer. The silence shouted at Vanessa. Eden answered when the waitress left.

"We make a special brand of honey called by most bee people, 'Mad Honey' because it is known to have a toxin called grayanotoxin. But we only use it to enhance flavors of other types of honey."

Vanessa scrunched her eyes. "Grayanotoxin? What does it do?"

Eden leaned closer over her food. "Rhododendrons and azaleas contain this toxin in leaves, roots, flowers and branches. It's known to cause serious problems if animals eat any part. In small amounts, it's not harmful. I guess in larger amounts the plants can cause illness."

"Like what?"

"From what I know, paralysis of the muscles impedes breathing and heart function." Eden gasped, rocked her head back and forth, and rolled eyes. "My god, what have I done. What if people are getting sick with the blending of it with other honey?" Her hands cradled a tearful head.

"Get me a sample. I'll have it tested. If anything matches, I'll let you know immediately."

"Nessi, I didn't mean to kill anyone." Vanessa reached across the table. She held a forearm.

"You haven't done anything wrong. Someone is selling a lethal brand of honey and tea laced with crushed rhodie leaves."

Eden regained her composure. Her eyes narrowed and her lips curled. "Nessi, who's coming to my farm? I want to meet with them before they arrive."

"Why?"

"I have to clear the air before they alert others. I'm not sure, but if I'm right, I might be able to help solve their case." Eden stopped talking and picked up part of the sandwich she had ordered. Taking a bite, she chewed a slow, contemplative pace. Vanessa knew the signs of a brain at work.

"Eden, they already may be there."

"Did you authorize them to come to my farm?"

"As I said, I have a detective working a case. One of my sergeants and the Portland forensics boys are working with him. I understand my sergeant's son and brother are helping. The brother is a deputy in Snohomish"

Eden placed the sandwich on the plate, finished chewing and swallowed. "You should eat." Vanessa stared at her sister who remained in a trance of thought. After a few seconds, the eyes focused and a smile brightened the farmer's face. "Please, eat."

They finished their meal without another word exchange. Vanessa clicked open her cell and started the phone app. She punched in a number and waited for a connection.

"I'm calling my detective. He might have an update for me." Eden stood and moved to an unoccupied part of the restaurant to make a call of her own.

When the other party answered, Eden asked, "Donna, has anyone from any law-enforcement organization arrived at the farm?" She listened. Satisfied with the answer, she ended the call and returned to the table.

Vanessa said, "Thanks," and clicked her phone app closed. "Nothing much to report. A request for testing of a teabag came in. A fingerprint was found but no match to anyone in our records."

Eden said, "We don't sell tea. What's the significance of a teabag?"

"It was found at the motel room where two flower delivery drivers died. That's the case my detective is working."

"Remember when Dad got sick. We thought he had heart failure. He took his medicine but never seemed to get better." Vanessa nodded a recognition of her memories. Giordano Montague had been a strong and resourceful man., building an empire which appeared to have taken its toll.

Malcolm Varian and Eden had married and worked with him.

Vanessa had left the farm to pursue her dream of being a cop. Her husband, Warren Christine, had died a heroic fire fighter. No children meant all energies consumed her ascent to Assistant Chief of Criminal Investigations.

"What are you thinking? That Dad's death may have been deliberate? Who would want him dead?"

"I don't know. Certainly not me or Malcolm. And Malcolm's death from heart failure. Do you believe in coincidences?"

"You suspect he died from toxic honey? I can ask a friend in Snohomish to pull the file so our coroner can take a closer evaluation of the evidence." The waitress left the billing on the table and hurried away. Eden placed a twenty in the folder. Vanessa also paid cash.

They left the restaurant as twilight claimed the afternoon. In the parking area, Eden said, "Come out to the farm, tomorrow. I may have a way of answering some of these questions."

"You called the farm to find out if anyone had come there, didn't you?" Vanessa asked. She clasped hands and continued. "If my detective or sergeant are there, don't worry."

"No one came. A young couple was there searching for plantings on their new property." Eden frowned as if to cry.

"I'll see about getting away from the office for a bit. Please, be calm and stay alert to anything you aren't sure about."

"Isn't that a little difficult? To remain calm and look for danger?" They smiled. Inside, neither was positive that all was well at Montague Wholesale House.

Eden watched as Vanessa departed for Seattle and her home. She had a shorter drive than Eden who lived near Sultan on Highway 2 which crossed the Cascade Mountains through Stevens Pass.

Arriving after dark at her house, Eden parked the car, not expecting anyone. The silence eerily surrounded her as she walked up the front steps to the house. Tomorrow, she had to ask about the young couple. Were they investigating the farm for signs of malfeasance? What questions had they asked? Did they make any purchases?

Late summer and early fall were not unusual times for customers looking to buy at wholesale prices instead of the markup at retail stores and nurseries. Her mind conjured a scenario of two people posing as customers and wanting to find criminals. Had they met with Chris or Bernice? Donna hinted at such an idea. Nothing was sacred anymore. Not life. Not friendships. Not business. Nothing.

Locking herself into the house, she closed curtains and secured windows. Alone had not been fearful until now. Vanessa's warnings and her suspicions isolated her. She feared a break-in when no one was around. The crew which lived on the property were all at their cottages. All the other workers had clocked out and gone home. Tomorrow, her investigation was to begin. She had no idea where to start, except in the greenhouses. Whom could she trust?

Trust. A devil of a concept. So easy to accept until broken. So difficult to rebuild when fractured. She prepared for bed, brushing teeth, combing hair, washing her face. Trust. Who could she ask for information and get the truth? Chris Colella? Bernice Harapat? Jorge? Donna? Any of the workers?

Sleep eluded her for a time until exhaustion overpowered her brain. Dreams invaded her slumber and crawled around her mind's creativeness. Malcolm and Giordano came to her as she studied her manager and her beekeeper in a dream as vivid as life. What did they want to tell her?

CHAPTER

41

Marc woke early and slipped from the bed, trying not to disturb Joan. His wife of nearly twenty years carried a heavy burden of worry about his safety. In the last few months he and his law enforcement family members had engaged a gang of drug dealers in three firefights in Everett, Washington and surrounding communities. Although the cartel had collapsed and the leader was dead, Marc and his father had suffered life-threatening injuries.

While on a vacation cruise to Anchorage, Alaska with their three children, the family endured the arms of the cartel octopus which refused to die. Someone poisoned both sons. Marc had received a head wound from a bullet meant to kill him. Several people were dead as a result of the activities of members of the smuggling operation working aboard the ship.

Now he was about to confront another of the tentacles when he and his cousin, uncle, and father were heading to a farm outside of Sultan, Washington. JJ had called last night informing him of his investigation of a potential source of the honey used to kill an unsuspecting author, a crew member, and attempted murder of his sons, Marcus and James, as well as the daughter of the shipboard medical doctor.

His plan was simple. Take Kaliana with him to the farm and have her identify anyone with whom she had any transactions. A female deputy was to accompany them as a security measure.

In the bathroom, he prepared for a shower. Joan wandered in before he stepped in. "I'm sorry. I didn't mean to wake you."

"You didn't. I must be at work early today. Are you leaving for Snohomish soon?"

Marc nodded. "I'll get the kids off to school, today." Joan finished her business and joined him in the shower.

"Please, be careful. Lately, it seems everyone is out to kill you or any of your family. Marcus was kidnapped again. And though he escaped, I'm not convinced someone won't try again."

"This trip is not to a battle scene." He hoped it was not, at least. They finished soaping each other and rinsing. Joan left the shower leaving Marc leaning on the wall with water cascading across his head and down his body. He was tired of one criminal organization occupying some much of his time. Sheriff Fellington warned him of the consequences of a lack of service to Kitsap.

The battles had been intense as the war against Andrew Pepper and his gang raged on. Elements of the gang survived, although Marc figured the number of combatants had to be dwindling.

He heard a ringing sound like bells in a faraway cathedral. His cell phone. He shut off the stream and exited the shower. Grabbing his towel and drying as fast as possible, he wanted to check who called. Joan walked in with phone in hand. "It's your uncle."

Standing naked he wrapped the towel around his waist and took the phone. "Good morning, Uncle Jerry. You're up early."

"Did I interrupt something?" Uncle Jerry asked.

Marc laughed, "No, just getting ready to leave." He walked into the bedroom and put the speaker on. Placing the phone on the bed, he dressed as they talked.

"We have a print from the teabag found in the motel room. JJ wants to match it with anyone at Eden Montague's farm in Sultan."

"That's the place he worked during college. Right?"

"Yeah, he feels something has changed since he was there. He and Regina sensed a tension between the principals of the business. Eden was not there, though."

"Who was he referring to?" Marc pulled up his pants and tightened his belt after buckling and zipping.

"Are you getting dressed? You sound like you're moving around, and I hear clothing."

"Guilty, Uncle. Now back to the question. Who was he talking about?"

"The supervisor and the beekeeper." Marc picked up the phone after slipping on socks and shoes.

"What kind of stress?"

Jerry cleared his throat, "He said the joy he remembered was gone. They interacted like frenemies, as he put it."

Marc walked down the stairs having turned off the speaker. "I'm bringing Kaliana with me to the farm. She can ID whoever is the one who sold them the lethal honey if we have the right property."

"What about Kerrine? She seems to be the boss."

Marc laughed, "Yeah, but she took the opportunity to attack me and somehow escape. I don't believe she'd leave her sister to rot. Kaliana's attraction to me means she'll stay."

Jerry said, "JJ and Regina are coming to my house. Tiberius is arriving with Manny Espinoza. The forensic twins are coming as well. Since the farm is in my county, I've been assigned the lead from my sheriff. He wants any remnants of the scourge infesting the county removed." They ended the call.

Marc awakened Sarah and James who complained like the teenagers they were. Joan was in the kitchen with a mug of coffee in hand and one on the counter for Marc. Lunches awaited the family. Joan had prepared them the night before.

Marc asked, "Have you eaten?" She nodded and pointed at a bowl in the sink. She had placed three more cereal bowls on the counter with spoons.

"Have cereal and juice. Nothing elaborate since we have to leave soon." She had three glasses on the table with a bottle of orange juice.

Marc placed a variety of cereals on the table and poured Wheaties into one of the bowls. Sarah and James arrived in time to say goodbye to their mother. She then kissed Marc and departed.

"Have cereal. If you want toast, make your own," he told his children. "Lunches are ready to go." He finished his preparations to leave for the Central Kitsap office of sheriff. Returning to the kitchen, he saw his children had bussed the table and departed for school. The house echoed an eerie silence.

At the office in Silverdale, Marc completed the paperwork for the transportation of his prisoner and arranged for the female deputy he requested the previous evening to accompany him across Puget Sound.

When Kaliana arrived at the departure door in a complete set of body chains, she asked, "What are we doing, Marc?" He ignored the request as he signed the log book for her traveling with him.

"Kaliana, we are going on a field trip. I think you'll enjoy it," he said to her. A smile broached his face. "Officer Tanaka will accompany us to keep us from detouring from our purpose."

"A three-way. I like your thinking, Marc. Officer Tanaka, are you up to the challenge of sating our lust?" The officer remained stoic. Marc had briefed her well.

Tanaka drove while Marc sat in the rear seating with Kaliana. His weapons were in a lock box on the front passenger seat.

"These chains are hurting me. Can't we take them off? I'm not running away. I have nowhere to go." Marc rocked his head from side to side.

Crossing from Kingston to Edmonds, the officers and their charge remained in the car on the main deck. Arrangements made for an early load place them in the front of the line of cars.

After driving off the ferry, Tanaka drove up the hill. "Where are we going?" Kaliana asked.

"We'll be there soon," was the only remark given.

"I have to pee," she said. "Can we stop somewhere so I can pee?"

Marc called the Monroe Correctional Complex to request a stop for a bathroom break. Tanaka altered course and headed to the prison in Monroe, Washington. The travel time changed but not the direction of travel since Monroe was situated on the same highway as Sultan.

After a brief respite for all three travelers, the journey to the farm commenced. Arrival was less than an hour away. Kaliana shifted in her seat in the car as an awareness sank into her brain. The area was familiar. She and Kerrine traveled here on several occasions to obtain their preferred elixir of death.

"Field trip. I get it now. To the farm we go." Kaliana chuckled. "You want me to rat out the person responsible for selling us our honey and tea. There's nothing wrong with buying honey and tea."

"Oh, but when it is a deliberate act of murder or attempted murder, then the wrong belongs to you and whoever provided the materials," Marc stated as calm as a man realizing his choice was correct.

In Sultan, the body of officers gathered at a local park before crossing the Skykomish River to confront Eden Montague and her staff.

JJ and Regina had submitted the honey for analysis in Everett, but results would not be available for another few days. Manny Espinoza came with Tiberius and the Portland scientists. He carried the report of the fingerprint on the teabag. An app on his phone would analyze each person who worked at the farm. Jerry played the role of officer in charge as a representative of the Snohomish County Sheriff's Office. Snohomish had jurisdiction for all reporting and records. No one cared so long as the contraband could be found and confiscated, and all persons involved detained for questioning.

"Let's do this," Jerry said. The automobiles moved across the highway to the bridge and destiny.

CHAPTER

42

The morning sun had yet to rise above the Cascade Mountains. Eden's sleep ended in a fit of dreamed rage. Nothing remained clear to her about the images of Chris and Bernice eating dinner with her and watching her warily. What was it they said? Drink your tea?

Sitting on the edge of the bed with head hanging down, she wondered if any of her thinking had any merit. Confronting Chris or Bernice had problems. Little, if any, evidence of wrongdoing existed. They had produced plants and various kinds of honey craved by a voracious public. She clicked a light on to better see her future.

From her bedroom window, the morning sky cast a hazy grey/blue sheen across the farm. The end of summer was near. She rose from the bed and went to the bathroom to prepare for another day. A shower cleansed her body and relaxed her mind. A clean break. Maybe she needed it.

In her kitchen, she made coffee and poached an egg. Toast completed her simple meal. She opened a new jar of honey her apiary expert concocted, a mix of several types of flower pollens.

She examined the jar for the ingredients. The label did not contain any rhodies or azaleas. Her mind slipped into a trance of what happened to the Greek warriors of ancient times who were slaughtered by the Turks after eating Mad Honey.

"No more," she murmured. After eating her meal, she turned on the television to catch an update on the weather. Gray skies were coming by the next week. Leaves on the deciduous trees were yellowing. Fall flowers were out for delivery and bulbs were in greenhouses for the winter. Shrubs and bushes would winter through.

Eden walked to the office. As the day grew brighter, sunlight streaked the clouds with orange and red. Some of the farm hands were about their tasks without any instructions from Chris. These workers knew the drill. It would be another hour before the migrants arrived, although most had departed for the eastern side of the state to harvest apples, apricots, plums, cherries, and other fruits.

She sat at her desk and punched in the password for the computer. Opening the financial records, she started transferring numbers from the truck hauls to the spreadsheets. All the data added up and made sense. "Why the paranoia?" she thought.

She opened one of the books Bernice gave her about bumblebees and their abilities. Her knowledge level needed this information if she was to relieve Bernice of her duties. She hadn't uncovered a reasonable cause to do so, yet.

She checked her watch. Time had crawled toward 8 AM and staff arrived for the opening of the retail parts of the farm. She decided to check on the availability of Chris and Bernice. Finding neither on the property, she walked to the retail store and found Donna.

"Tell me about the couple here yesterday afternoon." Donna scrunched eyes brows, then recalled JJ and Regina.

"They were here to find plantings for their new home. He said he worked summers here when he was in college."

"What was his name?"

"JJ. I think. Jefferson?" Eden remembered the deputy assigned to the case of Malcolm's death. His son had applied for a summer program working the fields. She didn't recall much about the son, but the father was seared into her history because he questioned Malcolm's death. When the autopsy declared it to be heart failure, he stepped back. Murder. He questioned their relationship. He questioned others and their intentions regarding the farm.

Eden asked, "What did they buy?"

"The woman bought some honey. They said they were coming back today. It was getting dark."

"Honey? What kind?" Eden's voice wavered.

Donna frowned, "Is something wrong?"

Eden smiled, hiding her concern. "Just wanting to know what's selling."

They separated, and Eden left the store. A car entered the parking lot and parked near the store. She watched a young couple exit the vehicle. The woman was attractive. The man had a familiar look but younger. She approached them.

"Welcome to Montague's." She reached for a hand. JJ accepted.

"Remember me?" he asked. "Oh, probably not. It's been a while since I worked here."

Eden cocked her head. "You're the boy whose father came when my husband died."

JJ grinned, "Jeremais Jefferson, Junior. My father is Sergeant Jefferson."

"And who is this young lady?" She shook hands with Regina.

"I'm Regina McDonald."

"You're Canadian."

"Yes, Ma'am."

"I understand you are looking for plantings for your property." JJ displayed his Snohomish Sheriff's badge.

"We're here on official business. Is there somewhere we can go? I have a few questions to ask you." Eden directed them to the house. As they neared it, two more cars arrived with the remaining members of the family and one guest.

Jerry approached Eden, JJ, and Regina. "Good morning, Mrs. Montague. I'm Sergeant Jefferson of the Snohomish County Sheriff's Department."

"I remember." She directed the four of them into the house. Tiberius and his crew vacated their car and spread about the property. Marc and Kaliana remained behind in his car to not attract attention.

Inside the house, Eden directed them to the living room. Vanessa's warning had become a reality. A bead of sweat formed and her heart pounded. "What's this all about? All these cops?"

Jerry said, "I am sorry for this invasion of your privacy, but we are seeking some answers which we believe you may be able to supply."

Eden sat still, as stoic as a statue. Then she said, "Where are my manners. Do any of you want something to drink? I have coffee or soda." Each shook a head.

Jerry asked, "Are you a producer of a honey with a nickname of

Mad Honey?" Eden lowered her head. A slight nod answered his query.

"We make it to mix with other honey to give it a unique taste. No one should be getting sick from it. One would have to consume a rather large quantity."

"I didn't say anyone was getting sick. Would you please explain why you said that? Has someone gotten sick from your honey?" Jerry asked.

A knock on the front door interrupted an answer. Eden rose and opened it to find a manacled young woman standing with another man dressed in coat and tie. He displayed a badge which had Kitsap Sheriff on it. "May I help you?" She stared at the restraining device around Kaliana and the uniformed female.

"I'm with them," Marc said. "I want to ask you a question."

She directed them into the room to join the other three. "You sure are full of questions today." Marc turned attention to his prisoner.

"Is she the person with whom you made transactions for honey and tea?"

Kaliana shook her head. "No, the lady was older, heavier set. She was a beekeeper, I think." Marc directed his next question to Eden.

"Who is your beekeeper? Is she here?"

"I don't know. She hadn't arrived before you came. I was in the office. Hers is next to mine. Why are you interested in my bees?"

Jerry stood and said, "Not your bees. Your honey. We need a sample of the honey your bees produce from the rhododendrons."

"We don't have any. It has yet to be produced. It takes several weeks to gain enough product for harvesting. The process is just beginning." She pulled out her phone and clicked Bernice's office number. The phone rang, but no one answered. "She may be in a greenhouse and didn't hear her phone."

Jerry repeated his earlier question. "Has anyone gotten sick from consuming your mad honey laced honey?"

"Of course not. I wouldn't be selling it if anyone got sick."

"May we look around your property?"

"What for? Do I need a lawyer?"

"I don't think so unless you have something to confess or hide from us." Jerry rather sneered as he spoke.

"I've nothing to hide." Jerry, JJ, and Marc headed outside. Regina and the deputy stayed with Kaliana. Eden pulled her cell again and dialed another number. She separated from the other females. As she waited on her porch, watching the three men walk across her yard, she noticed the other men, one in a uniform.

Vanessa answered as a message voice. "You were right. Several officers are here. Do I need a lawyer? Call me." She clicked off.

As she scurried to catch all the men on her farm, she saw Chris enter the gate. He parked in his reserved spot and vacated his car, staring at the cadre of strangers.

Marc approached and introduced himself and the others. He did not mention the three women in the house. Eden came up.

"Chris, I want you to cooperate with these men. They have some questions about our operations." He scanned the varied men

"Eden, what is this all about?"

"They'll let you know. Just be honest."

CHAPTER

43

Chris waited. Marc asked, "Is there a place we can go to get out of your public arena? I don't want customers scared away by the horde." Chris signaled for him to follow to the offices.

Jerry, Tiberius, Manny, Ryan, and Jeremy scattered across the property to speak with workers and to collect any possible evidence. Eden stood frozen as fear of discovery might jeopardize her future. Chris entered the office compound. She turned to reenter her house and ask a question which could clarify her status. As she did, a car approached. Bernice arrived for work.

Inside she asked Regina, "What are you expecting to find here?" She crossed arms over her chest. Her voice conveyed her tension.

Regina answered her, "We are not certain to find anything here. We are conducting investigations of several farms in the area which produce a certain type of honey."

"Mad honey, I assume."

"Yes."

"Why? Why me? What evidence do you have I've done something wrong?"

Kaliana interrupted their conversation. "That's her." She pointed out the window.

Regina and the Kitsap deputy followed the indication. Eden closed her eyes and exhaled. She knew. Anxiety heightened her breathing. Regina said, "Please ask that person to come here."

"Who?" Her question meant to deflect and delay the inevitable.

"Whoever is entering that building across the parking area. Get her now, please." Regina opened the phone app on her device and punched a preset number. She waited. "JJ, a woman just entered the building across the parking area. Bring her to the house. Kaliana seems to recognize her."

Eden said, "I can get her." She started for the door.

"Please, stay here, Ms. Montague. My partner can access her and bring her."

"You don't trust me to get her, do you?" Eden bulged a vein on her forehead, her voice lowered. "This is my property, and unless you have a search warrant, I'd like you all to leave. Now."

Regina placed a hand on Kaliana's chains but didn't move. "You gave us permission to search the premises. As a gesture of good faith, I will contact all of them to stop looking." She released Kaliana and called Marc. Informing him of Eden's temperament, she then contacted Tiberius.

JJ called, "Which person, Ginnie?" He stood in the parking area looking at greenhouses and the office complex.

"In the building which is not a greenhouse. A lady entered there as did Marc and Ms. Montague's foreman." She watched him nod and closed the call. He opened the door as Marc and Chris arrived. He related his task and Marc nodded. JJ entered while Marc and Chris returned to the house.

As the group gathered, Marc asked Eden, "Are you asking we stop surveying your property until we obtain a warrant to search?"

Eden asked, "What are you looking for?"

"Ms. Montague, we are conducting investigations of several farms in Snohomish and King Counties to ascertain if any of them have provided a toxic product capable of causing heart arrhythmia and possible death. We understand your farm produces a type of honey which may be capable of causing this to happen."

Another car pulled into the driveway and parked before Eden answered. As Tiberius and Manny crossed the lot, they stopped and spoke with the woman who vacated the car. Chief Christine followed them to the house.

Upon entering, Vanessa said, "Eden, are you okay?" Marc furrowed his brow. Tiberius cocked his head. Manny folded arms.

"How do you know Ms. Montague?" Marc asked. His arms rested on his hips.

"We're related." Vanessa's comment brought a collected hushed gasp.

Tiberius asked, "How are you related to this woman. And you knew we were heading here and didn't tell us. Don't you think we should have known?"

"My relationship to her does notimpede your investigation."

Manny spoke next, "Maybe not an impediment, but have you been apprising Ms. Montague of our progress regarding this investigation? Have you warned her so she can hide incriminating evidence?"

"Be careful what you say, Detective. You're accusing me of obstructing your investigation. I've done nothing to stop you." Her eyes narrowed.

Marc calmed the atmosphere. "Let's relax. We are not here accusing anyone of anything. We are exploring a lead."

Vanessa said to Tiberius, "You and Detective Espinoza do not have any reason to be here. I would like you to leave at once. This interrogation is over."

Jerry confronted her. "I'm sorry, chief, but this my jurisdiction, and I do have permission from my Sheriff to conduct this matter. Contact him, if you need."

Vanessa flinched but held fast. "Sergeant, you and Detective Espinoza are to report back to Seattle. Write a report about this and have it on my desk by the end of today." She saw the Portland forensic scientists walk up the front steps. "And take those two with you."

Marc intervened, "Chief Christine, these men are here because the head of the Washington State Crime Lab assigned them."

"They are assigned to work with Detective Espinoza. That means they are under Seattle. They are leaving." Ryan and Jeremy glanced at each other and the chief. What had they entered?

Jerry continued to support his position. "With all due respect, they can work this case as members of the Crime Lab. I can call and get that if you insist on taking this harsh stance. It seems incredulous to me when we are all seeking the same thing."

Ryan stepped into the fray. "Jeremy and I will see this through, Chief. We found something in one of the greenhouses which may be culpable. I suggest a follow-up."

Eden asked, "Why are you arguing. I have nothing to hide. I want a warrant, however. And my lawyer. So, unless you are buying any of my products, get off my property. I'd call the police, but you're already here."

Regina interceded regarding Kaliana's comment. "Excuse me, but a woman came on the property, and our prisoner recognized her. I would like to know who she is."

Eden answered her. "If you want to interrogate any of my workers, I want a warrant. Chris grinned as he followed the dialog. His time had concluded, nevertheless. He departed without a complaint from anyone.

Marc said, "Uncle, I think we're done here for now." He signaled the parade to leave and congregate at the park in Sultan. A cavalcade of vehicles filed out through the gate. By now many of the workforce had awakened or arrived and stared at the proceedings with confusion. No one hid from the law since each had proper documentation as legal immigrants or citizenship proof.

"Eden, I'm sorry I didn't get here sooner," Vanessa said. She knew her position in Seattle hit a wall. Explaining would be difficult. "Get ready for a return visit. I can't stop Snohomish or Kitsap, but my people will not be back."

"Nessie, I'm scared. I don't have any idea what they want from me. My honey isn't poisonous. Thanks for coming out here. I know how much this can jeopardize your career." Tears formed in lids unable to hold them. They hugged for a moment before Vanessa bade farewell and left for Seattle and an uncertain future.

Eden built her resolve to flush out the reason for such a raid. Something was rotten, and the only way to staunch the stench of soiled systems was to confront the two people who had control. A deep inhale and exhale started her march across the yard and parking to the office building. Donna came out to uncover the craziness. "Close the store and gate. We're closed for business today." Donna hesitated. "Now," Eden yelled and continued her march to find Chris and Bernice. Her father had instilled in her a resolve to secure any situation and conclude any challenge with a win. She needed his strength at this moment. She was, after all, a Montague.

Entering the office area, she called out. "Chris. Bernice. My office. Now." Her voice echoed the hallway. She did not wait to see either of them vacate their own offices. Her room was suddenly stark, devoid of remembrances of the business her family had built. She would change that. She sat at her desk and clicked on the computer and logged in. Chris entered the room.

"You called?" He seemed breathless as if coming to her office included a sprint. Beads of moisture shone on his head.

"Where's Bernice?"

"I don't know. You want me to go check her office?"

"No. I'll talk with her later. Sit down." Chris complied.

"What was going on at the house? Those officers seemed upset about something. What did they want from you?"

Eden put up a hand with an open palm. He stopped talking. "Chris, what have you and Bernice done behind my back that caused police from three different jurisdictions to show up at my front door with a prisoner who fingered Bernice as someone she recognized?"

44

Jerry said, "JJ, you and Regina explain what we need to a judge and get a warrant to explore that property, thoroughly." They nodded and left for Monroe and a District Court.

"Marc, you and Kaliana can return to the farm and find out who she saw. We need some answers."

"Tiberius, you and your gang can return to Seattle and get any forensic data from the lab. Leave the teabag with me. I'm going to monitor who enters and leaves."

Tiberius said, "I'm concerned my chief is colluding with Montague to thwart any investigation."

"Manny, have you ever had her act this way in the past?" Jerry frowned. The detective shook his head.

As the posse separated for various places, Tiberius remained skeptical. Was his Chief of Investigative Services a mole while they searched for truth? He had to confront her. "Manny, you, Ryan, and Jeremy, please follow the forensic evidence and I'll have a talk with our leader."

Manny asked, "What if she doesn't return to Seattle?"

"I'll find her."

⋈ ⋈ ⋈

Jerry drove to the property behind his nephew and his prisoner. He wanted no trouble but anticipated it. Something was wrong. As Marc, Officer Tanaka, and Kaliana entered the farm she parked the vehicle on the side of the road with a view of the parking lot and a greenhouse. They slid into a spot and Marc left the car. Kaliana remained in the back seat with the deputy in the driver's seat. He watched a worker approach Marc. The man pointed toward a building out of sight which he believed to be the office compound. Marc moved in the direction of the man's finger.

Jerry clicked his cell open and called Marc. When he answered, Jerry said, "Marc, leave your phone open. I'll record whatever conversation you have. We may not be able to use it in a court, but it might help us to solve what's happening out here."

"Good idea, Uncle. I'm looking for the beekeeper, but no one seems to know where she is." Jerry scrunched his eyes.

"Didn't someone come onto the property who Kaliana identified?"

"Yeah, but she didn't say any name. I'm not sure she knows who that was by name."

"Be safe. If anything happens, I'm on the road outside of the farm and can assist immediately."

"Roger that."

⋊ ⋊ ⋊

Marc placed his phone in his jacket pocket and entered the office area. He found Eden at her desk clicking keys on her computer. "May I have a word with you?"

"What are doing here?" Eden asked. "Do you have a warrant, already?"

"One is being procured as we speak. My concern is regarding the woman who was identified by my prisoner. I want to meet her and have her explain why a confessed killer knows her."

"She doesn't have to speak with you or anyone. I've called my attorney, and she advised me to keep you off the property. Get out of here."

Marc turned to leave, then faced her again. "If you want, I can have the State Patrol get involved. Maybe the FBI would be interested. How about the Food and Drug Administration? Think they may be interested in your honey?" He waited as she stood and walked around the desk.

"You can threaten me all you want. I have nothing to hide, but Gestapo tactics don't work here." She walked to the door, and held it open so he could leave. Marc gave a slight nod as he passed by her.

Chris came from another office as Marc entered the hallway. "May I have a word with you?" Marc asked.

Eden said, "You don't have to speak with him. Don't answer any questions."

Chris looked at her. "I don't have anything to hide." He turned to Marc. "Come on in and let's talk." Chris sneered at his boss. Eden closed her door with a loud thud.

"Have a seat." He pointed at a chair for Marc to occupy. "How can I be of help?"

JJ and Regina entered the Superior Court building situated next to the Washington State Fairgrounds in Monroe, just off Highway 2 which led to Everett and the site of the beginning of this war against the enemies of law enforcement.

At the front desk, he asked for Justice Weldon Chomsky. "I need a warrant made out to inspect a property near Sultan." The court clerk working the desk for the day nodded and opened a schedule ledger on the computer.

"He's in court for another half hour. I can send in a message. Do you have the warrant?" JJ shook his head and asked for a form to complete. The clerk pulled one from a file cabinet behind the desk.

He and Ginnie sat at a table in a side room to make the case for searching Montague Farms. "What are we looking for?" Regina asked. "Details are important."

JJ nodded, "Yeah, I know. Dad wants to find any paper trail which connects the farm to Andrew Pepper. Uncle Marc needs to connect the twins. I'm not sure what Uncle Ti wants. I guess the detective wants to find the murder weapon source and tie the twins to it."

"Do you think Eden Montague is guilty?"

"I don't know. We need to focus on the fact it is her farm. She must know what's happening. Wouldn't she?" He finished writing details on the form and signed it. Handing it to Regina, he waited for a response. He trusted her judgment, thinking of her as smarter about things than he.

"This looks good. Computers are an important item. Good choice.

Should we include all the greenhouses? We might find something in one of them." He added the greenhouses to the list.

"What about her house? She could keep records there."

"And anything else which might connect her to the twins and the death of those people."

"And the deaths on the ship." He added the house with specific items and places to inspect, as well as the house generally.

Chris leaned against his desk. "How can I help you?" He figured the property was soon to be crawling with cops, turning over all boxes, cabinets, and rooms. The small room below the one greenhouse had a well disguised entry. He would check it before anyone arrived. Only Bernice and two others knew about it. The two workers were compensated well and would not talk. Bernice was another question.

Marc looked up at the farm's supervisor and said, "Tell me about Eden."

After pursing his lips, Chris began a short narration. "Eden and I have worked together for more than twelve years. She is a fair and generous boss. She and her father worked hard to make this place a success. Her husband and she continued to grow the business after her dad's heart attack."

"I understand her husband died of heart failure, too."

"Yes, unfortunate because he seemed healthy." Chris sat in a chair next to Marc. He wanted to appear as calm as possible.

"Do you know what the autopsy showed?" A bead formed above a nervous eye. What did this man know?

"I don't think anything found suggested something other than his heart stopped." Marc stood up. Chris did the same. "Anything else?"

"Yes, the beekeeper. Has she arrived? I'd like her to meet someone."

"I can check her office." He picked up the intercom and punched a button. After a moment, he said, "Bernice, a detective wants to speak with you, if you have time." He listened again and hung up the receiver.

Marc placed hands behind hips. "Well, what did she say?"

"She said she would talk with you later. She's involved in a project right now." Marc nodded. He started for the door. Chris opened it for him.

"Thanks for speaking with me." In the hallway, he turned to leave and stopped. "Which is her office?" He scanned the area.

"Uh, she's not available." He attempted to block a possible move to her room, then thought better about it. He pointed at a room two doors away from his. The building housed only five offices and a storage room. Marc watched Chris's eyes.

"That one over there?" He indicated the room Chris had shown him. He walked to the door and knocked. Opening the door, he viewed the room full of many pictures of bees, awards and plaques, and a case full of books. The one thing he did not see was another person. Stepping back into the hall, Chris was gone.

Knocking on Eden's door, he heard, "What?"

He opened the door and entered. "Ms. Montague, I think we need to talk."

"I have nothing to say to you. Get off my property."

"I will. But first, where is your beekeeper. I just checked her office, and no one is there. And your supervising manager disappeared after he had a conversation with an empty room."

"What are you talking about?" Eden stood and approached Marc.

His phone buzzed. He answered it. "Good to know." He looked at Eden and smiled.

CHAPTER

45

Clicking his phone off, Marc said, "A warrant has been issued to search this property. My questions are simple. Why did your supervising manager run away from me after he pretended to talk with your beekeeper? And. Where is your beekeeper?"

Eden stayed quiet. Nothing made any sense to her. Marc clicked his phone on again and called Jerry. "Stop any cars which try to leave the property. We have the warrant and JJ and Regina will be here within the hour."

"What's happening?"

"I think the manager is going to run. He's hiding something or knows something." He closed the call and turned to Eden.

Eden asked, "What is it you want to know?" Marc walked closer to the manager's office.

"What makes an innocent person run?" He hesitated before finishing. "Nothing." He opened the door and scanned the room; no one was present.

A siren sounded outside drawing Marc's attention. He and Eden left the building to uncover the reason. Jerry stood by a car at the entrance of the property with a gun trained on Chris. He had tried to leave and got as far as the gate.

"Do you have a picture of your beekeeper. I want to show it to my prisoner." Eden returned to her office and retraced her steps to Marc with a photo. Marc accepted it from her. At his car, he opened the door and asked Kaliana to step out.

"Please, Marc, release me from these shackles. I won't run. I don't even know where I am."

"Really, and yet you knew someone on the property. Is that

because you have been here before and met this person to procure your toxic honey and tea?" Marc unlocked the foot restrains and released the waist chains. "Be a good girl, and I'll unlock the handcuffs."

She held out her hands so he could access the locks. He undid one wrist and then locked it on his left arm. "You and me. Isn't that what you wanted?" Her eyes narrowed, and her tongue crossed her lips. She thought better about spitting.

Jerry walked in with Chris whose arms were behind him, constrained by wrist straps. "Well, well, well. We have a suspicious person."

Marc placed the picture in front of Kaliana and asked, "Is this the person you saw earlier today?" She nodded. "Ms. Montague, we need to find your beekeeper and get some answers from her. But first, let's have a go with the manager."

"I've nothing to say." Chris glared at his captors. His mouth clamped shut.

Jerry leaned against the car in which Officer Tanaka sat. He signaled for her to vacate the car and take charge of Chris. The cuffs were unlocked from Marc's wrist and connected to Chris's wrist. Marc said, "Uncle J, call my dad and see if anything is back from the crime lab. Update him and Espinoza about the warrant and call for a search team to come here. After all, this is your jurisdiction."

"You sure are a smart ass." Marc and Jerry laughed.

Turning his attention to Eden, "Where might your beekeeper be?" He stood nearer dragging Kaliana and Chris with him.

Eden shrugged. "I don't know, but we can try the greenhouses. She might be working her boxes." Marc flashed a hand palm up and pointed for her to lead the way. They headed to the nearest one, a smaller building. Jerry followed with phone in hand and waved for Tanaka to follow along.

Inside the greenhouse a sweet aroma of fall blossoms permeated the air. A faint buzzing reminded them of the reason for the visit. No one appeared inside. "Wait here," Marc said. He walked toward the beehives with his hand on the handle of his pistol. Checking the neat rows for anything suspicious, he found nothing in the room. The buzzing increased as he approached the boxes, but the bees ignored him. A hat and jacket lay on the ground nearby, as if discarded hurriedly. He returned to the group.

"Is there another way out of here?" He directed the question at Chris.

"In the back behind the storage area."

"Where does it lead?"

"Outside to the fields." Marc directed Jerry to leave the way they came in. He asked Tanaka to take the prisoners to the car and stay with them. He and Eden returned to the back of the greenhouse to exit out the back and trail a missing Bernice Harapat.

⋈ ⋈ ⋈

Tiberius and Manny sent Ryan and Jeremy to find any evidence from the Crime Lab. Meanwhile, they went upstairs to the Crime Investigative Services Department. A visit to the chief's office seemed appropriate. She needed to explain her interference with Eden Montague. Her secretary informed them she had not returned from a visit with a friend up north. Tiberius asked, "Did she say who the friend was?"

"No, Sergeant. She called to say I was to tell you nothing." Tiberius flailed his arms in frustration.

Manny interceded, "Nothing about what? We just left her in Snohomish County. What is she not wanting you to tell us?"

"Well, detective, if I say, then I will not be following orders." Tiberius turned and left. Manny followed.

"What was that about?" Tiberius said. His phone buzzed. Seeing the caller's name, he answered. "Tell me you have good news."

Jerry said, "We have a warrant, an identification, and a possible suspect." His voice had a negative lilt in it.

"Bro, do you have bad news?"

"I do have some bad news. We don't have the beekeeper. She's gone."

"We'll be out there as soon as possible. Our chief has not returned, yet."

"Any evidence returned from the crime lab?" Jerry asked.

"Ryan and Jeremy are checking into it."

"Okay. Get here as soon as possible."

"Manny, we haven't gotten off to a great start, but there is a common goal. We need to get to the bottom of what our boss is up to."

Vanessa neared the pair as they spoke. "What I'm up to is none of your business." Marc stared at Manny and then at his chief.

"Chief, you showed up at an active investigation site. We have questions." Tiberius cocked his head. Manny folded arms across his chest.

"In my office, now." Chief Christine marched to her room trailed by her officers. As she closed the door, she signaled them to sit. They waited as patient as dogs stalking squirrels. She walked to her desk and leaned against it, keeping her position above them. "Neither of you has anything to worry about. Someone is coming who can explain all to you. Be patient."

A knock on the door alerted them to the arrival of another person. Manny and Tiberius twisted around to see the mystery person. Vanessa pushed away from the desk and walked to the door. Opening it, she said, "Come in, I have a couple of men who are interested in my involvement in their investigation." She stepped aside to let the person enter.

Tiberius stood as he recognized the guest to the conversation. Manny did not know the visitor but realized the importance of the person.

"Sergeant, I believe you have met my guest. Manny, I'd like you to meet a very good friend of mine. Olivia Breckenridge is part of the FBI here and has worked undercover to destroy the cartel in Everett. As Jefferson knows, she was aboard the cruise ship as a nurse and helped Sergeant Jefferson and his son to break up a group which transferred drugs and other materials into the United States.

Tiberius asked an obvious question. "How long have you been playing us?"

Olivia laughed a small and short guttural sound. "Fair question. No. I have not been playing you. Vanessa and I have been in touch with each other about criminal activity in Seattle. The cartel in Everett had little connection until the trail included your son and brother. We decided to keep an eye open and swatch you professionals pull the threads of this riddle until all the answers showed."

Vanessa said, "My sister is deep in the abyss of whatever remains of Pepper's web. That said, I don't think she knows."

"Knows what?" Manny asked.

"She doesn't know what's happening on her property. Someone is supplying her honey to people bent on using it for deadly purposes. We haven't yet identified who is involved."

Tiberius added, "That may change since one of the twins IDed someone, a female, on the property."

Vanessa said, "That would be the beekeeper, Bernice Harapat. She has the expertise to strengthen the abilities of her bumblebees to handle the highly toxic pollen from mutated rhodies and azaleas."

Olivia continued, "And the property supervisor has the training and experience to hybridize plants."

"Which means they are the main people of interest we should be interrogating." Manny whispered his comment as he thought about the morning excursion to Montague's.

Tiberius interrupted. His phone had buzzed again, and he had answered it. "Seems the beekeeper is missing, and the property manager is in custody for attempting to run away from Jerry and Marc."

46

JJ and Ginnie arrived with the needed warrants and served them to Eden Montague. Eden had called her attorney, Paula Cross, who lived in Sultan and arrived at the same time. Marc said, "Can we get to unraveling what is happening here?" Eden handed the document to Paula, who read through it.

"This is limited in scope to greenhouses and the offices." The attorney said. JJ handed a second document which dealt with the house. "Why do you need to tear apart the house?"

"Precautionary," Marc said. "We're not sure where the evidence is. We just know it's here." Paula nodded to Eden. The search commenced with the county search team, which had been called and waited until the warrants were served.

As the teams of deputies and dogs scattered, Marc turned to Chris Colella. "This goes a lot faster with cooperation. Mind filling in the details of how you, the beekeeper, and Ms. Montague worked this honey scheme?"

He remained silent and scowled. Eden protested her involvement. "I have nothing to do with any honey scheme. All our product is safe and approved by the FDA."

Deputy Tanaka oversaw the prisoners, Chris Colella and Kaliana, who sat on the front porch of the house. A search team entered and began the process of dismantling all possible hiding places seeking evidence in the form of papers, tea, honey, files, pictures, and computer documents.

Other teams entered greenhouses and storage buildings. One team commenced to searching the offices. After an hour and a half Marc asked Eden, "If you're not part of the business of providing toxic honey and tea, who would be suspect?"

Her face, set as stone, glared at him. "Don't assume anything is going on here about which I don't know. And nothing illegal is happening. I run a legitimate business." Her attorney placed a hand on her arm and waggled her head. Paula whispered something to Eden. "I'm to remain quiet according to my attorney," she said. "Direct your questions to her."

Two automobiles arrived on the scene, allowed to enter by the sheriff's deputies assigned to block customer traffic to the farm. When they parked Tiberius, Manny, Ryan, and Jeremy exited one vehicle. Olivia and Vanessa left the other. Marc raised his eyebrows at the sight of his FBI cohort from the cruise ship.

"Welcome to the farm," he said, greeting her with glee. "What have you unraveled which brings you to this place?"

Olivia said, "I've been in touch with Chief Christine for a couple of years, working the cases which had ties to Andrew Pepper in Everett. There weren't many until our experience aboard the Salish Sea."

"You didn't tell us about this at your house when we were there and had captured the Asian woman who attempted to kidnap my son." Marc placed his hands on his hips.

"Nothing to tell, until now. By the way, we have secured warrants to inspect Colella's house and Harapat's condo. From the porch, Chris gasped. His shoulders collapsed without notice by Marc. Officer Tanaka watched the concern exhibited, noting Chris's head drop. She left the porch to inform Marc of her observation. He looked up at the unfortunate pair.

Olivia answered her phone as Marc ascended the steps to ask Chris about his emotional setting. She called out. "Marc, I have a surprise for you. Mr. Colella has been holding out on us." She spoke in her phone, nodded, and clicked off the call. She joined Marc on the porch.

"What surprise?" He asked. She directed her next comment to Chris.

"You've been a bad boy." Chris looked at her with weepy eyes and a slight tilt of the head. "She's still alive," Olivia said and turned to Marc. "Our prisoner from the other night is at this man's house. She was found staggering around when my team of special agents arrived and entered the house. It appears Colella fed her honey and tea. EMT peesonnel who accompanied the team administered a stimulant."

"The Asian woman?" He looked at Chris. "I guess you do have reason to be concerned about your future." Eden came up the steps and approached them.

"You son of a bitch. What have you been doing on my property?" She attempted to slap her manager, but Marc restrained her.

"Careful, Ms. Montague. No one wants charges of assault filed." He released his grip as he directed her away from the prisoners. A sergeant from the Snohomish search team approached Jerry and said something to him. "Marc, they found something of interest." Jerry signaled for his deputy to lead the way. Tanaka stayed with the prisoners as Marc and Eden followed the small body of people to a greenhouse.

Inside they were directed to a small hatch-like opening in the floor at the far end of the building. Descending the staircase, Marc and Jerry saw the object of interest. A body lay on a tarp. Marc turned to Eden and asked, "Is this your missing beekeeper?"

Eden wailed and grasped her head. "What happened?"

Marc spoke with a medical technician who explained the cause of death to be strangulation. Evidence indicated she had been killed in the room and placed into the refrigeration unit for storage or an attempt to change the time of death.

"Can you get a read of when she died?" Marc asked. He shook his head but stated that it must have been very recent.

Turning to Eden whose eyes cascaded wetness, he asked. "When did you last see her alive?" She blinked her lids and wiped the tears from her cheeks.

"This morning when she arrived. We were in my living room. I didn't see her after that." She turned and gazed up the stairwell to the greenhouse floor. "Chris went to find her after you all had left. He said something about finishing business." She started up the stairs, skipping steps. Marc chased after her.

She ran across the floor of the greenhouse and punched through the door. Marc ran after her. She bounded up the steps of the house and stopped when Tanaka pulled her weapon and pointed it at her. "You bastard. You didn't need to kill her." Marc arrived in time to hear the conversation. "Why? Why kill her? What have you two been doing here?" She turned to Marc. "I trusted them." She collapsed on the steps and cried. Another call came to Olivia from another FBI team at Bernice Harapat's condo. Records of offshore accounts indicated she accumulated an exorbitant amount of money. A list of customers for honey included the names of the twins. Agents were sent to uncover the whereabouts of each of the named people.

Paula Cross sat with her friend and client. Nothing remained intact on the family estate. A lifetime of building unraveled in a matter of hours. Eden stopped crying and turned as she sat. "You killed him, too. Didn't you?" She directed her remarks at Chris. "You eliminated any competition. He had the goods on you, and you killed him so he couldn't say anything." Chris remained stone-faced.

"Detective, I made a regrettable mistake a couple of years ago. I had an affair with him." She pointed at Chris. "I didn't think much about it and broke it off before Malcolm found out. After my husband died, we started up again. I knew it was wrong and stopped it again. He's tried to convince me to let him be part of my life. I've resisted. My concern is about how my husband died. I think it may have been more than a mere heart attack."

Ryan and Jeremy overheard her statement and approached Tiberius who had returned from the greenhouse. "Marc, these guys have some compelling information about what Ms. Montague just said." Marc came to Ryan and Jeremy.

"What do you have?" Ryan held out a folder with a Washington State Crime Lab logo.

"We got these in Seattle before returning here. They are the results of the tests done on the teabag from the hotel and a return to the death of Malcolm Varian."

Marc read the information and handed it to Olivia who gave it to Vanessa. "Well, this does make for an interesting read. No information regarding the fingerprint on the bag, but a definite change of cause of death for Mr. Varian."

Jeremy also had a folder. "Marc, this was rushed through after being obtained from your Mountie. It is honey purchased here and sent to the lab yesterday." Regina came closer with JJ.

"What did the lab find?" she asked. Marc read the report and handed it to her. She and JJ perused it and closed the folder.

JJ said, "Nothing much to tell except for the trace amounts of grayanotoxin."

Eden lifted her head while she remained sitting on the steps. "We mixed it with other types to enhance flavor. Nothing much. It shouldn't have killed anyone."

Marc looked at her. "We don't believe your commercial grade jars of honey were laced with enough rhodie honey to be dangerous. However, the amount of grayanotoxin found in tissue samples from your husband's body tells a very different story."

CHAPTER

47

Approaching the front of the Kitsap Sheriff's office housing Kerrine, Cassandra Camacho scanned for external cameras. Her hat pulled down to conceal her face; she walked around to the rear door which deputies used for entry to the secured part of the building. She carried a mask and quick acting neuro-agents to cause a near-immediate sleep. She wore protective gloves and clothing. She had but one target for her assault on the facility.

A female vacated a car after arriving as Cassandra neared the door. "May I help you?" Cassandra smiled and answered.

"Yes, please. I was asked to wait here for a friend of mine who works inside. He was supposed to be out a few minutes ago."

The officer responded, "Please return to the reception room, and I'll have him meet you there. This is a restricted area. He made a mistake asking you to meet him here." Cassandra turned as though she was acknowledging the request. The officer asked, "What's your friend's name?"

"Oh, yes. Of course." She faced the woman and sprayed her with the neuro-agent which incapacitated her within a few seconds. Cassandra had not wanted to be exposed to discovery but needed somehow to get through the door. Taking the identity badge from her belt, Cassandra swiped the scanner, unlocking the mechanism which operated the door release. As she opened the door, she placed the mask over her face and walked to an area of the building housing other officers and staff. She pulled the cap of a bottle of the neuro-agent and placed it near an intake vent of the air heating system. Waiting for the gas to disperse throughout the building, she checked nearby rooms and found them empty. Another door was labeled locker room. She opened it and found two men crumpled on the floor.

In another part of the facility, she found staff members collapsed at desks. She opened the reception room office door. A deputy sprawled across the control desk. Pressing the jail door release, she entered, propping the door open. Two inmates were sleeping on the hard metal beds covered with a thin mattress. She found her target.

With the press of another button at the entry to the confinement section of the sheriff's office, the cell doors opened. Reaching down for Kerrine, she injected a counter-acting agent. Removing her mask, she waited for her friend to awaken.

A groan escaped from Kerrine. "Welcome to freedom land," Cassandra said. "We must get out of here before the rest of them wake up and before other officers get back off duty or come in with prisoners."

Kerrine sat up and looked at Cassandra. "That fool has her with him."

"Kaliana? I know. We're getting her next." After destroying the recording of her visit on the monitoring equipment, she assisted Kerrine out of the building. Driving to the rental house in Wendlesburg for a change of clothing from county orange to a more suitable fashion, she explained what happened at the farm of Eden Montague.

"I didn't get too close, but I did follow the younger Jefferson and his Mountie girlfriend after leaving them a cryptic note when we were on the ferry together. I led them to a house in Edmonds and pretended to stop as though I lived there."

"They'll run your plates and the address of the house." Kerrine was fully awake.

"I'm sure they will. And the people in the house will be as surprised as the officers who interrogate them." She made a quick meal to refresh their hungry bodies since the next possible meal was another day away.

"What are we doing next?" Kerrine asked.

"We're off to see our nemesis family and make an offer they can't refuse." Kerrine grinned. Enough stark video nature of a young, vibrant teenage girl could be a strong deterrent to acting rashly. Kerrine had mentioned it to Marc and made a promise. Now she was free to implement the threat.

⤢ ⤢ ⤢

Marc's phone buzzed in his pocket. He retrieved it and noticed the number. "What now?" he mumbled. Answering, he said, "Marc here."

Glenmore Fellington growled his response, "We've had an assault on the Central Kitsap station. No one is hurt, but you're not going to like what happened."

"Glen, I'm not in the mood for games. What happened?"

"Someone broke out your girlfriend." Marc's shriek alerted the rest of the crew. "They used a type of sleep-inducing agent. The only prisoner not here was Kerrine."

"What about the security system? Did you get a look at the assailants?" He began a nervous pace around the grounds of the farm. He listened to the answer from his sheriff and groaned. "Alright, send a car to my family and get them out of harms way. That will be the next place they'll go." He knew it was already too late. He ended the call with Fellington and called Joan.

Jerry approached to ask what occurred. Marc held up a hand as the phone went to message. "Call me as soon as you can, Joan."

"What's happened?" Jerry whispered.

"Kerrine broke out and I'm afraid she may go after Joan and the kids. I've got to get back to Kitsap." He signaled Tanaka to come to him. She left her charges, still manacled together. "We have to get back to Kitsap. There's been an assault on the Central Kitsap office." He pointed at Kaliana, who understood and grinned.

Jerry said, "Leave her with me. That way no one will get to her. If they can't find her, they can't have her." Marc nodded an agreement. The Kitsap contingent left for a ride to Edmonds and the next ferry to Kingston.

Time crawled as they flashed lights to part the traffic impeding their flow. In Monroe Tanaka exited Highway 2 for Highway 522 and a shorter triangulation to Edmonds through Kenmore and Bothell. Marc radioed the State Patrol office in Edmonds to hold the ferry closest to their estimated time of arrival.

Officer Tanaka maneuvered through the heavy traffic in Bothell with siren and lights, attracting the attention of local law enforcement which radioed assistance and learned the need for their hurried pace. Intersections were blocked to halt cross traffic, and traffic lights became less an impediment.

The next ferry was soon to arrive in Edmonds and traffic interfered again as they wound through Kenmore and Lake Forest Park to Highway 104. Drivers pressed to the side of the road as they approached. Crossing under Interstate 5, Marc called back to various police entities and thanked them for their help with cars.

The lanes ahead contained many more vehicles which squeezed to the side of the road so they could pass. Marc called the Patrol to let them know they were near to the landing. Along the waterfront, Marc saw the white bridges of the ferry. Tanaka turned onto the approach to the loading dock stopping behind the line of cars waiting for the emptying of the ferry.

Marc vacated the car and spoke with one of the ferry attendants who directed him to the office ahead. He ran up to the gate and spoke with another person who garnered what he requested.

When the last of the cars was off, bicycles loaded, then motorcycles. Walk-on passengers crossed the gangway above. With the last of the two wheelers on Tanaka was signaled by an attendant to move forward and park at the head of the line. Lights extinguished, she placed the car in park and set the emergency brake.

Marc followed in the unorthodox method of running the auto gangway much like Michael Douglas in the movie 'Disclosure' when he was leaving Bainbridge Island for Seattle.

They remained in the cruiser as the ferry loaded cars and trucks. He radioed the central office in Port Orchard to ascertain what damage had resulted from the escape of Kerrine and the gathering of his family and their safety. Joan and the children were not in the care of any deputies. He called Joan again. Her phone went to message again. He told her what had transpired at the Central Kitsap office and the danger she, Sarah, and James faced.

Puget Sound was not as wide between Edmonds and Kingston as it was nearer Seattle and Bainbridge, but the ride was still thirty minutes of agony. He got out of the car and stood at the rope across the bow. Two ferry workers approached.

"May we be of any assistance?" one of them asked. Marc shook his head but offered a short explanation of the urgency of the police business which enveloped his day. They left him to watch the waves and the approaching town of Kingston.

His cell phone buzzed in his pocket. He saw a familiar number and answered it. "Joan, I need you to listen. You're in danger. One of the twins escaped and may be heading to you. Get to the sheriff's office with the kids. Please hurry."

A calm, Hispanic voice answered him.

CHAPTER

48

Marc listened to the words of warning. Kerrine was clear. She had Joan and would swap for Kaliana. He wrote a note for Officer Tanaka which requested her to call his father in Snohomish and apprise him of the situation.

When she stopped talking, Marc answered her request. "Kerrine, your sister is at the farm where you bought the honey. Any harm befalls my wife or children, and I'll see to it you never have any contact with her. Who broke you out?"

"Marc, it is not wise to threaten me. You know what I can do. One at a time I will destroy your family. You've already destroyed mine. So, I have no regrets seeing your wife suffer a painful, agonizing death." Marc scribbled another note to Tanaka requesting a call to Fellington.

"Don't you think this war has gone on long enough? I'll meet with you, and we can arrange for the transfer of our prisoners. I want to speak with my wife to be sure you have her, and she is unharmed."

Tanaka wrote a note and showed it to Marc. His children were secured and safe from harm.

"I want my sister transported back to Kitsap. If you want to see your dear little wife again, get Kaliana here within the next three hours. You can speak with your wife when I see my sister."

"And where is here?" Kerrine remained silent. "I need to know where I should be for this exchange to happen."

"When my sister is in your custody, call me. Remember, you have three hours." The call ended, but the GPS app on Marc's phone located her phone at the house. Joan had returned home to intruders.

As the ferry docked, Marc paced the deck until the last of the motorcycles departed. He then sat in the car and Tanaka drove off the boat. "Detective, we'll make this better. You can't lose hope." Marc simply stared out the windshield.

As they drove through Kingston toward Bond Road, Marc clicked open his cell phone and punched in the number for his father. "Dad, bring Kaliana back to Kitsap to my house. I need to make the exchange for Joan. Kerrine gave me three hours to comply."

"Marc, you need leverage, so Joan remains safe. I'll bring her and my brother. The rest of us can keep searching the farm for evidence." The call ended with assurances of keeping Kaliana as a prisoner and rolling Kerrine back into custody. The unknown factor was the person helping with the escape and the possible kidnapping of Joan.

Marc's cell buzzed. Tom Knudson's number shone on the screen. "What's up partner?"

"We got a probable location of a rental near your house. A lady rented it a week before you returned to Washington. She gave her name as Cassandra Camacho. Paid cash for a month's rent."

"Camacho? She gave her name as Camacho?"

"Yeah. Why? Mean something to you?" Marc nodded as he answered.

"The cruise director aboard the Salish Sea was named Camacho. I can't believe this person is so cavalier as to use her real name, if she's related."

Tom continued, "I'm sending a unit to the address to check it out from a distance. Plainclothes and no sheriff markings."

Marc nodded again. "Good, let me know what you find. Kerrine may have Joan at my house. Check it as well."

"Will do." They ended the call. Tanaka maneuvered the traffic with blaring siren and flashing lights. Poulsbo was within minutes and then on to Wendlesburg.

Marc formulated a course of action for the liberation of Joan and the incarceration of Kerrine and the other person helping. He had no information about any other people who might be watching or securing the surrounding neighborhood.

Bond Road ended at the light on Highway 305 as they turned to drive up the hill to Highway 3 and south to Wendlesburg. His cell buzzed again with an unknown number.

"Hello," he said as calm as a cougar waiting to pounce.

"Hey, cousin, we got a hit on the license of the car on the ferry with us. It belongs to a Cassandra Camacho who lives in Edmonds near the address of the house she stopped at."

"Thanks, she has to be related to the cruise director. Has Dad left to bring Kaliana here?"

"He left right after you called."

"Good. Our fathers are quite a team." The called ended as siren and lights created a lane of passage. After several agonizing minutes at high rates of speed, the exit for his house came into view. Tanaka drove to the light slowing to allow for cross traffic to clear or stop for her passage. They arrived at Marc's house within five minutes. She parked on the street.

"Stay here," he said. He observed Tom Knudson sitting in an unmarked car across from the house. He approached to garner any information. Tom got out of his automobile.

"Anything happening at my house?"

"Nothing I've seen. Want me to go with you?"

"Yes, take the back. I'll enter the front. If anyone leaves, shoot them."

"Bit harsh, isn't it?" Tom grinned.

"Yeah, a bit harsh." Marc snarled.

Drawing weapons, the pair took their positions. Marc signaled for officer Tanaka to join him at the front door. She complied. He tried to door, but it was locked. He removed his house keys from his pocket and slipped the correct one in the lock. Leaving it dangling, he opened the door enough to ascertain any booby traps. Finding nothing, he pushed the door open and entered.

Except for a refrigerator motor and heat flow, the silence told a tale of abandonment. Inside the living room a phone buzzed on the table. It belonged to Joan. With a stylus he punched the app to answer.

"Glad you made it home, Marc." Kerrine's voice haunted his brain.

"You placed another camera in my house." He searched until he saw two on a window sill, one pointed to the street. The other into the room.

"I realized from the very beginning of our escapades you were smart. Be a good boy and have your friends leave. We don't need them in this act of our play. They can come later to pick up your corpse."

"And Joan? Is she a corpse or living?" He holstered his weapon and turned his back to the camera. Mouthing his words, he asked Tanaka to get Tom. "Well, is she still with us as a live body?"

"What did you tell your deputy?" He turned to the camera and glared at it. "Is my sister on her way?"

"Kaliana will be here within three hours. Let me speak with Joan, or I'm coming to get you." A rustling sound peaked attention to activity on the other end of the call. He took the opportunity to collect the cameras. Finding a battery compartment, he disabled them.

"Marc, I'm alright for now. But don't," Her comment was unfinished.

"Joan had to go. I'll call you in another hour. Wait at home. I will know if you leave." More cameras, he thought.

Tom Knudson and Officer Tanaka entered from the kitchen. "Tom, I don't know if they have audio, but these cameras were in plain sight for her to know when I returned here. She says she'll know if I leave, so there may be more."

Tom acknowledged the information with a nod. "Want me to get a team here to scour again?"

"No, I'm guessing she planted those only to see me return so she could call Joan's cell." He pressed a couple of keys which revealed where her phone had traveled. The house was the last destination. The phone number of the last call gave him a clue, but time was short. He needed to get a trace and had no ability for securing what he wanted.

Tanaka said, "I can take your wife's number to the station and have them ping the last call cell towers to at least get an area to search."

Marc answered her. "Thanks, but I think I know where they are. Do you have the address of the rental?" Tom nodded. "Do we have anyone on site?" He nodded again. "Then let's join them and decide how best to assault the place and take prisoners. No casualties, please." Joan had to be the target of rescue while the attack commenced.

As they left the house with Joan's cell phone and a clear idea of what had to happen, Marc called his father to get an ETA. "We're waiting for a ferry to arrive," Tiberius said.

"Good. We're going after Joan." Tiberius grunted his apprehension with the idea. "It's okay, Dad, we'll get her before any harm comes to her." He wanted his brain to believe his words. But he had doubts. Still, he couldn't just sit and let the ladies dictate terms.

They traveled on foot since the other house was only three blocks away. A sheriff cruiser sat around a corner keeping an alley escape covered. Another unmarked car sat across the street from the target. Two deputies were in plains clothes, dressed as though they were missionaries with materials to hand out. They waited to enact the play until Marc arrived.

Out of sight line of the house, he signaled them to start the ruse. Marc maneuvered his small team from house to house until he could see any activity at the front door. Tom Knudson and Officer Tanaka were in the alley behind the place. His fellow officers walked up the steps and knocked on the door.

CHAPTER

49

Marc watched the door open. An unfamiliar face appeared. He snapped a picture with the camera which had a long-range telephoto lens. His mind seemed to play tricks as he envisioned another person with similar features. Who was this person who conjured deep memories?

He waited as the two undercover officers left their pamphlets and departed for another house. The ruse had to continue to other properties in the event someone monitored the unexpected activity. After several homes received materials or declined interaction, they gathered at the alley to display anything which may have been relevant to the actions.

The deputies laid out the recordings they gathered. Video confirmed the pictures Marc snapped. Audio presented another familiar aspect which conjured more memories for him. "She sounds just like a woman on the cruise. And she looks like the same person I interacted with while sailing to Alaska."

Tom asked the obvious question, "Who?"

Marc answered, "Our cruise director." He studied the image from his camera. "Jarina Camacho died of a gunshot wound inflicted by our Mountie when she was going to shoot me." He stared at Tom for a second. "We should find out if she has any family members."

Tom directed one of the deputies to return to the station house and start the search process for any other Camacho family members. The investigation had little chance of success in a short period of time, since Camacho could have been a family name, married moniker, or adopted name for secretive reasons. Only time would tell, and they had none.

Tom asked, "What do you want to do? There is no visual confirmation of Joan or Kerrine being in the house. The person answering the door was defensive, but that could be attributed to a lack of interest in the propaganda."

"I need to get inside, but that may not happen unless I have Kaliana with me. And that is not happening. If I show up with her and no backup, I'm as good as dead."

"What if we stage a raid?" Tanaka offered. "Not one which would get your wife killed, but a quick invasion which throws their response time out the window and gives us an opportunity for rescue and containment."

"It's worth thinking about. The problem is not knowing how many are in the house."

Tom said, "We have the heat sensor at the main office in Port Orchard."

"Take too long to get it here. I'm going to chance a move they won't kill me right away if I show up at the house." Marc paced as he spoke.

"What if they have Joan at another location. If they expect we are searching for them, they might have anticipated we would find this location." Tom continued, "The trap may be set for you to get in the house and become a prisoner."

"I know you're right. I can't sit and wait for something to happen." Joan's phone buzzed again. The same number display as unknown caller. He answered.

"What do you want now? I want to speak with Joan," he said.

"Oh, Marc, don't get so testy. She is fine. You have a very strong-willed wife. It will be a shame for her to die because you won't follow directions. I said you were to stay at your house. And now you have all those people wandering around the rental house we procured so we could watch you squirm." He gritted teeth as he realized Tom was right and they were anticipating his every move.

"Alright, you know what I'm doing. Your sister is awaiting a ferry in Edmonds. She will be here within two hours. Now let me speak with Joan."

"I guess it can't hurt." A silent period ripped into his heart. A rustling awakened his brain to listening.

"Marc." Joan's voice quivered with a sound of stress. "I'm fine.

No one has hurt me, and the kids are safe. She has promised to let me go when her sister is here." Silence returned.

Kerrine resumed her speaking. "Marc, that will be the last time for you and wifey-pooh to speak. I will present her with a nice cup of tea laced with a delicious honey sweetener, if I do not have you and my sister within the next hour. You hear me?" A quiet rage rattled through the phone.

Marc set his jaw tight and grimaced with eyes shut and lips parted, exposing teeth. "I'm guessing you're not at the house with the other lady." He paused a mere second before asking a futile question. "Who is the lady in the house. She reminds me of our cruise director, Jarina Camacho."

"Marc, so many questions. Time is ticking. Get those people away from the house and allow my friend to leave without being followed." Kerrine disconnected the call. Frustration racked his temperament.

"Did you get the tracker on her car," he asked one of the deputies who had approached the house as a missionary. He nodded. One positive note for a pageant filled with misdirected action. "Let her go after we enter the house and have a short dialog with her." The remaining deputies affirmed his words. Taking positions in front and back, they waited as he approached the front door and knocked.

><< ><< ><<

Joan complained about the restraints around her ankles. She had free hands but no ability for walking. The plastic ties cut her skin and droplets of blood pooled near her toes. Her feet were bare. Most clothing was removed. She sat on a chair in bra and panties. The strap around her waist kept her tightly attached to the backrest of her seat.

"Do you plan to let me go when you have your sister? Or is this another attempt to wipe out the one person who is a thorn in your side? He will not let you get away with this. You know it, and I know it. He will hunt you to the ends of the earth before he lets you best him."

Kerrine's hand flashed across her cheek with a smack. The contact rocked her head as pain wired her brain. "Shut up, bitch. He must pay for what he has done." Kerrine raised her hand again. Joan winced in anticipation.

"He's not giving you your sister. You'll have to kill me and then she dies, too. Next, he'll hunt you like the vermin you are, and he'll kill you. Probably nice and slow." The hand traversed the space to her other cheek in the form of a fist. Joan blanked for a moment as sparkles flashed in her eyes. Her jaw moved to one side and she suspected a dislocation. Noting the severity of response to her comment, she played 'possum.

Kerrine clicked the hammer of the small caliber pistol and planted the barrel on Joan's temple. "I should pull the trigger and end this misery. He can't get you without me messing up your face, and I still get to pop him." Joan remained in a state of false unconsciousness, listening and waiting for a chance to strike like a cobra. No one else was with them at the motel on Kitsap Way. How could she signal Marc a location? She had to think, and no chance presented a clear way for her.

Cassandra Camacho opened the front door with a glower as she looked Marc eye to eye. "My sister needn't have died except for your interference." Marc shoved his way into the house. Tom and Officer Tanaka followed him with weapons drawn.

Marc said, "Your sister was running an illegal operation aboard the cruise ship, and she was about to shoot me. Self-defense is what the law calls it."

"Why? Why shoot her?"

"I didn't, but the person responsible for the wounding and subsequent demise of your sister acted properly and legally." Marc clasped Cassandra's arm and forced her to a nearby seat. "Tell me where my wife is, and I won't have to hurt anyone else."

Cassandra rubbed her arm where Marc squeezed it. She said nothing.

"Silence, eh. Okay, we'll do this the hard way." Joan's phone buzzed again. The same unfamiliar number emblazoned the screen. He answered.

"Marc, I asked a simple request from you, and you have

disobeyed. My friend is to leave without any interruption." A loud thwack echoed through the ear piece. "I guess I should provide more evidence of what is happening to her pretty face." Joan's phone buzzed as a picture replaced the phone app. Seeing his wife bleeding, with swollen eyes and mouth, raised his ire to a fever pitch.

He clicked off the call and pulled his service weapon. Pointing at Cassandra he aimed at her hip. "Tell me where they are, or I put one in you."

"You won't shoot me in front of witnesses." Her breathing pace increased as sweat beaded on her forehead.

"You have ten seconds to decide if you want to be a cripple for the rest of your life." The phone buzzed again. He holstered his pistol and answered the call. "Marc, let her leave. And shooting her will cause your wife to be disfigured." He closed the app. Another camera. He waited a moment and then lifted Camacho from the chair. With every movement monitored, he decided another course of action was needed. He explained it to Tom as they left the house with Cassandra Camacho in custody.

Placing her in the driver's side of her car, he entered the backseat. "Drive."

CHAPTER

50

A medical examiner approached the group. She had studied the body of the late Bernice Harapat. All eyes focused on her.

Jerry asked the one question which intrigued them. "How'd she die?"

The M.E. answered, "She was strangled. Looks like somebody with strong hands. He left his mark around her throat."

"Do you have enough to make a definite identification of the hands and fingers?" All ears concentrated to hear her answer.

"She put up a struggle. We have DNA from under her nails. Should be able to give a defined answer with that evidence. Anyone have scratches on them?"

Eden looked at Chris. Nothing showed. She started to move to him, but JJ stopped her. "Let me do what you want to do." As he moved toward him, Chris glared.

"I didn't do anything." JJ checked his neck, arms, and face. Nothing was scratched.

"Open your shirt." Paula Cross approached.

"Before you have him do that, has he been advised of his rights?" JJ turned to his father. A nod relieved a growing tension. Paula backed away.

Chris unbuttoned his shirt which had a tear along the side under his left arm. He opened it and exposed his chest. No scratching was discerned. Lifting the shirt to one side, three small welts shown crimson. One had broken the skin. A small amount of blood had coagulated.

"Care to explain how you injured yourself?" Marc asked.

"You don't have to answer him." Paula Cross stated firmly.

"She's right. And a warrant might be advisable for DNA analysis of you. I would suggest, though, that answering the question might be considered as cooperating with a police investigation. Not answering might mean you have something to hide."

Chris hissed. "I have nothing to say."

A Snohomish deputy assigned to search the grounds came near with an evidence bag which contained what appeared to be a bone and tissue. He said, "We found this buried in a tree root ball. I don't think it's human. But it has been cut from an animal of some sort. We also found three other root balls with animal remains."

Jerry looked at Eden and then at the examiner. Ryan came up to look at the bag. "I'd have to examine it more closely, but it looks like a cat femur." Jerry faced Eden.

"Is it a common practice to place animal remains in tree root balls. Is this a type of fertilizer I've not encountered?" Eden shook her head.

"We don't put animals in our tree balls. Each ball should contain fertile soil and water retention pellets to feed the root system."

JJ asked, "Dad, do you think it possible for a body to be dismantled and sent away a piece at a time in a root ball. That way no one would be able to trace the disappearance of a person." They turned and looked at Chris. JJ continued, "I can imagine someone cutting a body into small pieces and sending the body all over the northwest. No one would ever be the wiser."

Olivia approached and said, "I've asked for our lady friend to be brought here to confront her lover about his mistreatment of her. She wants to press charges."

"Will she get a deal?" Jerry asked. "She did kidnap my nephew for ransom."

"We can hold her on that charge after we get information from her about him." She glanced at Colella. "No need to bother her about it now."

Jerry came up to Chris and asked, "Were you practicing how to rid yourself of a body? Who was your intended victim? Eden? Or Bernice and she, being now dead, would have to disappear without a trace." Colella sneered. "When we find evidence on the beekeeper which links her death to you, nothing is going to keep you out of jail for the rest of your life." Paula Cross held out a hand.

"That's enough. You might want to concentrate on that warrant for Colella's DNA." Eden walked up with a glass in her hand. She held it out for Jerry to take.

"What's this?" he asked.

Eden answered, "Chris was drinking from this glass earlier today. Could it help?"

Paula said, "It's not admissible. His things are not evidenced without a warrant."

Eden looked at her. "The glass is mine. If he killed Bernice, I want him to pay for what he did." Jerry reached out to a deputy for an evidence bag.

After sealing it and filling in the information, he said, "Well, Mr. Colella, last chance at redeeming something of value for your life."

Eden asked Chris, "Did you kill Malcolm? How about my father? They died from the same thing. Heart failure." Chris flicked his eyebrows but said nothing.

A breeze filtered floral aromas toward the mass of people in Eden's yard. Reminded of the ease with which a natural ingredient such as honey could be used as a murder weapon, Jerry spoke with Olivia. "Everything is in place. All we need is enough evidence for a conviction. Will Mai Ling provide us with what we need here?" Olivia nodded aa Jerry continued, "With Kaliana in custody, an identification of Bernice as the sales agent for the honey, and the DNA on her to prove Colella's involvement in her death, this about wraps up the Andrew Pepper investigation started over two years ago. Maybe now you and Randolph can finish your plans for a future together."

"We'll see. I'm not sure everything is complete. I'll feel better when the Crime Lab verifies what we believe to be the truth."

"Let's hope everything in Kitsap works out for the better." Jerry turned to another deputy and instructed him to keep watch on Chris Colella.

Vanessa Christine said, "One problem remains. No evidence of any honey or tea was found. It could be because all of the materials are expended or removed."

Olivia answered her. "As soon as Mai Ling arrives, we can ascertain from her any process she knows about operations."

"I hope Tiberius and his prisoner arrive in time to keep Joan from harm." Jerry looked as if he had exhausted the last of his energies. He buzzed his brother to get an update on the trip to Kitsap. The ferry had just left for Kingston.

"Miss Montague, you have overseen a large operation for many years. How is it you are unaware of the murder for hire trade of toxic materials by employees? Why didn't you suspect something was wrong?" Jerry's questions aroused tears in her eyes. "The only reason I can fathom for this lack of oversight is that you are the ringleader."

Vanessa growled. "She had nothing to do with any illegal operations. In a matter of a few years, she endured the death of her father and her husband. Now we may have to investigate those deaths as homicides. She would not be a willing accomplice in killing our father nor her husband." Chief Christine pointed at Colella. "He, on the other hand, has ample reason for wanting them out of the way."

Olivia chimed in on the verbal assault. "Killing your cohort leaves little doubt about your ability for mayhem." Chris Colella just stared at the ground.

An officer approached Jerry with a box. "We found this in the underground bunker, buried beneath one of the shelves." The metal box was large enough to hold several items. Gloving his hands, Jerry opened the box and pulled out folders with dates and names written on the tabs. He perused some of the documents and then looked directly at Chris. Walking closer to him, stopped and smiled.

"A bit callous on your part to leave all of your records in such an easy place to find."

"They're not mine." He looked at Jerry. "Bernice kept the records of all of the honey we produced. I venture to think those are the records." Jerry turned to Eden.

"You signed most of these documents."

"I've signed thousands of bills of sale, production records, invoices, payments, salary and wage checks."

Jerry faced Colella. "Did your co-conspirator handle all of the paperwork? Did she leave you with the mess to clean up and that is why you killed her?"

Before he answered, Vanessa's cell phone sang a lovely song. All eyes focused on her. "Thanks," was the only word she uttered. The other officers waited impatiently for a clarification.

"Well," Jerry asked, "what did you find out?" A smile crossed her face as she went to Colella. His eyes widened.

"I do believe a fine piece of evidence just arrived at your beekeeper's house." Vanessa faced Olivia and Jerry. She then smiled at her sister, Eden. "The beekeeper had an envelope mailed to her from a remote location not far from here. The postal stamp is Covington." She stood by Eden.

"What was in the envelope?" Eden asked.

Facing Chris again, she spoke words to which his face scrunched with a recognition of the meaning for him. He had little recourse left for any possible escape from justice through legal means. Bernice had outsmarted him after all.

CHAPTER

51

As Cassandra drove to the motel and an uncertain fate, Marc pondered the need for so much drama in his life for the last several months. All he wanted for himself and his family was quiet. The war had to end. The octopus had to die.

"Tell me, Miss Camacho. What prompted you to involve yourself in the lives of these vicious sisters? Do you enjoy the thrill of killing innocent people?" She didn't respond. "I'm guessing your sister's activities excited you. She was enjoying a rich life aboard a cruise ship while you remained at home living a dull life."

"We're here." Her voice quavered.

"Don't move a muscle until I say so." Marc scanned the scene of the Wayside Motel, a seedy place of known prostitution and drug dealings. "Which room are they in?" Cassandra began to point. "Just tell me. Don't indicate with your hands."

She placed her hands in her lap. "Room 219." Marc found the number on a second-floor door. Before leaving the car, he called his father to gain a time of arrival of Kaliana. With the information he needed he called Tom and Officer Tanaka who had followed them. The tracking device worked its wonders for the other officers who had instructions to stay out of sight but within assault range.

"Tom, check with the manager of the motel and find out who rented 219 and which other rooms are occupied and by whom. I want to know if anyone has more than one in their name. Tanaka, stay in the car until we need you for backup." Clicking off the call, he directed his conversation to his prisoner. "Shall we investigate where my wife is?" They vacated the car and climbed the staircase to the second-floor outdoor walkway. He directed Cassandra to lead the way to Room 219.

At the door, he pulled her away from knocking, instructing her to say only she was outside wanting in. Marc removed his weapon and rapped on the framework. No sound responded. Trying the door, he found it locked. Placing his ear to the door, he heard nothing. Directing Cassandra to call out, he waited for a response. Nothing. They walked away from the room and descended the stairs to the parking area.

The reception room was at the entrance to the horseshoe shaped buildings of the motel. They walked the short distance to discover what Tom had uncovered. As he approached the office, he scanned other rooms for anyone peering out of a closed curtain. He saw nothing.

In the reception area, Tom turned as they entered. "The room you asked about is occupied by Joan Jefferson. Paid cash for a week."

Marc frowned, "I don't think she did it willingly." He pulled out pictures of Joan and Kerrine and asked which one paid. The girl behind the desk did not recognize either face. "Who else works this desk?"

"Bobby and Joanie are the other desk managers. They have evening and overnight shifts." She said.

Looking at the ceiling, Marc noticed a camera. "The surveillance system work?" She shook her head. Get me the addresses of your staff. They need to help find a missing person." She departed to another room and returned with an older gentleman and a binder.

"I understand you want to find someone," he said. "Shelly said you're with the police." Marc and Tom showed credentials. Cassandra sat quietly in a chair away from the door as she was told to do. Marc showed him the pictures and asked if he had seen either of the women within the last day. He studied them for a moment and pointed at the picture of Kerrine.

"She rented two rooms as I remember."

"And used the name, Joan Jefferson. Did you ask for identification to verify her name?"

"She paid cash. I didn't ask."

"What other room did she pay for?"

He used the computer and looked up the information. "Room 219 and 217."

Marc scowled. "Are they adjoining rooms?" He nodded. "We need entry to both rooms."

"Do you have a warrant?" the manager asked.

Marc wanted to reach across the counter and pull the man over and beat him. "We are investigating a kidnapping of a woman and possible assault. If you want to have this place crawling with cops who will roust all the illegal business happening here, I can have that happen in a matter of minutes. My officers are awaiting the signal. Now get me entry to those rooms." The man swiped two key cards on the machine.

"Tom, get Tanaka so she can watch Camacho. I'm going to get my wife."

Marc raced up the staircase and stopped at 219. He used the key card to unlock the door. Crouching down, he pushed it open, pointing his weapon inside. No one occupied the visible space in front of him. He entered. After inspecting the closet and bathroom, he checked the connecting door to room 217. It opened with a slight push. The room was empty, as well. On the bed lay a phone and a note. No one had used the room.

Without picking up the note he read the message. "Use this phone to call me."

⋈ ⋈ ⋈

Kerrine glanced at her phone. Joan watched her. She was as antsy as a caged animal. "He's coming for you," she said to her captor. "He's figured out where you are, and he'll be here before you get your sister."

"Shut up, bitch."

The straps around her waist and chest were not as tight as before and having dressed so they could move to this other room, Joan had played with them. Joan sat tied to another chair, her feet free to move. Her hands were behind her back. "Kaliana is not coming." The pain in her jaw throbbed as she tried to speak. She moved her mouth as little as possible. A ring alerted them both to a call. Kerrine clicked open the phone.

"So glad you found the phone, Marc. Sorry, we weren't there to greet you. Has my sister arrived?"

Kerrine imagined Marc's face as a frustrated frown at being duped. "Very clever of you to not confide with Cassandra what your real intentions were. Kaliana has arrived on this side of the pond and will be here shortly. Of course, I have no idea where to deliver her."

"Use the phone and let me know when she arrives." The call ended.

Joan wriggled in the chair, "He won't let you have her. Not until he has me. Alive." Kerrine glared at her. She moved about the room, pacing in random patterns.

"You'll be alive, but I can't guarantee in what condition you'll be." Joan winced with her words. "I never imagined this getting so far out of control. He should have died on the ship. Now he must die for me to save my reputation."

The ties holding Joan's wrists together behind her cut into the skin. Pain increased as the bindings caused the flesh to swell. Joan needed to distract Kerrine from her obsession with killing Marc. "You need to focus on the good you and your sister have in life. Between the two of you, a family bond exists as no other person can experience without a twin of their own. Why lose that because of a failure to kill Marc? Why be separated for the rest of your lives because of convictions for the crimes you've supposedly committed?"

"Supposedly? You have no idea what we've done. And no one else did either until your husband interfered in Andrew Pepper's operation and destroyed all which meant the most to us. He must pay for the very reason that family bonds are not always blood-related. Some family bonds exist because of the relationships which come together and are strengthened through fire and tribulation. Marc has to lose his family bonds because he destroyed mine."

Her phone buzzed on the table where she had placed it. The number displayed was the burner she left in room 217. "This better be good news, or I'll just let your pretty wife become an ugly hag."

Marc said, "Kaliana arrived a couple of minutes ago. Do you want her in one piece? Or shall I begin dismantling her finger by precious finger? Let me speak with Joan or the next sound you hear will be the first removal."

Kerrine placed the phone next to Joan who said, "Marc, I'm alright. Let her have her sister so they can leave. She doesn't want to finish her deed." Kerrine pulled the phone away.

"Now you have it. I get my sister, and you get your wife. We leave town, and you'll never see us again. Deal?"

Marc paused before answering, "Deal." Kerrine clicked off the phone before anyone spoke another word.

"He is such a liar." Kerrine gritted her teeth as she spoke.

Joan furrowed her eyebrows. "He agreed, and you don't believe him?"

"Why should I? He's sworn an oath to uphold the laws of the land, and we've broken quite a few. He will deliver Kaliana to me. Then I will let him know where to find you. Any other arrangement and I'll harm your children in ways that will cause loss of respect and honor. We have videos of your dear daughter doing things which she wouldn't want her friends to see." Joan paled at the mention of the probable recording from the time in the house before the discovery of the hidden cameras.

"Why didn't you ask to speak with your sister? I thought you had a bond like no other. Is your tightness failing?" Kerrine grinned.

"Good point. Where are my manners? He wanted to speak with you. I should require him to allow me to speak with Kaliana." She called the cell and waited for Marc to answer. Nothing. Was he playing a game of cat and mouse? She clicked off the call and turned to Joan. Raising the pistol and pointing it at her, she said, "Time's up."

CHAPTER

52

Tiberius and Kaliana arrived at the Wayside Motel as Marc spoke with Kerrine. He thought it odd she did not want to speak with her sister but dismissed it as a minor incident. He did not hear the buzz of the phone which lay on the bed in the motel room. Tiberius and Kaliana stood with him.

"She didn't explain where to find Joan, and I'm tired of this game of hide and seek," Marc said to his father. Turning to Kaliana, he continued, "If you have any information about where she is, I want it now."

"I don't know where she is," Kaliana said.

Tiberius said, "Marc, we have the needed evidence for closing several cases. The Montague Farm is the source of the honey and tea. Eden Montague probably was not aware of what was happening on her property, but her sister will have some explaining to do about her involvement with feeding information to her."

"I need to find Joan," Marc said. "Right now, Kaliana is the leverage I have to pry open the last of the cartel and kill the octopus." He removed his weapon from its holster and pointed it at her. "Do you suppose your sister wants holes in you? Or will you tell me what I want to know." Tiberius opened his mouth to speak, but remained quiet as Kalaina gasped and ranted incoherent words.

"She's at the house. No, you know about it. She must be around here, but you've searched the place. I don't want holes in me. She wants you, not Joan. I can't imagine the state of mind you're going through. I don't want to die."

"Shut up," Marc yelled. He holstered the weapon. "She has it right about one thing. Kerrine wants me."

"Has the motel been thoroughly searched?" Tiberius asked. Marc shook his head. "Who was the other lady in custody in the office?"

"She's the sister of the cruise director on the Salish Sea. She might know more than she's telling." Marc picked up the burner on the bed and noticed the unanswered call. "Shit."

"What?" Tiberius asked.

"I missed a call from Kerrine." He punched the redial and waited. After a couple of rings, his adversary answered. "Sorry I missed your call. What did you want to tell me about your location?"

Kerrine's voice growled at him. "Times up. Let me speak with Kaliana or I'm putting a bullet in your lovely wife's face." He put the phone next to Kaliana.

"Kerrine, I'm okay. Tell him where you are." He pulled the phone away.

"Now that we have established I have your sister, let's exchange our guests and get on with our lives free from each other."

"I agree. Get Camacho and tell her something for me. Then let Kaliana and Cassie go. Once I have my sister with me. I'll call and let you know where to find what's left of your wife."

"What do I tell Camacho?" He listened. Then ended the call. "Let's go to the office."

"You shoot me, and he will hunt you to the ends of the earth, and your sister will die before he does." Joan examined her adversary for any hint of her following through with the threat. The gun lowered.

"I know. All I want is to escape from here with my sister."

"Call him and set up the swap. Leave me here with a phone to call him when you get her. I promise to be a good girl and stay until then."

Kerrine wandered the room lost in a morass of her creation. Another death meant nothing to her, except for the consequences of executing this one.

"Do you want to live or die?"

"I want you to shut up so I can think."

Joan grinned as Kerrine peeked out the window at the walkway across from rooms 217 and 219. She looked up at the doorway to see Marc, Kaliana, and Tiberius exit and come down the stairs and head to the office. So close to success. So far from victory. The room had a small patio accessed by a sliding glass door. She could leave anytime and fade into the mists of time. Life without Kaliana was possible, but she would regret not helping her to escape. Camacho was expendable. She picked up the phone.

Marc answered on the first ring. "Have you let my sister leave? On her own. Without anyone tailing her?" He responded with questions of his own.

"Where is Joan? Is she unharmed? May I speak with her."

Kerrine paced as she spoke. "Let her leave, and I will tell you where to find your wife."

Marc said. "We're not making any progress. I want assurances she is alive and well."

Tiberius spoke with Tom Knudson. "We need to get people here to search the remaining rooms. She may still be here."

Tom nodded but said, "Marc wanted to keep the others in a perimeter noose, but I agree with you." Marc ended his call.

"She won't budge."

Tiberius asked, "What if she is still here in another room?" Marc smiled.

"I love you, Dad." He turned to the manager. "Which rooms are occupied?"

The manager's head beaded as he looked up the occupants.

"Only six others." He printed a list and handed it to Marc.

"Tom, get some help in here and remove these people to safety. If Kerrine is here, she won't go quietly." He left to gather a force. "Are any of these people working?"

"What do mean? Working?"

"I do believe you understand my words. Are any of these people known to you to be in the trade?" He looked at the list and rocked his head side to side. To his father, he said, "We have civilians. Once they're out, we search all the rooms. I'll call Kerrine and keep her occupied."

At his request, the manager radioed the staff to gather in the office. He had called the other desk personnel and reached the other girl, Joanie. Bobby had not answered his call. Marc radioed a deputy to pick up both people and bring them to the motel.

When all the workforce had gathered, Marc asked them if they recognized either of the women he presented. One maid affirmed that she had seen Kerrine.

Tom returned with five deputies. Marc directed the manager to give them master key cards and then ordered them to remove the occupants, forcibly if necessary. When that operation was completed, they were to open every door and inspect the rooms. Caution was the order of the day.

Tiberius stayed in the office with Cassandra Camacho and relieved Tanaka to aid in the room search. Marc directed Kaliana to accompany him as he returned to rooms 217 and 219. He wanted to search for any other telltale signs someone had been there. Other than the phone and note on the bed.

From the walkway they watched the officers knock on doors and escort people away from the rooms. They then entered room 217. "Your sister is very clever, as I know you are. But she isn't getting away from me. I have you, and you are an ace in the hole. If she wants you, she must come get you, and I will take her down. If any harm has come to my wife, I will see to it you are held as complicit. This is the end of your reign of terror."

"She won't surrender. I think she would rather die than be confined in prison. I prefer freedom but want to live. I admire what you have. A good marriage, children, friends, and freedom to do what you want." Tears accumulated and dropped. "I'm sorry." She spoke while he investigated the room. He found nothing more than the note. The other room was just as empty of clues. These women were thorough in keeping evidence at a minimum.

Kerrine peeked out the curtain and saw the cadre of officers escorting others from their rooms. It was only a matter of time before this hiding place became compromised. She had to finish her task and escape. Marc had to pay for his endurance and tenacity chasing after her. Her choices were limited. She made a fateful decision and called the number one last time. Marc answered.

"Are you releasing my sister?" She heard him say "yes" and did not believe him. His leverage would melt away with letting Kaliana go. He asked for Joan's location. "You will know soon enough." She clicked off.

To Joan she said, "I guess we're finished here. I'm sorry you must be the one to pay for his malfeasance, but he is not returning my sister. It is just as you said. He will not give up his leverage." Joan inhaled. Dreading the next action of her captor, she pleaded once more for sanity to rule.

Kerrine raised the revolver and aimed it at Joan. The end was inevitable.

CHAPTER

53

Marc watched the progression of officers opening and checking rooms. SWAT led the way. Each clearance fostered an all clear until one room on the single floor side of the motel.

"Marc," said the lead SWAT investigator through his radio, "you need to get over here. Now." The urgency in his voice shook Marc's thoughts. Had he found Kerrine and Joan? No gunshots had alerted anyone. The next call was for a medical team and hospital transportation.

Marc hurried from the office leaving Kaliana with Tanaka and Knudson. At the room medical preceded his entry. They were working on a body slumped in a chair. He did not discern who the person was.

The lead SWAT officer said, "She's alive, but someone smacked her in the head pretty hard." As Marc looked again, he recognized Joan's face and hair matted with blood. Kerrine was not present.

"Where's Kerrine?" he asked.

"As far as we can ascertain, she left by the sliding glass door." Marc saw the opening in the curtains. He then turned to observe the work done on his wife. She sat unconscious and limp as medical techs checked her vitals and affixed an IV drip in her arm. Although her arms hung by her side, she remained strapped to the chair.

"Find her." He directed the comment to the SWAT commander. His eyes narrowed as he hissed, "Find her and bring her to me at the hospital. I'm going with my wife when they transport."

"I'll get a canine search team." The commander and two others left the room to trail the missing twin. Marc paced the room until the medical techs cut the straps holding Joan to the chair and

In the Garden of Eden   259

moved her to a gurney. After strapping her to it, they removed her to a waiting ambulance. Returning to the motel office, he directed Officer Tanaka and Tom to return Kaliana to the holding cell in Wendlesburg. He then followed the EMT truck to the hospital.

At the emergency room, he waited for attendants to diagnose Joan's condition. Pulling out his cell phone, he called her parents' house to apprise them of the situation. They agreed to make the journey to the hospital with Sarah and James.

Marc called his tracking team about progress finding Kerrine. She had used a pepper spray to disorient the dogs and vanished like a mist on Sinclair Inlet. The team had called off any further work. All ports of departure were contacted to be on the lookout. Officers were at the rental house, the Jefferson family home, and ferry terminal watching for her to show.

Marc retraced his attention to Joan and her hopeful recovery. Violence for the sake of violence irked him. But his mind conjured ways to inflict pain so egregious Kerrine would know the pain she inflicted on him. His law and order attitude regarding her died with the injury sustained by Joan.

Justice would be served without the need for courts or attorneys or procedure. A medical technician approached as he thought of ways to torture this current nemesis. He stared at her anticipating terrible news and awaiting a positive one.

"Mr. Jefferson, we are moving your wife to surgery to relieve some pressure building on the brain. She will be on the fifth floor for a while. You can wait here or in the lobby area." She handed him a paging unit. He stared at the machine like it was a pariah stealing his future. Life without Joan had little or no meaning for him. Their differences of opinion about his work chinked their armor but did not cause any real emotional destruction of their love for each other. She was his reason for ridding the world of dangerous and evil people. Safety for his family was paramount, but one person and his nefarious organization had entered his world and upset the equilibrium of life.

He put the pager in his pocket and left the building. Although the signal did not have a long range, he didn't care for the moment. He had to find the last of the cartel and the only lead sat in a Wendlesburg jail. Joan's parents could see to the needs of their daughter and care for his children. He set a goal to wrench information from the one twin in custody.

⤨ ⤨ ⤨

Jerry sat in Eden's house interviewing Mai Ling about her relationship with Chris Colella. He thought it remarkable she spoke with glowing words about her feelings for the man who attempted to kill her. Chris remained within earshot of her answers to the questions, saying nothing and remaining stoic.

Jerry asked, "What places are familiar haunts for the twins? You know, places you have frequented with them." She didn't answer. "Who are their other friends?" No answer. "Have you ever participated in one of their sexual escapades which ended in the death of the exploited person?" She didn't answer, but telltale eye flinches gave him answers. "When did you meet Mr. Colella?"

Mai Ling answered, "We met a couple of years ago. He was at a party which I attended."

"Did he pay attention to you right away or did you solicit him to buy your services?"

"He approached me and asked about my professional status. We came to a mutual agreement, and he became a regular."

Olivia came near the interrogation, heard Jerry's question and Mai Ling's answer, and asked, "When did he become your boyfriend?" Mai Ling studied her adversary, tilting her head.

"We became a steady item after the collapse of Andrew Pepper's enterprise when the Jefferson family raided it. You were the nurse who patched up injuries which needed not to be reported."

"Can you assess why he wanted to kill you?"

Mai Ling looked at Chris and back at Olivia. "I don't know. We had a good thing together. But I was a problem he didn't want. He complained about his employer and the beekeeper hindering his lifestyle. I didn't know I was also a hindrance." Tears accumulated in her eyes and spilled over her lids.

"You will have to account for kidnapping the Jefferson boy."

"I wasn't going to hurt him. They wanted leverage to get that detective to cooperate. All I had to do was hold him for a while. He surprised me when he attacked me. I wasn't expecting him it." Her head drooped as she spoke. "What happened to his family?"

"That's police business." Mai Ling nodded.

Jerry asked Chris Colella, "Do you have anything to say about your actions today?" He stared at the sergeant and then looked away. Turning to another officer, Jerry said, "Take him to lockup in Monroe. We'll transfer him to Everett, later, for arraignment."

Turning toward Eden and her sister, he continued, "Ms. Montague, I am sorry for the invasion of your property, but I do believe we have concluded our business here. I may have some follow-up questions later, especially regarding a review of the deaths of your father and husband. For now, we'll clear out and leave you to continue your operations, hopefully without any further misuse of Mad Honey."

"Thank you," Eden said. "I never would have guessed my supervisor and beekeeper were involved in helping others to kill people." She clung to Vanessa's arm as if a fortress of strength.

Jerry signaled to the officers and forensic team to gather their materials and vacate the estate. Pulling out his cell, he called his nephew. Marc answered and explained about Joan's condition and the vanishing Kerrine. Jerry asked about Kaliana. Marc stated he had interrogated her, discovering the escape plan they had devised for leaving Kitsap County, Washington State, and the United States. The plan was executed by only one.

"Do you think Kaliana will turn on her sister and let you know where she is?" Jerry asked.

"I don't think so. The twins might have contingencies for a separation. Without any help, though, I don't know how Kerrine can get Kaliana out of prison. She's headed for a secure lockup. The only time she would be vulnerable is during a trial when transfer from jail to court could leave an opening for Kerrine to strike."

"How about the Camacho woman?"

Marc said, "She came across as an adjunct part of their attempt to finish me off. I think the twins convinced her I was the reason for her sister dying aboard the Salish Sea. She's cooperating with us."

Jerry said, "We're finishing here at Montague Farms and will be in Everett soon. I'll come over with Lydia and we can wait with you until Joan is out of harm's way."

The call ended. Jerry had begun the assault on Andrew Pepper over two years before and began a string of events which endangered his family and friends. The end was bitter sweet. However, he smiled and relaxed for the first time since acting out his suicide to distract his enemies. The last of Andrew Pepper's cartel was finished. The octopus was dead, except for one elusive tentacle.

ACKNOWLEDGMENTS

Writing a manuscript has many starts and stops as a writer crafts the plot line from a planned outline or straight from the brain. Many people become part of the process as the story develops. Friends ask about the progress. People who have read other books ask about the progress. Family members ask about the progress.

And so, a writer keeps the development of the story, characters, dialog, and action growing from the first nugget of an idea through to the final line of the last chapter. To help me craft a great book I rely on various people to provide the needed feedback to glean from the story what should be improved or eliminated.

My first reader is my wife, Sandy, whose holistic ability to decipher the global manuscript from the pieces of the story provides a first line reading for interest and desirability. She gives me a chapter by chapter accounting of the development and offers advice about dullness settling in like a dusty room with no filter. She is invaluable to me.

My second line of defense is the group of beta readers who read the raw words and provide feedback in much the same way Sandy does. The added benefit comes in the notes made in the margins of pages which suggest helpful changes and corrections. These people are my loyal critics and first set of editors. Tovi Andrews, Becky Bauer, Sheila Curwen, Elizabeth Moorhead, Maggie Scott, Susan Wall have read all or some of the manuscripts in raw form and have highlighted the necessary parts of the story requiring upgrades and improvements.

Because this book is the third tale which began with 'Jerry's Motives', published over three years ago, and because the second tale, 'Death Stalks Mr. Blackthorne', elicited a need to understand honey, bees, and processing, I want to again thank my friend and fellow Episcopalian, Barbara Stedman, for allowing me to interview members of her staff.

My pharmaceutical friend, David Smith, originally investigated the toxic results of consuming rhododendron and azalea plant parts or the honey made by industrious bumblebees. He has continued to assure my proper use of the pharmacological aspects of my stories about the war with my fictional Andrew Pepper and his cartel of drug running thugs and conspiratorial agents of crime.

When a story expands beyond the usual one book and becomes a trilogy of mayhem and thrilling action, a writer might become lost in the development of the characters and who they are in each story. I have worked to keep faith with each of the main characters and to hold a steady plot line with the sub-characters and minor plots weaved into the fabric of the tale. Each person has a life of importance to themselves, as I see it. Although one person may not be as fully understood or able to be known by an adoring readership to a greater degree, be content to know that I, the manufacturer of the character and the developer of their lifeline attempt to maintain a believability for my reader to accept and enjoy.

An author undertaking the daunting task of writing and publishing must rely on the people who will finish the work and produce a viable book. I want to thank Tim Meikle of Kitsap Publishing and Printing for his tireless work formatting my manuscripts into useful files which are then sent to IngramSpark which oversees the printing of physical books. I have designed the covers of my last three books using licensed photos and visuals images from Shutterstock.com. I have enjoyed the creation and testing of my ideas to design an intriguing and attractive cover.

I am also grateful to the members of two organizations of which I am a member. The first is Kitsap Literary Artists & Writers. We are a loose collective of writers who support efforts to build an audience through marketing. We have engaged the services of the local television access channel. Bremerton Kitsap Access Television, to produce and air a weekly interview broadcast in which a member will interview a local writer, artist, or musician. KLAW has also undertaken airing Halloween and Christmas shows in which authors read from their materials, stories, and books.

KLAW also spearheaded an author event at Kitsap Mall in Silverdale, Washington and the sponsoring of a booth at the annual Blackberry Festival in Bremerton. More future events are planned.

The other organization is the Northwest Independent Writers Association. Organizing and staffing booths at various fairs, expos, and events has led to the introduction of my books to a wider distribution than I could attain on my own.

Character names can be difficult to cull from the deep recesses of my brain. However, as I travel and meet people, they offer me a chance to use their names. For this reason, I thank Chris Colella and Bernice Harapat, Alaska Air flight attendants I met on a flight to Las Vegas. I explained my newfound profession of writing, and we agreed their names suited being characters. The name for the Assistant Chief of Criminal Investigations came about when I began following an Instagram account and asked if I could use her name as a character. Her answer? "Feature me." So, I did. I do want to meet her in the future but probably will not. The name Eden Montague is entirely my idea, but Malcolm Varian is a combination of my grandson and a former student. Eden's attorney name came from a friend who is my son, David's, case manager, Paula Cross.

To my loyal readers, I say thank you. I enjoy crafting my works and sharing them with you. Your feedback has helped me to be a better writer. I will endeavor to continue improving the quality of my books and to enliven your world with better entertainment.

ABOUT THE AUTHOR

Peter Stockwell is a retired middle school teacher embarking on his next career telling stories. After 32 years of guiding mind and emotions of preteen and teenage students, he left the classroom to relax and enjoy the rest of his life with family and friends. Instead, he wrote a book and published it. The fun began when he learned the next step, marketing his creation to the world.

He lives with his wife, Sandy, and two cats in Silverdale, Washington. He has five children and eight grandchildren who are a source of great joy. He is member of Pacific Northwest Writers Association (PNWA), International Thriller Writers (ITW), and Northwest Independent Writer Association (NIWA) and Kitsap Literary Artists & Writers (KLAW). He publishes through his company, Westridge Art.

Each month Peter and another KLAW member, Mark Miller, record and produce a television show in which they interview northwest authors, artists, musicians, and publishers. Production of the show is in conjunction with Bremerton Kitsap Access Television (BKAT).

Contact Peter at stockwellpa@wavecable.com
Follow Peter on Facebook, Instagram, and Twitter

CPSIA information can be obtained
at www.ICGtesting.com
Printed in the USA
FSHW010905290419
57669FS